FLINTLOCK:
PITCHFORK PASS

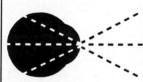

This Large Print Book carries the
Seal of Approval of N.A.V.H.

FLINTLOCK: PITCHFORK PASS

WILLIAM W. JOHNSTONE
WITH J. A. JOHNSTONE

THORNDIKE PRESS
A part of Gale, a Cengage Company

Farmington Hills, Mich • San Francisco • New York • Waterville, Maine
Meriden, Conn • Mason, Ohio • Chicago

Copyright © 2018 by J.A. Johnstone.
The WWJ steer head logo is a Reg. U. S. Pat. & TM Off.
Thorndike Press, a part of Gale, a Cengage Company.

ALL RIGHTS RESERVED

Following the death of William W. Johnstone, the Johnstone family is working with a carefully selected writer to organize and complete Mr. Johnstone's outlines and many unfinished manuscripts to create additional novels in all of his series like The Last Gunfighter, Mountain Man, and Eagles, among others. This novel was inspired by Mr. Johnstone's superb storytelling.
Thorndike Press® Large Print Western.
The text of this Large Print edition is unabridged.
Other aspects of the book may vary from the original edition.
Set in 16 pt. Plantin.

**LIBRARY OF CONGRESS CIP DATA ON FILE.
CATALOGUING IN PUBLICATION FOR THIS BOOK
IS AVAILABLE FROM THE LIBRARY OF CONGRESS**

ISBN-13: 978-1-4328-5544-4 (hardcover)

Published in 2018 by arrangement with Pinnacle Books, an imprint of Kensington Publishing Corp.

Printed in Mexico
1 2 3 4 5 6 7 22 21 20 19 18

FLINTLOCK: PITCHFORK PASS

"Yup, Lefty Kelly was a high-strung feller to be sure, but a couple of barrels of buckshot to the belly calmed him down right quick."

"He's as dead as hell in a preacher's backyard," Sam Flintlock said, his eyes moving to the corpse slung across the back of a mustang horse. "A man can't get much calmer than that."

"And you just said a natural fact, mister. I'd say truer words were never spoke," the old man said. "A dead man sure don't feel any excitement. Well, Lefty Kelly's outlaw days are over and the news will come as a relief to the honest citizens of the Arizona Territory and a warning to them as ain't honest."

Fat black flies buzzed around the dead man's head as Flintlock said, "Are you the one cut his suspenders?"

"Yes, I did. Lefty was a fugitive from

justice and he paid the price, poor feller." The man leaned forward in the saddle and extended his hand. "Name's Ebenezer Stone, originally out of the Texas Llano River country, but now I reside right here in the Territory. As you might have guessed, I'm an officer of the law, at least some of the time."

"I'm Sam Flintlock." He took the man's hand. "And this here is O'Hara, who rides with me."

Stone gave O'Hara a long look. "Half-breed, ain't you sonny?"

"Seems about right."

"Seen that right off. I'd say your ma was Apache and with a name like O'Hara your pa was an Irishman."

"So I'm told," O'Hara said, his face stiff.

Stone nodded, his long, white hair moving across his broadclothed shoulders in thin strands. "I got an eye for these things," he said. "Knew you was a breed and I said so, didn't I?" He looked at Flintlock. "And I've heard of you. Heard about that tattoo on your throat. And mighty unusual it is, I must say."

"It's a thunderbird and it goes back a ways. Barnabas, my old grandpappy, had an Assiniboine woman put it there when I was a younker. He figured it was a fine way for a man to make his mark, folks would remember him, or so he said." Flintlock shrugged. "I was raised rough."

"And folks remember you favorably, I trust." Stone smiled. "That was the marshal in me talking, Mr. Flintlock. Feller who wears a star takes stock o' men like you who were raised rough."

"Well, lawman, so you know, here's how I stack up. I'm pegged in place by differing opinions. Some say pretty bad things about me. I've been called out for a mean bounty hunter, gunman, outlaw when it suits me and a wild man who's never chosen to live within the sound of church bells. All that is true, of course. But when you flip the coin you'll find that I have never betrayed a friend or turned my back on a crying child. I don't abuse dogs, horses, or women and when all the talking is done and guns are drawn, I never show yellow." Flintlock grinned. "At least I haven't so far."

Stone said, "Jibes with what I was told, some good, some bad. I heard tell that you're riding all over the frontier trying to find your long-lost ma. Am I right or am I wrong?"

"You got it right."

"And I heard you're a fair to middling gunhand and that you have a reputation as a bounty hunter who always gets his man."

"For me, bounty hunting is only a some-times thing. On any given day, it kinda depends on which side of the law I happen to be on."

"And what side are you on today?" Stone touched the brim of his battered black top hat. "If'n you don't mind me asking."

"The side that wonders why you gunned the feller behind you, hanging belly-down across a mustang hoss."

"His name's Lefty Kelly, or did I tell you that already?"

"You told me that already," Flintlock said.

"Well, since explanations seem to be in order, I'm not a federal marshal or a county marshal, just the city marshal of a town to the northwest of here they call Dexter, after the tinpan who founded the place. There was a gold mine there once, but it played out after a year or two and the town played out with it. Now there's only about a hundred people left and a few of them are sickly. Long story short, Kelly robbed the Dexter bank and rode off with all the money, a grand total of a hundred and seventy-three dollars and eighteen cents, and a ham sandwich, the bank president's lunch."

"And you went after him for that?" Flintlock said. "Less than two hundred dollars."

Stone shrugged. "The bank president is also the mayor and he set store by that sandwich. I had my orders."

"So, the bottom line is that you gunned the poor son of a bitch over a ham sandwich."

"Yeah, I did, but it didn't need to be that way. Mistakes were made. I told you he was a mighty skittish feller and prone to errors in judgment."

"What kind of mistakes, and who made them?" This from O'Hara, whose sour expression made it clear that he didn't much like lawmen in general and this one in particular.

Stone scratched his stubbly chin. "Well, sonny, seems like Lefty Kelly made all of them."

"Tell us. What were they?"

"Injun, are you suspicioning me? You think I murdered him?"

"You could say that. You told us that you're a lawman but you're dressed up like an undertaker and I don't see a badge."

"Listen, sonny, a town with less than two hundred dollars in the bank don't give out silver badges. But in the eyes of the Arizona Territory I'm a sworn peace officer, lay to that. Hell, son, you're giving me sass and

11

making the same mistakes Kelly did."

"O'Hara, let the man talk," Flintlock said. "He's a half Indian and he don't know any better. But, Stone, if you did murder that man we'll take you back to Dexter. Recently O'Hara and me have fallen on hard times and there might be a reward for bringing you in."

"And good luck trying to collect it. Anyhoo, the Injun is right. I dress the way I do because I'm the town undertaker and man and boy I've always been an undertaker," Stone said. "I only act as city marshal. It's what you might call an honorary post and that means it's unpaid except for a per diem allowance for feeding prisoners and the like. Only I never have no prisoners."

"So, Kelly robbed the bank and you were acting as honorary, unpaid city marshal when you went after him," Flintlock said. "At least that's what you're telling us. Then what happened, since me and O'Hara are chasing a reward, like?"

"Well, sir, Lefty rode a few miles out of town and then camped in the pines, bold as you please, on account of how he figured nobody in Dexter would have the sand to come after him. Fact is, he was bilin' coffee when I came up on him in my capacity of officer of the law. 'Howdy,' says I. 'A fine day, huh?' Well, he didn't answer and it was shortly thereafter that the mistakes I was talking about earlier began to be made."

"Kelly's mistakes? Or yours?"

"His. I don't make no mistakes. Leastways, in my undertaking career I never planted anybody by mistake. Anyhoo, it seems that Kelly took me for a preacher or maybe a drummer, I don't know. But what he said was clear enough. 'Ride on,' he says. 'There's nothing here for you.' Says I, 'Smelled your coffee.' Says he, 'Beat it. I only got enough for myself.' Well, that was downright unsociable and it was Kelly's first mistake. His second was that he'd taken off his gunbelt and holstered revolver and laid them by his sideprevious."

Stone looked at O'Hara and then Flintlock. "Are you gents catching my drift?"

"So far," Flintlock said. "Get on with your story. It seems plausible enough so far, him not willing to share his coffee, an' all."

"Yeah, that was downright mean, and bad manners to boot. Somebody didn't raise that boy right, if you ask me. Well, I'm advanced in years, but lucky for me I'm quick," Stone said. "An undertaker has to be quick . . . box 'em and bury 'em afore they stink, you understand?"

Flintlock said, "So, you're quick. How quick?"

"Quick enough that it was only the matter of a moment to slide my shotgun from the boot under my knee and point the muzzles at Lefty's middle. 'On your feet,' I said. 'And no fancy moves.' But alas . . ."

"Alas, what?" Flintlock said.

"Alas, Lefty made yet another, and this time fatal, mistake. He underestimated my skill with a shotgun and my resolve to bring him and his ilk to justice. With one bound, he grabbed his revolver and was on his feet. Then, uttering a vile profanity, he readied himself to shoot. But I was resolute and felt no fear. I let him have both barrels of the Greener in the belly and a great cloud of blood erupted around him and he fell dead on the ground. I broke open the shotgun and I'll always remember taking out those two, bright red, smoking shells." Stone shook his head. "I recall thinking how little lead it takes to kill a man and take away his past, present and future."

"Two barrels of buckshot in the gut will just about do it every time," Flintlock said. "Where's the money you recovered from Kelly?"

"Right here." Stone reached into his coat pocket and produced a small canvas sack that bore the legend DEXTER BANK & TRUST. "It's all here," he said, jingling the coins in the bag. "And the bank makes a profit of three cents, the money that was in Kelly's pocket."

Speaking to O'Hara, Flintlock said, "I tend to believe him. He even speaks like a lawman."

"Yeah, he's telling the truth," O'Hara said. "The Kelly feller was too slow on the draw and shoot and that done for him." He glared at Stone. "Had it been me, your scattergun would've never cleared the boot."

"I take it that you've no intention of robbing the Dexter bank?" Stone said.

"No," O'Hara said. "Not much profit in it, even with the dead man's three cents."

"Then we'll never find out if my scattergun would or would not have cleared leather, will we?" Stone said. He gathered up the reins of his rawboned nag and the mustang's lead rope. "It's been a pleasure talking with you gents, but now will you give me the road?"

Flintlock drew his horse aside to let Stone and the dead man pass. But the marshal drew rein and said, "You boys headed west?"

"Seems like," Flintlock said.

"Then I got a warning for you."

"We know it's mighty rough country

15

between here and the Painted Desert. Is that what you were going to tell us?"

Stone shook his head. "No. Anybody with half a brain already knows that. My warning is about a man, well, maybe he's a man, maybe he's something else. But he's pure pizen, and that's my warning."

"We've bumped into outlaws before," Flintlock said. "Most of them were friends of mine."

"The Old Man of the Mountain is nobody's friend. He's at war with the world and everybody in it," Stone said.

O'Hara's face changed from studied disinterest to shock. "He rides a tall black horse and carries terrible weapons, two Colt revolvers and a Winchester rifle that cause death and destruction wherever he goes. The Old Man of the Mountain can command the thunder to roar and the lightning to strike and he sits on a throne made of black iron, surrounded by the skulls of his enemies. He is very old, older than the rivers and the mountains."

"Ye don't say? Then you know more about him than I do," Stone said.

"The Apache knew and feared him," O'Hara said. "The Old Man once made war on the Mescalero and killed many people."

"Well, I don't know about all that," Stone

16

said. "But I can tell you that just about every stage holdup, train robbery and busted bank in this part of the Territory and West Texas can be laid at the Old Man's feet, to say nothing of scores of rapes and murders. Five years ago, in the spring of '81, a cavalry major by the name of Obadiah Sutherland resupplied his men in Dexter and then led forty troopers west into the Balakai Mesa country where the Old Man is supposed to be holed up. He promised the townfolks he'd bring back the outlaw's head on the point of his saber. But it was the major's head that came back, dumped on the mayor's doorstep by a galloper in the wee hours of the morning. Nothing more was heard of the troopers, as I recollect, all of them young, lively lads."

"Thanks for the warning," Flintlock said. "But last I heard my ma is headed west and I aim to find her. The Old Man of the Mountain won't stop me."

Stone shrugged, a dismissive gesture. "Your funeral." He kicked his horse forward. "Well, good luck to you both."

Flintlock said, "Yeah, thanks, Stone. And good luck to you, too."

CHAPTER TWO

"O'Hara, I don't see any need for a scout," Sam Flintlock said. "Set and have a cup of coffee. We'll spread our blankets here tonight and head out at first light."

"Them the same grounds you used this morning that you'd used the previous night?" O'Hara said.

"Yeah, but they'll still bile up strong enough after two, three hours on the fire."

"That's what you said this morning."

"So how was the coffee?"

"Coyote piss."

"O'Hara, there are times when you can be a right fussy man. Strange, that. I mean, you being half Apache, an' all."

"What's being half Indian got to do with it?"

"Nothing. But it's just strange."

"Geronimo liked his coffee. You ever hear that?"

"No, I never did."

18

"Arbuckle, biled up with honey when he could get it. He was much addicted to it."

"Didn't sweeten him none," Flintlock said.

O'Hara led his horse from the moonlit ponderosas where there were patches of graze. "I aim to ride west for a spell, take a look-see."

"The undertaker feller got you spooked, huh? All that talk about the Old Man of the Mountain and them soldier boys."

"No, I'm not spooked, I just don't want any unpleasant surprises come morning," O'Hara said.

Flintlock took the bubbling coffeepot off the coals. "I'll let it stand for a spell, settle the grounds." He looked up at O'Hara, who'd swung into the saddle. "Know what I think? My guess is that them soldiers weren't bushwhacked by the Old Man of the Mountain. I reckon they bumped into bronco Apaches and got themselves massacreed."

"Why would the Apaches return his head?"

"Indians take on some mighty strange notions. Maybe they did it just to be sociable. Who knows?"

"Enjoy your coffee, Sam," O'Hara said. "If I'm not back by first light get the hell out of here."

"Can't do that. I'll come looking for you."

"As the undertaker lawman said to us . . . it's your funeral."

O'Hara swung his horse away and rode into the blue twilight of the fading day. Flintlock sat among the pines and watched him go, worry nagging at him.

There was just no telling what trouble O'Hara might get himself into when he wasn't supervised.

Sam Flintlock rubbed his hands together in delight. His coffee was starting to smell almost good. But then the rubbing slowed to a halt . . . it wasn't his coffee he smelled, it was wicked old Barnabas, Sam's dead grandfather. The old mountain man stood at the edge of the pines watching him, a smoking tin cup in his hand.

"Hot as hell, bitter enough to curdle a pig and as black as mortal sin, the way I like it, boy," Barnabas said. "I'd give you some, Sam'l, if I wasn't such a selfish son of a bitch."

"I thought I'd gotten rid of you," Flintlock said. "You haven't showed up in months."

Barnabas sipped from his cup, steam rising, obscuring his bearded face. Only his green eyes were visible "Well, let me tell you . . . there was a big tidal wave in the

South Seas, an' all kinds of people drowned and there was a lot of cannibals to be welcomed. You-know-who had a hell of a time getting them settled down, had to teach them that they can't take bites out of the other guests. I mean, we got full-time demons to do that sort of thing."

Flintlock sighed. "What do you want, Barnabas?"

"Well, first off to remind you that you're an idiot. And secondly to warn you that your redskin friend is riding into a heap of trouble. No, don't get up. It will be full dark soon and you'll never find him."

"Is it the Old Man of the Mountain?"

"Who?"

"The Old Man of the Mountain. We were warned to stay clear of him."

"Why? Speak up, boy. Cat got your tongue?"

"Because he's a rapist and a murderer and a vicious outlaw."

Barnabas shrugged, an irritating habit he'd picked up from the emperor Napoleon. "The Old Man sounds like a fine fellow to me. No, it's not him."

"Glad to hear that," Flintlock said.

"Maybe you shouldn't be. But I guess you'll find out soon enough."

"What's going to happen with O'Hara?

21

Barnabas, tell me."

The old mountain man made a childish face. "No, I won't. And you can't make me." Then, "I see you still got the Hawken."

"It's the only thing you ever gave me." Flintlock touched the thunderbird tattoo on his throat. "Well, apart from this."

"Still holding a grudge because I didn't give you my name, huh, Sam'l? Find your ma and get your own handle."

"That's why I'm here in the Arizona Territory. You know that. And you could make it easier for me. Tell me where Ma is."

"I don't know where she is."

"I thought you knew everything, past, present and future."

"This is good coffee," Barnabas said, drinking from his cup.

"Answer me, old man. Where is Ma? And when you're done, tell me why you sent me into the bear cave that time. I never got the straight of that from you."

"On your tenth birthday, wasn't it, Sammy? I can't quite recollect."

"I was nine and it wasn't my birthday. You planned to winter in the cave and sent me inside to make sure it wasn't occupied. It was."

"Why worry over old times and old wounds, Sam'l?"

"I'm the one with the old wounds, Barnabas. The scars are all over my back. O'Hara saw them a few weeks ago when I was taking a bath in a rock spring up on the rim. 'I never knew somebody went at you with a bullwhip, Sam,' he said. I said, 'It wasn't a whipping. One time when I was a boy I tangled with an old she-grizz who was sore at being wakened from her winter sleep. She tore me up good before Barnabas shot her.' "

"Yeah, now I recollect," the old man said. "Sure, now I remember, Sammy. As things turned out that was a right cozy cave and we had bear meat enough to last for weeks."

"Damn it, you almost got me killed."

Barnabas gave his irritating shrug. "As that old undertaker lawman said, mistakes were made."

"You heard him?"

"Of course I heard him. I was there, or thereabouts."

Flintlock raised his coffeepot, thumbed the lid and sniffed. Now he couldn't smell much of anything. He put the pot back on the fire and said, "All right, you didn't give me a direct answer to the cave question, so I'll ask the first one again: Where is Ma?"

"And my answer to that one is the same — I don't know. I can see some things, but not others. Your ma, I can only catch a glimpse of her now and again, like she's walking in a mist. You-know-who knows she's my daughter and it amuses him to torment me." Barnabas smiled. "He's real good at his job, knows where to stick the pitchfork, if you catch my drift."

"But Ma's still in the Arizona Territory?"

"Yeah, somewhere west of here, I think." Barnabas sighed. "I've already had too much coffee and I got a full cup. Well, I'll just get rid of it."

The old man tipped his cup and Flintlock yelled, "No!"

Too late.

A brown cascade of Arbuckle splashed on the grass.

Barnabas grinned. "I got to go. So long, Sammy."

He vanished from sight and Flintlock yelled, "Who is the Old Man of the Mountain?"

His only answer was a derisive laugh that immediately became one with the harsh cawing of the ill-tempered crows quarreling among the pines.

Flintlock stepped to where Barnabas had poured out the coffee. The grass still steamed. He shook his head and decided that the unrepentant old sinner richly deserved to be in the place where he was.

The coffee Flintlock poured into his cup was the color of swamp water and tasted just as bad. He drank it anyway, rolled a thin cigarette and stared into the gathering darkness . . .

Where the hell was O'Hara?

CHAPTER THREE

O'Hara rode west from Pleasant Valley into a vast, empty land of long, piñon-covered mesas, red sandstone cliffs, huge open valleys and deep, mysterious canyons. For centuries, the Hopi, Navajo and Apache had hunted and warred across this land but had left no mark, and over the course of tens of thousands of years the only thing that ever changed was the sky.

When night fell, O'Hara spread his blankets within a stand of pine and juniper that had enough sparse grass to graze a horse that was used to roughing it, and his paint made no complaint. During the remaining daylight hours after he left Flintlock, O'Hara had not seen another human being. Once he startled a small herd of mule deer and then a jackrabbit bounced in front of his horse for a few yards before vanishing into the brush.

Of the Old Man of the Mountain there

was no sign, and O'Hara closed his eyes safe in the knowledge that he had been on the scout for a Mescalero legend . . . just another scary boogeyman the squaws used to keep their children quiet at night . . .

That and nothing more.

O'Hara fell asleep to the sounds of darkness. An owl asked its question of the night, coyotes yipped as they hunted squeaking things among the rocks and a south wind whispered secrets to the piñon.

He woke to the dawn . . . and to the hard steel of a Winchester rifle muzzle jammed firmly between his eyes.

"On your feet, Injun," a man's voice said. Then, spiked with impatience, "Now! Or I'll blow your eyeballs through the back of your skull."

O'Hara blinked, stared into a tough, bearded face, and said, "Go to hell."

That statement brought its own reward, a swift kick in the ribs from a square-toed boot. Two other men cursed, brushed the rifleman aside and hauled O'Hara to his feet. One of the three wore a patch over his right eye that partially covered a vicious, livid scar that ran from his cheekbone to the corner of his mouth. This man, O'Hara later heard him called Mort, said, "What's a thieving Indian like you doing in this part

27

of the Territory?"

O'Hara met the man's reptilian eyes and said, "I'm only half thieving Indian. My other half is thieving Irishman."

"Then you're a damned dirty breed," Mort said.

"I'm a damned clean breed," O'Hara said.

"You're a funny man, huh?"

"No one ever said I was funny."

O'Hara's revolver was in the rifleman's waistband and that caused him a deal of disappointment.

"Know what I do to funny men?" Mort said.

O'Hara shook his head.

"This!"

Mort backhanded O'Hara across the face. The blow sounded like a pistol crack and was powerful enough to send O'Hara staggering on rubber legs before he thudded onto his back, dazed, the taste of blood in his mouth.

"I can't abide a lippy breed," Mort said. "I can't abide any kind of breed."

"Looks like a full-blood Apache to me, Mort," the rifleman said, shoving his rifle muzzle into O'Hara's belly. "I thought all them scum was in the Florida swamps someplace."

Mort was a big man, well over six feet,

heavy in the chest and shoulders and strong. He effortlessly yanked O'Hara upright. "Look at my face, breed," he said. "What do you see?"

A trickle of blood ran from the corner of O'Hara's mouth and his right eye had started to close. "I see a son of a bitch," he said.

A series of back-and-forth, open-handed blows bobbed O'Hara's head on his shoulders, and saliva flew from his mouth in scarlet strings. Mort shoved his face close to O'Hara's and paced his words. "Do . . . you . . . see . . . the . . . scar?"

"Yeah, I see it." O'Hara was barely clinging on to consciousness.

"An Apache buck did that, cut me up afore I could put a bullet into him and I've been searching for him ever since," Mort said. "Look at me. I'm death on Apaches."

"I'm looking at you and I still see a son of a bitch," O'Hara said.

"Still the funny man, huh?" Mort said. He threw O'Hara to the ground then turned to the rifleman and said, "Deke, build us a fire."

"What's your thinking, Mort?" Deke said.

"If all this damned Apache sees when he looks at me is a son of a bitch, better he doesn't see anything ever again."

"What you gonna do, Mort?" Deke said, grinning his amusement.

"Burn his damned eyes out. That's what I'm gonna do."

It took Deke only a few minutes to start a small fire, just big enough to burn the end of a twig that Mort had sharpened into a point.

The third man, a tall, lanky drink of water with sad, hound-dog eyes and a Colt holstered high on his left side, said, "Mort, maybe we should take the Injun to the Old Man for questioning, like. I mean, what's he doing out here? Is he scouting for the army? Could be, you know."

"Well, Clem, if he is, his scouting days are over, and anyhow, since when was the Old Man afeard of the army?"

"Since never, I reckon," Clem said.

"Then there's your answer. We'll take the Old Man the breed's scalp."

"Yee-haw!" Deke yelled. "Another scalp fer Custer."

Mort placed the end of the twig in the flames and grinned. "Yes, it is. I do declare."

The way Mort said that last made it a good joke and his two companions laughed. But they didn't laugh for long, since no sooner did Mort's words leave his mouth than a .50 caliber ball drilled through the crown of his hat and took off the top of his skull.

Chapter Four

Sam Flintlock saddled his buckskin at first light. O'Hara had not returned and that was worrisome. Wishful for coffee, sourdough bread and bacon, but having none, he put the thought out of his mind and mounted. Hunger was not new to him. Flintlock called it by name since it returned at regular intervals like an unwelcome guest.

Apart from the finer points of drinking and whoring, old Barnabas and his fellow mountain men had taught Flintlock how to track a man and when the tracking was done how to kill him. He put those skills to good use now.

Despite his vaunted half-Apache ancestry, O'Hara left an obvious, meandering trail like the heading-home of a drunk Irishman. His shod pony had left scars on the land that were easy to follow, even in that rocky country. There were a couple of spots where O'Hara had dismounted, turned and checked his back trail. On both occasions, he'd smoked a meager cigarette, a habit he'd recently acquired since reading in an eastern newspaper he'd picked up in Fort Defiance that smoking was an excellent strengthener of the heart and lungs. O'Hara had gathered up the telltale butts, however he'd left other sign, the gray ash that still lay on the ground.

After an hour on the trail and as the morning brightened, Flintlock crossed a wide, dry wash, spared a glance for the lank, white bones and skull of a long-dead burro, and then skirted around the outer wall of a horseshoe-shaped bluff, the red sandstone rim rising a hundred feet above the flat. This was lost, lonely country and the still air smelled of sagebrush and warming rock and the ever-present odor of dust . . . and of something else . . . the tang of woodsmoke. And close.

Flintlock drew rein. By nature, he was not an overly considering man, but he was sure that O'Hara, with nothing to boil on it, would not start a fire this early in the morning. That left two possibilities: he'd fallen in with coffee-drinking men or the fire belonged to strangers. Strangers being the most likely, Flintlock was suddenly wary. The Territory's mesa country was not the haunt of honest men, but a haven for outlaws and all kinds of frontier riffraff on the make, a wild, lawless place where a man could easily get dry-gulched and just as easily die.

There was no wind, so the fire was close, the smoke barely drifting. Flintlock swung out of the saddle and led his horse forward. He made his way through some knee-high brush and descended into another wash, this one narrow with a sand and pebble bottom. Schooled by mountain men who were more lobo wolf than human, Flintlock had the instincts of a predatory animal and he stepped carefully, making no sound, his great beak of a nose raised, testing the air. He left the wash and crossed twenty yards of open ground, ahead of him an escarpment the height of a tall man separating the bluff as though it had been cut in two by a knife. Now that he was close enough to the source of the smoke he heard voices, the harsh talk of some rough and mighty unfriendly characters.

Suddenly Flintlock knew with certainty that O'Hara was near . . . and in trouble.

He let the buckskin's reins trail and slid his .50 caliber Hawken from the boot. On the opposite side of the saddle hung a .44-40 Winchester, a far superior weapon, but that unrepentant old sinner Barnabas, with many a curse, cuff and kick, had taught Flintlock the ways of the plains rifle and his much-abused student was deadly with it at under a hundred yards. A fair hand with a revolver but no great shakes with the Winchester, without a second thought he left the cartridge rifle with his horse and stepped on cat feet to the point where the bluff abruptly dropped to a slope that ended in a jumble of talus rock.

Keeping to cover, Flintlock made his way through some fair-sized boulders and then looked out into an area of open ground surrounded by trees. O'Hara lay on the ground, his face bloody, and a man stood over him. The man was big, bearded and huge in the chest and shoulders, and he said something that made his two companions laugh.

Still unseen by the three men, Flintlock's gaze flicked to the big, grinning man, then to O'Hara and back to the man again.

It was never said of Sam Flintlock that he was a contemplative sort of gent. Rather, without much ado, he made up his mind and acted. He threw the Hawken to his shoulder and triggered a shot. High and to the left. He'd aimed for the big man's temple but the errant ball blew off the top of the ranny's head. The big man went down without a sound, his holed, bloody hat rolling away from him when he hit the ground.

Flintlock dropped the Hawken and pulled his Colt from the waistband.

"You two stay right where you're at," he said to the dead man's companions, walking forward, closing the distance between him and them. "I ain't in the mood for talking polite, so I won't tell you again."

But then the two men surprised the hell out of Sam Flintlock.

He had the drop. His gun up and ready, and he'd caught the pair flat-footed . . . but they tried to draw down on him. Stranger still, in the instant before he shot them both, he wondered at their expressions, tranquil, almost serene, like the faces of a couple of nuns in church on Sunday.

Hit hard in the chest, one man fell immediately. The other, a tall man who wore his gun high and unhandy on his waist, was gut-shot. He staggered back, his face twisted, triggered a shot that missed by a yard, and then collapsed like a puppet with its strings cut when Flintlock plugged him again.

"What the hell?" Flintlock said, the actions of the two men puzzling him. They must have known they didn't stand a chance on the draw and shoot, yet they went ahead

36

and did it anyway. Why would they do such an idiotic thing? It didn't seem . . .

"I'm just fine, thanks," O'Hara said. "Real good of you to ask."

Flintlock helped O'Hara to his feet. "Are you bad hurt?"

"Beaten up some, but I'll survive."

"Your face is bruised."

"I reckon."

"What happened?"

"They jumped me when I was asleep."

"Asleep? Why were you asleep?"

"Because I was tired."

"And you let them three jump you?"

"Sure did."

Flintlock shook his head. "Damned careless of you."

"They sneaked up on me. Some white men can sneak up as good as any Indian."

"Any idea who they were?"

"Their names were Mort, Clem and Deke. That's all I know."

"Mighty unsociable, them three."

"Unsociable enough that they were going to burn my eyes out."

"Yeah, that's mighty unsociable. All right, let's have a look at them boys."

A search of the bodies revealed one thing for certain — they weren't punchers. Their duds, boots and gun leather were of good quality, more expensive than any puncher could afford, and each man had five double eagles in his pocket, indicating they'd just been paid.

"Paid for what?" O'Hara said.

"A hundred dollars is top gun wages," Flintlock said.

"Didn't do much to earn their wages today, did they?" O'Hara's bruised mouth and split lips made his words sound thick. "Hey, look here."

O'Hara kneeled beside the body of Mort and held the man's arm for Flintlock to see. "Look at his wrist."

On the inside of the dead man's wrist was a tattoo of three blue triangles rising from a red baseline. Flintlock inspected the other two and said, "They all got the same thing."

"It's the Indian sign for a mountain," O'Hara said. He looked troubled.

Flintlock immediately grasped the significance. "The Old Man of the Mountain?"

"Seems like. And you just killed three of his boys."

"Three of his gunhands," Flintlock said. "O'Hara, I had them two over there dead to rights. Why the hell did they draw down on me?"

"Hell if I know," O'Hara said. "I saw it, but I couldn't believe it. I still don't."

"It's like they were willing to die."

"Yeah, even with death staring them in the face, they wouldn't accept defeat."

"Did the Old Man make them that way?"

"Sam, how the hell should I know?"

"I thought you knew everything."

"When it comes to a reason for men to throw their lives away, I don't know a damned thing."

"Maybe the Old Man has a hold over a man that doesn't allow him to think straight," Flintlock said. "I mean, that could be."

"Maybe," O'Hara said. He looked around at the breathtakingly beautiful but pitiless land. "If those three rode for the Old Man then he's close. We better get the hell out of here."

Flintlock said, "The undertaker lawman said he was from a town —"

"Dexter."

"Yeah, Dexter. I say we take the dead men's horses and traps and sell them there."

"Sam, if we do what you say, we'll never come back into this country," O'Hara said. "You know it, and I know it. You want to find your ma before her trail grows cold again, so the decision is up to you. Do we carry on or go back to Dexter and then take another route around Balakai Mesa and the

Old Man of the Mountain?"

"We'd waste days, weeks, maybe," Flint-lock said.

"That's the worst thing I've ever heard," O'Hara said. "But as I said, it's up to you."

Flintlock made his decision. "Unsaddle the horses and turn them loose. They'll find their way back to the Old Man." He glanced at the three sprawled bodies. "Then he can come bury his dead."

"That's how you want to play it?" O'Hara said.

"It's the only way to play it," Flintlock said. "My ma is close. We keep on going until we find her."

CHAPTER FIVE

Shanghai, China. July 1855. Twenty years before the Old Man of the Mountain established his outlaw stronghold among the peaks and arroyos of Balakai Mesa.

Jacob Hammer, as he was known then, left the teeming, clamoring streets of the International Settlement and climbed the winding, mile-long path that led upward through groves of plane trees to a *siheyuan,* a Chinese courtyard mansion built in the traditional style, a large quadrangle surrounded by buildings on all four sides. From there, the Whangpoo River, a tributary of the Yangtze, was seven miles distant, but still, Hammer smelled its familiar stench, a mix of fish, seaweed and if some reports were to be credited, decomposing human bodies.

Jacob Hammer was thirty-nine years old that summer, the American first mate of the fast English tea clipper *Rochester* out of

London town. In three days, she would set sail again and arrive at the Thames one hundred days later with a full hold after exchanging her cargo of Indian opium for tea, porcelain and spices.

But as he neared the mansion, Hammer gave little thought to the tea trade. He had come to the home of the rich merchant Sun Yu on a much more important mission . . . in search of the Tibetan potion that gives the imbiber eternal life.

"Aye, Mr. Hammer, it's a legend right enough and maybe that should be an end to it," Captain Miles Davies said as he and Hammer stood on the *Rochester*'s quarter-deck and looked out on the city's waterfront and business and financial district. Close by, a massive British ironclad, HMS *Devonshire,* lay at anchor, its great turret guns pointed landward. Sampans and junks scuttled everywhere, men, women and children in cone-shaped coolie hats manning their decks, thin dogs standing in the bows, barking at everything.

Captain Davies, a big-bellied man with side whiskers and a huge walrus mustache, offered Hammer his silver flask. Hammer declined and Davies took a swig, recorked the flask and said, "Mind you, I heard that there are lively young lads running around

Shanghai who drank of the potion and claim to be a hundred years old and more." Davies smiled, revealing the bad teeth of the longtime mariner. "But I put no stock in that story. Chinese people believe what they dearly want to believe, magic potions being one of those things."

Hammer, who'd learned the seaman's trade in the hell ships sailing out of New York, was a hard-faced man with ice-blue eyes, a wide, cruel mouth and a volcanic temper. As a third mate, he'd once beaten a sailor to death with his bare hands for spitting on the deck and it was rumored, but never proved by the San Francisco police, that he'd strangled a whore in a Barbary Coast brothel. At six foot four and two hundred pounds of bone and muscle, a boot and skull fighter who was good with the gun, knife and billy club, Jacob Hammer was an elemental force to be reckoned with and even tough men with scarred faces stepped carefully around him.

"Cap'n, I'm told a merchant by the name of Sun Yu has the potion," Hammer said.

"Who told you that?"

"A whore by the name of Chenguang. She said Sun Yu uses her from time to time when he needs a diversion."

"She's a whore at the Seven Seas on Nanjing Road?"

"Yeah, she is. Maybe you know her."

"I know her. In English, Chenguang means 'Morning Glory.' As you probably know, there is nothing glorious about her first thing in the morning. Damned unwashed hussy."

Hammer said, "She told me that Sun Yu showed her a golden bottle that held the potion. He told her that if she was real nice to him, one day he would give her a slug."

"Nobody can lie like a Shanghai whore, Mr. Hammer. They're famous for it."

A fat seaman wearing a white apron had been standing at the deck rail of the British ironclad, a slop bucket in his hands. He waited, his gaze constantly searching the coffee-colored water that lapped against the hull. At last he saw what he'd been looking for, a sampan that had steered too close to the ship, the man at the sculling oar distracted as he argued with a woman at the bow. The seaman grinned, tipped the sloshing contents of the bucket over the boat and was rewarded by a string of Chinese curses from both the male and female. The sailor gave the pair a derisive salute, then stepped away from the rail, whistling.

Jacob Hammer had watched the little drama play out with no display of emotion.

Now he said, "I want to talk with Sun Yu. How do I find him?"

Captain Davies seemed alarmed. "After a visit to Sun Yu, do you know the first thing the Chinese do?" Hammer made no answer. "They touch their heads to make sure it's still on their shoulders. He's the most dangerous criminal rogue in Shanghai, maybe in all of China. He controls prostitution, gambling, the opium dens, the police, operates a murder-for-hire enterprise and gets a cut from every porcelain bowl or ounce of spice that's loaded into the hold of a clipper ship, including this one. Take a piece of advice from an old China hand, Mr. Hammer, stay well away from him."

"I still want to talk with him."

"Do you really think he can give you immortality? For centuries, Chinese emperors tried to find the secret of eternal life, and they're all dead. The only immortality is through our Blessed Savior and I advise you to visit a church instead of a brothel and trade the pox for piety."

Many years after the events recorded here, the retired Arizona lawman Chester Monroe said that the Old Man of the Mountain had outlived his eyes, that they'd died decades before his demise, and the gaze Hammer turned on Captain Davies gave truth to that statement.

"Sun Yu. Where can I find him?" Hammer said again.

And Davies, a religious man after his own fashion, met that stare and caught a glimpse of hell. "Take the main road out of the International Settlement and after a mile you'll come on the gravel track that leads to the *siheyuan* of Sun Yu." And unsaid: *And may God have mercy on your soul.*

Captain Davies watched Jacob Hammer as he walked along the dock toward the business district, his first mate's stride fast and purposeful. He nodded to himself, reaching a decision. There was no doubt that Mr. Hammer would eventually leave Shanghai . . . but it would not be on the good ship *Rochester.*

CHAPTER SIX

Jacob Hammer left the path and the plane trees behind and stepped through the open gate to the entrance to the building ahead of him. Since the Ming dynasty, most Chinese mansions faced south and Sun Yu's was no exception, a structure with a red-tiled roof, its façade decorated with ornate carvings of dragons and other mythical beasts.

Hammer walked into the entrance and was stopped by a screen wall of rust-colored brick. Passage beyond was limited to a corner opening that led into a single small courtyard. Larger, wealthier houses had three or four, lined up one behind the other, each entered by a gate, but since Sun Yu's mansion had only one, it suggested that for all his wealth the crime lord lived modestly.

The main house in front of Hammer was almost identical to the entrance structure but more ornate. It had a carved wooden door, painted red, and he walked in that direction, only to halt in his tracks when a harsh yell came from a columned porch on his right. Four Chinese men rushed toward him, their faces tight and hostile. Each carried a British .702 Lee-Enfield rifled musket and had a *dao,* the deadly Chinese saber, belted at his waist.

The Chinese angrily jabbered to Hammer in a language he did not understand, but they didn't seem too threatening until they searched him and found the .36 Navy Colt tucked into his waistband at the small of his back, hidden by his peacoat. Immediately the situation turned dangerous when one of the Chinese slammed his musket butt into Hammer's chest and, caught off guard, the big white man stumbled and fell on his back.

Hammer saw a glint of steel as a sword slicked from its scabbard and he scrambled to his feet, ready to fight for his life.

Then the bull bellow of a man's voice froze everyone in place.

A massive white man wearing a cream-colored suit and pants, a wide-brimmed straw hat on his great nail keg of a head, bullied his way between Hammer and his assailants. The big man yelled something in Chinese and one of the guards answered him, jabbing his finger at the Colt, and then backed away. His blue eyes blazing, the man turned on Hammer and in a heavy German accent said, "Why did you bring a pistol into the home of Sun Yu, *mein Herr? Bist du verrückt?* Are you insane?"

Hammer's anger flared. "I always carry a gun. Who the hell are you?"

"My name is Herman Wegberg. I am the Honorable Sun Yu's personal secretary."

Hammer gave the German a once-over. The man was as tall as Hammer, but at least fifty pounds heavier, little of it fat. Fists, sunburned and covered in blond hair, hung as big as hams at his side and above his clipped military mustache was a flattened nose that had been broken many times and never reset. A dueling scar stood out as a livid white gash against his brick-red left cheek and his eyes were small and slightly protuberant, like those of an intelligent pig. Hammer had been around powerful, dangerous men all his life and he now marked down Wegberg as one of them. It was obvious the man had been hired for his muscle, not his secretarial skills.

What Jacob Hammer didn't know then, but would learn later, was that Herman Wegberg was an emotionless killer who had beaten eight men to death with his fists, all on the orders of Sun Yu, and he stood ready to murder another eight if his master so desired.

The big German spoke again. "What is your name and what is your business with the lord Sun Yu?"

"My name is Jacob Hammer and my business with Sun Yu is my own."

"You have an impudent tongue, *mein Herr.*"

"You asked and I told you."

"See you keep a tight rein on your tongue if and when you speak with Sun Yu, or he will have it cut from your head. By your accent, you are an American?"

"Yes, I am."

"Good. Sun Yu has no love for the British."

"Then I can see him?"

"Perhaps. I will ask if he wishes to speak with you. If he does not, then you will leave this house and never come back. Do you understand?"

"Perfectly."

"Then wait here. The Chinese will do you no harm."

Before Hammer could comment, Wegberg turned on his heel and walked into the house. He was gone for several minutes and then stood at the door and beckoned Hammer to come.

"Before we go inside, I remind you again to watch your manners," the German said. "Sun Yu is a great lord and is not to be insulted. Be a dummkopf, *mein Herr,* and you could lose your head."

Hammer smiled. "I'll be most respectful."

"See you are," Wegberg said. "Your life depends on it, American."

The German led Hammer through a dark hallway dedicated to Sun Yu's ancestors, dominated by an ornate shrine where small pots of incense burned. An open doorway led from the hall to the crime lord's audience chamber. After the strong sunlight of the courtyard, Hammer's eyes had not adjusted to the room's darkness and he stopped, uncertain of what to do next.

Beside him, Wegberg's voice fell to an urgent whisper. "Kowtow, damn you. Do as I do."

The big man dropped to his knees and touched the ground with his forehead. It was a craven, submissive gesture that didn't sit well with Hammer, but he needed the Chinese and had no choice but to follow suit.

"Rise now," the German said. "Stay where you are and under no circumstance approach Sun Yu."

Hammer's eyes adjusted to the darkness. He was in a large room, unfurnished but for a raised dais where the Chinese man sat in a high-backed, thronelike chair. Sun Yu wore Chinese garb, but his *changshan,* the traditional long tunic, was plain brown in color and bore no embroidered decoration. Hammer had half expected to meet an older man, but to his surprise Sun Yu looked to be in his early forties, a slender man with wide shoulders, the thin, straight hair that fell over his shoulders still black as ink. His eyes were dark, widely spaced and, unusual for a rich Chinese, he wore no beard or mustache. The man's slim, long-fingered hand waved Wegberg forward.

The German stepped to the dais, spoke to Sun Yu in Chinese and then showed him Hammer's Colt. After Wegberg stopped talking, he beckoned to Hammer that he should come to the dais. "Bow," he said.

Hammer bowed from the waist and then waited while Sun Yu's black eyes studied him. After what seemed an age, the Chinese finally said in good English, "Why do you wish to kill me?"

Hammer said, "I have no wish to kill you."

"Lord Yu," Wegberg said.

"Then why did you bring a revolver?"

"I forgot I had it, Lord Yu."

"You are an American?"

"Yes, Lord Yu."

"Then if you did not come into my home to kill me, what was your purpose? Do you wish to rob me?"

"No, I came to seek the potion that gives eternal life."

The Chinese was silent for a while and then said, "A man's life is a candle in the wind or hoarfrost on the tiles. It is short. That was ordained by the gods many, many years ago."

"I was told that the potion can make a man's life last forever, Lord Yu."

"American, this potion of which you speak, if I were to give it to you, what will you give me in return?"

"A hundred English pounds."

Sun Yu smiled, as though he thought this an impudence. "I have so many English pounds and German marks and American dollars that on cold nights my servants light the braziers with them. Nor do I lack for gold and silver."

"Then what can I offer you in return?" Hammer said.

"A favor," Sun Yu said. "That is how much of the business is conducted in Shanghai. I do you a favor, you do one for me in return."

"Name it, Lord Yu."

"Suppose I asked you to put your revolver to good use, what would you say?"

"I would say . . . put me to the test."

"You would do me a favor?"

"Anything you ask."

"Very well, I will ask it. On the eastern shore of the Huangpu River there is a dyer's shop owned by a man named Zhang Tao. His wife and son, whose names are unimportant, work with him. I loaned this man the money to start his cloth-dyeing business and it now returns a fine profit, but Zhang Tao refuses to repay me and has beaten and cursed my agents, telling them that the interest is too high. It is very vexing. So, American, what would you do with such a man?"

Hammer smiled. "Seize his business, Lord Yu."

The Chinese spread his expressive hands. "Yes, I can do that but it would be too light a punishment. Many people owe me money and they must be taught a lesson before Zhang Tao's open defiance can bring out a horde of devils."

Sun Yu fell silent and Wegberg said to Hammer, "Ask the lord Yu what service you can provide that will settle this matter."

Hammer figured that the Chinese man heard this as well as he did, but Sun Yu

54

remained silent. "What service can I provide that will settle this matter?" he said.

"It can be resolved simply," Sun Yu said. "You will eliminate Zhang Tao and his wife and son without mercy. Let there be no surrender. One cannot pull a white cloth from a dyeing vat."

"And when I do, what then?"

"Then we will talk again." Sun Yu rubbed his temples. "Now I grow weary and must let my women tend to me. You are dismissed."

Once out again in the sunny courtyard Wegberg said, "I will tell you how to reach the shop of Zhang Tao. Do this task well and you will be richly rewarded."

"Rewarded with the potion of eternal life?"

"This, I do not know," the German said. "But a word of warning, American. Fail, and before you breathe your last you'll die a hundred deaths each more painful than the one that went before."

"I won't fail," Hammer said. "Now, give me back my pistol."

Jacob Hammer did not fail. But his quest for eternal life was doomed to failure.

"You have done well, American. Zhang Tao and his wife and son are dead, and even my women rejoice. But there is no potion of eternal life," Sun Yu said. "Even the emperor, though fabulously rich, cannot buy one extra year. But the remedy for dying is living well. If you will be my retainer for two years I can teach you how to cram a thousand lifetimes into one life. The secret is wealth and power and with me you will learn how to acquire them both."

It was then that Hammer made a decision that would change his life forever. In exchange for his expertise as a conscienceless paid assassin, he learned from Sun Yu how to finance, organize and run a criminal empire and how to use money, drugs and women to control men. In two years Hammer killed nineteen people for the Chinese crime lord, one of them Herman Wegberg, whose freelance protection racket had not been sanctioned by Sun Yu. The German was eating dinner when Hammer shot him, and it amused him to stuff a bratwurst sausage into the big man's mouth for the police to find.

After his criminal apprenticeship was over, in the summer of 1857, Jacob Hammer set sail for the United States, eager to put into practice what he had learned.

"Remember," Sun Yu told him before he left for the dock, "make yourself impregnable. Remain in your stronghold, be it in the city or the country, but let your influence spread far and wide. And always bear this in mind, no matter how upright and honorable he may be, the man does not live who cannot be bought."

In the years that followed as Jacob Hammer grew in riches and power, he still smarted at being denied eternal life, but he turned his disappointment into a joke and called himself the Old Man of the Mountain. His dark, malevolent shadow spread over the entire nation, from San Francisco's Barbary Coast in the west to New York in the east. His criminal tentacles spread far and wide; opium, prostitution, gambling, protection, extortion, robbery and murder for hire all came under his sway and with two hundred traveling gunmen on his payroll no one dared stand in his way . . .

That was until the Old Man crossed paths with a saddle tramp in a buckskin shirt with no name of his own and a half-breed former army scout who knew not whether he was an Indian or an Irishman. Sam Flintlock and O'Hara were an unlikely pair to take on a mighty empire that reveled in its evilness, and later the reason President Theodore Roosevelt would give for their audacity was, "Those boys didn't have a lick of sense between them and they just didn't know any better. But, by God, sir, they had sand."

CHAPTER SEVEN

"Damn it all, Sammy, I'm getting scared," O'Hara said. "I know we won't starve to death, because dying of thirst comes a lot sooner."

"If the horses don't get water soon they won't last much longer," Sam Flintlock said through cracked lips. He drew rein. "One thing is for sure, my ma didn't come this way."

"Just figured that out, huh?" O'Hara said.

"We're on what they call a wild-goose chase," Flintlock said.

"Who told you she came this way?"

"Well, Barnabas, for one. He said she was headed west."

"And you believe Barnabas?"

"Some of the time."

"He works for the Prince of Liars."

"I know. I wish he would stay dead and keep away from me."

"Maybe once you find your mother he'll leave."

"Yeah, maybe." As was his habit, Flintlock raised his nose and tested the wind. "What do I smell?" he said.

"Probably me," O'Hara said.

"No. It's bacon. O'Hara, somebody is frying bacon."

O'Hara sniffed. "Hell, Sammy, you could be right."

"Can you follow it?"

"Follow what?"

"The smell."

"Hell, I don't know."

"I thought you were a half Indian."

"Look at my nose. It's an Irishman's nose."

Flintlock shook his head. "You're a sore disappointment to me, O'Hara." Then, pointing to the northeast. "The smell is faint, but it's coming from that direction. I'm sure of it."

"Well, we'll follow your nose, Sam." He regarded Flintlock's great beak. "I guess that means we got a long ways to travel."

Flintlock and O'Hara crossed rugged, broken county five miles north of Balakai Mesa and then looped south around the 7,500-foot bulk of Black Mountain. The frying bacon smell faded quickly, but as they crossed a dry wash they were rewarded by a thin column of smoke that rose straight as a string from a small rock cabin nestled at the base of a sandstone bluff.

Flintlock drew rein. "This looks promising," he said. "Maybe they'll feed us and let us water our horses."

"I don't see a well," O'Hara said. He pointed. "But I do see that."

Flintlock looked and saw what O'Hara saw, a crudely lettered wooden sign that read:

I GOT A BIG 50 POINTED RITE AT
YORE HED SHOOTIN GOIN ON
AROUND HERE

And under that:

~ ABE MOORE, ESQ.

"That notice doesn't apply to us," Flintlock said. "We're honest travelers . . . well, fairly honest, depending on circumstances."

"Go right ahead, Sam," O'Hara said. "I'll follow you."

"How does this look?" Flintlock said.

"How does what look?"

"My friendly, going-to-meet-kinfolk grin."

61

"You look like the fox that just ate the chicken."

"O'Hara, you're a discouraging man. Watch how it's done."

Flintlock kneed his horse forward a few yards and then drew rein. He pasted his grin back in place and raised his right hand. "Howdy!" he called out.

The answering .50 caliber bullet came close to clipping the nail of Flintlock's middle finger, a miss near enough that he dropped his hand as though it had just been stung by a hornet.

"Here!" he yelled. "That ain't true-blue."

Then a harsh male voice from the partially opened cabin door. "State your intentions or suffer the consequences. By nature, I'm a shootin' man."

Flintlock was about to raise his hand again but decided against it. His nails were trimmed close enough. Instead, he motioned to O'Hara and said, "Me and him, we're honest travelers seeking to water our horses and we could use a bit of grub if you have any sich to spare."

"You two don't look like honest men to me, a pair of desperadoes more like."

The cabin door opened and a graying man with a thin, sensitive face, wearing knee-high boots, baggy pants and a collarless shirt stepped outside, a scattergun in his hands.

"Come closer so I can take a look at ye," he said.

Flintlock beckoned to O'Hara and the two rode forward. When they were twenty yards from the gray-haired man he motioned with the shotgun that they were close enough.

"You boys come up through Pitchfork Pass?" he said.

"Never heard of it," Flintlock said, smiling, determined to be sociable.

"Maybe you have, maybe you haven't. That remains to be seen," the man said. "Did he send you?"

"He, who?" This from O'Hara, who tended to like or dislike people on sight. He didn't like the man with the scattergun.

"The Old Man of the Mountain, that's who. Don't tell me you haven't heard of him, either."

"We've heard of him," Flintlock said. "Lawman we met told us to steer clear of him."

"Then he gave you fair warning."

"Are you him?" O'Hara said.

"Hell, no." The man jerked a thumb over his shoulder at his cabin. "If I was, would I be living in a hovel?"

"I don't know. Would you?" O'Hara said.

"No, I wouldn't. They say the Old Man is the richest ranny in the country, richer than John Jacob Astor or William Henry Vanderbilt or all the other robber barons ever was. He lives like a king, no, like an emperor, south of here in Balakai Mesa."

"Why did you think we work for the Old Man?" Flintlock said.

"Because he wants my cabin . . . or what's in it."

"What's in it?" Flintlock said.

"Something more precious than all the gold in the world. Well, to me, at least." The man stared at Flintlock and then wiggled his forefinger at his own throat. "What the hell you got there?"

"It's a thunderbird."

"Tattoo?"

"Yeah, it's a tattoo. An Assiniboine woman did it when I was a younker."

"Mister, she didn't do you any favors."

"Seems like a lot of folks say that," Flintlock said.

The gray-haired man was silent for a while, then said, "I guess you pair are all right. Now I study on it, you're too raggedy assed to be the Old Man's gunmen anyhow. Name's Tom Smith. You might not think it, but I'm a poet. Now light and set. There's a rock spring behind the cabin where I keep

64

my dogcart and mule. You can water your horses and there's a patch of graze nearby. It isn't much, and your animals will have to share with the mule, but in this country any water and grass is better than none at all. When you're done, come back around to the front of the cabin."

The rock spring was a thin trickle of water that fell from a narrow fissure in the bluff and splashed into a sandstone basin. The supply was meager, but the horses drank their fill and there was enough left for Flintlock and O'Hara to slake their thirst and fill their canteens. Range grass, what little there was, covered about two acres of flat ground and competed for growing space with a few scrub oaks. If the horses thought the vegetation sparse and the mule unfriendly, they didn't let it show and began to graze as Flintlock and O'Hara left them and stepped to the front of the cabin.

What was that?

Flintlock stopped in his tracks as he reached the door. He thought he'd seen a flash of light among the rocks to the south. It was there for a moment and then gone.

O'Hara's gaze swept the burning distances of the shimmering landscape, no rock formation, ridge or stand of brush escaping his scrutiny. He saw no movement and said, "Sam, what did you see?"

Flintlock shrugged. "Nothing. Just a trick of the light."

O'Hara might have questioned more, but the cabin door swung open and Tom Smith stepped outside. "Come on in, boys," he said.

Flintlock turned . . . and his eyes almost jumped out of his head.

CHAPTER EIGHT

A girl stood beside Tom Smith, and Sam Flintlock took her to be about seventeen, more beautiful than any woman he had ever seen or remembered. The girl shaded her eyes against the sun and studied Flintlock, her gaze openly curious but not bold. The long hair that cascaded over her shoulders gleamed in the light like molten gold and her hazel eyes were the kind that would change from amber to emerald green, depending on her mood and desires. She wore a yellow blouse with a high collar and wide sleeves buttoned at the wrists and her green skirt was flounced, fuller at the bottom to accommodate a hoop if she wanted. The hem of the skirt was ankle high, revealing bare, dainty and dusty feet, and a wide-brimmed straw hat, hurriedly dropped on top of her head, completed her outfit.

Flintlock was stunned that beauty like hers could exist in such a wilderness, like

67

finding a perfect pink rose in a desert.

"This is my daughter, Louise," Smith said. "Louise, say howdy to the gentlemen."

"Welcome to our home," the girl said. She smiled.

To Sam Flintlock those four words sounded as though they had been set to a melody . . . accompanied by a smile so dazzling it set the sun to shame. His heart sinking, he was all too aware of what the girl saw when she looked at him. He was forty-four that summer, not forty as he claimed, a stocky man of medium height, who was as rough as a cob. A shock of unruly black hair showed under his battered straw hat and his eyes, gray as a sea mist, were deep set under shaggy, untrimmed eyebrows. Under his great, Roman nose his mustache was full, in the dragoon style made fashionable by the Texas Rangers. What Louise Smith didn't see was that Flintlock was tough, enduring, raised to be hard by hard-edged men. But there was no cruelty in him and he had much honesty of tongue and a quick, wry sense of humor. He'd killed fifteen men, three as a cow town lawman, a career that had lasted only a single violent year, the remainder since he'd turned bounty hunter. None of those dead men disturbed his sleep o' nights, and the only ghost he ever saw was that of villainous old Barnabas.

Flintlock, sounding hoarse, said, "Thankee, young lady. It's a real pleasure to be here." Then, remembering his manners. "And I'm sure my friend O'Hara agrees."

The trouble was that Flintlock had grown used to O'Hara. He'd forgotten that to others the breed looked like an Apache buck, a mirror image of the warriors who'd played hob in the Arizona Territory just a couple of years before.

A wisp of an uncertain smile touched Louise's lips, but O'Hara saved the awkward situation when he gave a little bow and said, "Pleased to meet you, Miss Smith."

The girl found her tongue. "You are most welcome, Mr. O'Hara."

"Well, let's get inside out of the sun," Tom Smith said. He smiled. "You, too, Mr. O'Hara."

Sam Flintlock used a piece of bread to sop up the last of the gravy on his plate, chewed, sighed his appreciation for his full belly and then said, "So that's why we're here, me and O'Hara. I was led to believe my ma was headed this way. Now I find it hard to figure why she would."

Tom Smith and his daughter exchanged glances, and then Louise said, "A woman

69

did pass this way and not too long ago."

Suddenly interested, Flintlock sat forward in his chair. "Did she say why she was here?"

"Yes, but she swore us to secrecy," Tom Smith said.

"Did she tell you her name?"

"Miss Brown."

Flintlock's disappointment showed. "That was all, just Miss Brown?"

"It wasn't her real name," Louise said.

"Did she say her real name?"

"No. She didn't."

"How old was this woman?" O'Hara said.

Tom Smith answered. "Late fifties, I'd say. But she looked wonderful, very slim and, I say this as a poet, still quite beautiful."

O'Hara looked at Flintlock. "It could be her, Sam. How old was your ma when she had you?"

"About Louise's age," Flintlock said.

"Then she'd be in her fifties by now," O'Hara said. "It adds up."

"Tom, I know she swore you to secrecy, but I think she could be Ma. Why was she here?"

Smith and his daughter looked uncomfortable, and the girl said, "Can I tell him, Pa?"

"I'll tell him, Louise," Smith said. "Miss Brown was a Pinkerton agent."

Flintlock's jaw dropped. "My ma . . . a Pink?"

Smith smiled. "The woman who rested here for a couple of days worked for the Pinkertons, but we don't know that she was your mother."

"What was a Pinkerton, and a woman at that, doing here?"

"Risking her life," Louise said. "She'd been hurt by a bullet, just a flesh wound on her right shoulder, but it caused her some pain and we took care of her for a while."

Tom Smith read the shocked expression on Flintlock's face and said, "A couple of outlaws tried to waylay her in a dry wash a few miles east of here. Miss Brown said she killed one and wounded the other and he took flight."

Flintlock's brow creased in thought and then he said, "Did the woman say where she'd learned to shoot like that?"

"Yes, she did," Louise said. "Miss Brown wasn't keen to talk about herself."

"Secretive, you might say," Tom Smith said.

Louise said, "But she did say her father was a mountain man and he taught her to shoot as soon as she could hold a rifle."

Flintlock's voice broke in his throat as he said, "Was her father's name Barnabas?"

"She didn't say," Smith said. "As I told you, she was very tight-lipped about her past." He smiled. "I guess all Pinkerton agents are like that."

"I think Miss Brown is my mother. In fact, I'm sure of it," Flintlock said. "Why was she here? Did she tell you?"

Again, Smith looked uncomfortable, and then he said, "It was all to do with the Old Man of the Mountain."

"Hell, that name keeps coming up," Flintlock said.

"And no wonder, he's the richest, most powerful man in the Territory, if not the entire country. The situation is dire enough that President Arthur called in the Pinkertons," Tom Smith said. "Miss Brown decided she could trust us enough to tell us that she and seven other agents were ordered to track the money trails in and out of Balakai Mesa. She said that the Old Man's revenues come in from his criminal activities in two dozen major cities and then goes back out again."

"Out to where?" O'Hara said.

"Some of it to pay his hundreds of employees, everybody from accounting clerks to opium dealers to hired toughs, but a large part goes to line the pockets of the crooked politicians who see to it that the Old Man stays in business. He grew richer after the Apaches were defeated and the railroads reached Flagstaff and Kingman and made it easier for his agents to travel across the country. Without the trains, the Old Man would be unable to conduct his affairs from his haven in the Arizona Territory."

Flintlock said, "And how was my ma, I mean Miss Brown, involved in all this?"

"Of the seven male agents, four were murdered, two disappeared and one was badly crippled when he was beaten by a gang of toughs in Flagstaff. Miss Brown was ordered to Flagstaff to talk to the injured man and then things took a strange turn." Smith lit his pipe before he turned to his daughter and said, "Louise, that night before bed Miss Brown told you what happened in Flagstaff. You can tell it better than me."

The girl looked down and smoothed her skirt over her shapely thighs and when she raised her head again her beautiful, flirtatious eyes were serious.

"Miss Brown said the Pinkerton agent was at death's door and his face was so badly smashed by boots and clubs he could hardly speak," Louise said. "But he managed to whisper the name Molly Meadowlark, and died a few minutes later. I remember the name because it was so unusual. Miss Brown made inquiries and discovered that Molly Meadowlark worked as a prostitute at a house of ill repute and she had a story to tell."

The girl fell silent, marshaling her thoughts, remembering . . .

Flintlock's place at the table gave him a view through the cabin's only window. In the distance, he saw a cloud of dust rise, still far off, two riders, maybe three. The sky was a mass of broken cloud, and thunder rumbled among the canyons to the south. Suddenly Flintlock felt uneasy, as though something was about to happen, but what it might be he couldn't imagine . . . unless the horsemen rode closer and then all bets were off.

Louise was talking again, refocusing Flintlock's attention.

". . . he told her he was headed back north to the mesa country and —"

"Who was he?" Flintlock asked. "Sorry, I wasn't listening."

Tom Smith smiled. "Watching the dust, huh? I'm keeping an eye on it myself."

"I reckon two or three riders," Flintlock said.

"Seems like. It could be tinpans, a few of them hereabouts, always hunting in the washes for the motherlode and never finding it."

"Or the Old Man's gunmen," Flintlock said.

"Not like them to come this far north of the Balakai, but stranger things have happened." Smith smiled when he said that, but lines of concern showed on his face.

"Is anyone listening?" Louise said, frowning.

"Yes, I'm listening," Flintlock said. "Please, go on."

"Well, one of Molly Meadowlark's . . . ah . . . customers told her his name was Maxwell St. John and he'd just got back from a week's stay in Carson City. He said he was headed back to the mesa country where he'd pick up money and go back on the road, probably east this time. 'I work for the world's richest businessman and he treats me right,' the man said."

"What manner of man was he?" Flintlock said. "The customer, I mean."

"Miss Meadowlark told Miss Brown that Max St. John had a lot of money to spend, enjoyed gambling and carried a Colt's revolver in a leather-lined pocket sewn into his frock coat," Louise said. "When he got drunk, he said he'd killed seven men with the revolver and he let Miss Meadowlark

75

touch it. That's all Miss Brown told me about him."

"Sounds like a hired gun to me," Flintlock said.

O'Hara said, "I recollect a 4th Cavalry corporal out of McAllen, Texas, by the name of Maxwell St. John. I don't know anything about him, though."

"It's an unusual enough name, so it's probably the same man," Flintlock said. "I guess he swapped a dirty blue shirt for a frock coat."

Louise said, "When St. John rode out the next morning he was accompanied by another man, and Miss Brown went after them," Louise said. "She tried to arrest them but they fled and she later got into a running gunfight with those two and killed one of them."

Flintlock smiled. "Yup, sounds like she could be my ma, all right."

O'Hara nodded. "I think we're finally on the right track, Sam."

Tom Smith said nothing. He stood and stared out the window. He crossed the floor, picked up his shotgun and said, "Louise, you stay inside." His voice sounded hollow, his face showing the sudden strain he was under.

Flintlock turned and looked out the window. Three riders had just uprooted the shooting sign, placed there by a previous occupant of the cabin, not Smith, and had remounted. Now they rode toward the cabin at a walk, three gun-belted men on blood horses, Winchesters under their knees, riding with the easy self-assurance of fighting men who were sudden and dangerous and knew it.

Smith opened the door and then turned. "Sam, you and O'Hara stay inside. I reckon this is about me and Louise and you've no call to get involved. It's not your fight."

Smith stepped outside, the shotgun in the crook of his left arm.

Flintlock looked to the riders, to Smith, and back again, not liking the signs that were there to be read plain. If this confrontation came down to a shootout, Smith was outclassed in every way a decent but untrained man could be when faced with three seasoned, hard-faced gunmen who'd no doubt killed more than their share.

Ignoring Smith's order to stay inside, Flintlock stepped through the doorway, and O'Hara took up a position on his left.

For long moments, no one moved and there was no sound but for the chime of a bit as a horse tossed its head. The three gunmen slowly took measure of Flintlock and

O'Hara, found them wanting, and dismissed them. One of the three, a big redhead with a hard-boned face and savage eyes, untied a burlap sack from his saddle horn and then tossed the bag at Smith's feet. The heavy sack made a chinking noise when it hit the ground.

The redhead said, his tone clipped and arrogant, "There's a hundred double eagles in there for the girl. Bring her out and we'll be gone."

Smith's anger flared. "Tell whoever sent you that my daughter is not for sale. Now take your money and go."

The man with the red hair and vicious eyes shook his head. "I'm not here to bandy words with a damned squatter." He turned to the man beside him. "Steve, go get her and tell her to pack whatever women's fixin's she needs."

The rider called Steve, a tall, lean man with a thick mane of yellow hair, was about to swing out of his silver-studded saddle when Flintlock's voice stopped him, freezing him in place.

"I wouldn't do that, Steve." Flintlock's Colt was in his hand and his expression was none too friendly. "From here, I can shoot you right out of that fancy saddle."

The redhead looked at Flintlock as though

seeing him for the first time. "What the hell are you?" he said.

"Your death, if'n you choose that path."

"Big-talking man, ain't you?"

"Nope. I'm just saying things as I see them."

"Ragamuffin man, that's what you are. What's that beside you?"

"An Injun."

"He's a breed."

"A rare breed, the kind that's a hundred different kinds of hell in a gunfight."

The redhead spat over the side of his horse. "Mister, you're all talk. Steve, do what I told you, bring the slut out here."

Steve stayed where he was, his shoulders stiff and tense. "Charlie, he'll plug me for sure. I can see it in his eyes."

The redhead's anger blazed. "You damned yellow-belly, I'll do it myself."

Then Charlie took Flintlock and everyone else by surprise.

He hollered a rebel yell, slammed his roweled spurs into his horse's flanks and drew as the startled animal reared and hurled itself forward. Like a thrown lance, Charlie aimed his speeding mount straight at Flintlock.

Then, a moment of dusty, hell-firing chaos.

Flintlock snapped off a fast shot. A miss. He was aware of O'Hara firing. Charlie's horse hit Flintlock a glancing blow that knocked him on his back. He looked up, saw the redhead lean from his bucking mount and draw a bead on him . . . and in that split second Flintlock knew he was a dead man.

But he was not destined to die that day.

A moment of time contracted into a single heartbeat as a startling fan of blood haloed around Charlie's head, followed by the distant report of a rifle. The big redhead fell out of the saddle and crashed onto the ground just feet away from Flintlock, the front of his head missing a chunk of bone.

Flintlock jumped to his feet and took stock of his surroundings. The man called Steve was sprawled in the dirt, a victim of O'Hara's gun. The remaining rider, big and bearded, sat his saddle, his face ashen. His arms were raised and he desperately clawed for handfuls of sky.

"I'm out of this!" the man yelled. "Let me be."

Flintlock, his narrow brush with death stoking his anger, thought about drilling the son of a bitch but Tom Smith's urgent voice stopped him.

"No, Sam! He's done. He's surrendered."

It took a while as Flintlock battled his baser instincts, but finally he forced himself to relax and holstered his gun. A few quick steps took him to the bearded man's horse and he reached up and hauled the gunman out of the saddle by his belt. Flintlock shoved the man against the flank of his mount, grabbed him by the shirtfront and slammed a fist into his belly. All the breath hissed out of the gunman, and Flintlock hit him again, a looping right to the chin that dropped him to his knees. His blood up, still angry at letting the redhead outsmart him, he dragged the bearded man to his feet and backhanded him, a brutal slap that buckled the man's knees. Flintlock hauled the gunman erect and, almost nose to nose with the man, he said, "Who sent you here?"

"Sam, let him alone. We know who sent him here." This from Tom Smith, who stood at Flintlock's shoulder. He pushed in between Flintlock and the gunman, allowing him to drop to the ground. "The Old Man of the Mountain sent him."

Flintlock blinked, calming down now. "He wants your daughter?"

"Yes, he wants a bride," Smith said.

Louise opened the door and stepped outside, walking through the dust cloud that still hung in the air like ragged burlap. She overheard what her father had told Flintlock and said, "Pa, I'd kill myself before I'd become that monster's wife."

Smith smiled reassurance. "It won't come to that. We're leaving this place and going back East. I've taught you all I can, Louise, and it's time you started on a proper education."

The girl looked crestfallen. "But, Pa, you love it here and your poetry . . ."

"I can still write poetry in Boston. Besides, that's where my publisher is."

Flintlock suddenly felt empty, washed out, the stress of the gunfight and his close call rebounding on him. Who had fired the rifle shot that killed the redhead? He'd find out later. Right now, he had a task to perform.

He picked up the money sack from the ground and said to the bearded gunman, "Git on your hoss." Unsteadily, the man climbed into the saddle and Flintlock said, "Tell the Old Man of the Mountain that I'm keeping his money. Now see you get my name right. Tell him Sam Flintlock — got that? — Sam Flintlock took it and he's not giving it back, not now, not ever. You understand what I'm saying?"

Blood trickling down his chin from a split lip, the man said, "I'll remember. And you remember this day. Mister, you've just signed your death warrant."

He swung away and set spurs to his horse.

Flintlock watched the man until he was out of sight and then stepped to Louise. He held out the money sack and said, "This will help pay for your education back in Boston town."

The girl shook her head. "I don't want it, Sam. It's blood money."

Flintlock nodded. "Yes, it is, and that's why I'm giving it to you. You will put it to good, honest use." He smiled. "Louise, you're beautiful and you're smart. You'll make your mark one day and this money will help."

"Louise, we can't give it back," Tom Smith said. "I never thought I'd hear myself say this, but keep the money. As Sam says, it's yours now."

The girl nodded, but said nothing. She carried the sack to the door and then turned to her father and said, "Until now, I'd never seen a dead body before."

"The fight was of their choosing," Flintlock said. "They're not the kind of men I'd mourn over."

"I regret the death of any man," Smith said. His smile was slight, weak. "But perhaps some more than others."

"These two were fighting men," Flintlock

said. "They both knew that one day they'd meet a man faster on the draw, or just luckier, and they accepted that fact. Well, me and O'Hara got lucky. On this particular day that's how the dice rolled." Flintlock looked around him. "Speaking of O'Hara, where is he?"

Tom Smith said, pointing, "Look there, he's heading our way."

Flintlock watched O'Hara come, closing distance with the easy, graceful lope of an Apache warrior. "Where the hell have you been?" Flintlock said.

"Up on the ridge back there," O'Hara said. "That's where the shot came from that saved your life, Sam." He dropped an empty cartridge casing into Flintlock's hand. "It's a .44 from a Henry rifle." As Flintlock examined the shell, O'Hara said, "Saw boot prints up there on the ridge. They were made by a small man or a woman. My guess is a woman." He held up a small cigar butt. "She must have been looking down on us for quite a spell, long enough to smoke a cheroot before she made the shot that killed the redhead."

Flintlock's brow furrowed in thought, then, "Can't be my ma. She wouldn't smoke cheroots."

"I don't know what she did in the past,

84

but she sure as hell smokes them now,"
O'Hara said.

CHAPTER NINE

That night Flintlock and O'Hara dragged the two dead men away from the house as Tom Smith and his daughter prepared to leave at first light the following morning.

"Tom, those boys left rifles and pistols and two good horses that will take you fast and far," Flintlock said. "Fill your canteens and keep your guns close."

"What about you, Sam?" Smith said.

"O'Hara and me will hold on here at the cabin for a spell, see if my ma shows up."

"You're sure it was her up on the ridge?"

"Pretty sure. But O'Hara is convinced she's the one fired the shot that saved my life."

"I sure hope that's the case," Smith said.

"That makes two of us," Flintlock said.

Come first light Tom Smith and Louise mounted and headed east under a clear, lemon-colored sky. Before she left Louise kissed Flintlock on the cheek and thanked him for saving her, and Smith shook his and O'Hara's hand in turn. "If you're ever in Boston town . . ."

"We'll look you up. A famous poet shouldn't be hard to find."

Flintlock knew it would never happen but it was something to say, sincere but empty words to ease the parting and show confidence that father and daughter would survive the long and dangerous trail back to civilization.

Flintlock and O'Hara watched them go until they disappeared through a break in a sandstone bluff where scattered piñons grew.

"Think they'll make it?" O'Hara said.

"I'm worried about them. It's a long way to Boston town."

"I reckon Smith can give a good account of himself in a fight. It took sand to leave the city and live all the way out here."

"Louise spoke with my ma." Flintlock shook his head. "That's something I've never done, that I can remember anyway."

"Pretty girl, Sam."

"Uh-huh, she's all of that. Some nice young city feller will come a-courtin' and sweep her off her feet. They'll get married and have lots of young 'uns."

O'Hara grinned. "That's how it's gonna happen, huh?"

"Nope, that's how I hope it happens," Flintlock said, and O'Hara saw the concern in his eyes.

The morning, so bright with promise, gave way to a gray, overcast afternoon and the air held an ozone tang, the harbinger of a thunderstorm. Out in the rocky, sunbaked badlands nothing moved, but far in the distance almost invisible against darkening clouds a buzzard quartered the sky and scanned the ground below with eyesight so sharp it put the best French field glasses to shame.

Flintlock and O'Hara had carried out a pair of wooden chairs from the cabin and now sat outside, sharing a bottle of rye that Tom Smith, a reformed drunk, had bought but never opened.

"Maybe we should holler," O'Hara said.

"Holler what?" Flintlock said.

"Ma," O'Hara said. "Holler for your ma."

"It wouldn't do any good. She ain't planning to show."

"How do you know?"

"I just know."

"Well, maybe hollering for your ma wasn't such a good idea. The Old Man of the

Mountain might hear us."

"Hell, O'Hara, after we let one of his men go, don't you think he knows we're here?"

"Yeah, I'm sure he knows. But why hasn't he attacked us?"

"He's in no hurry. He figures we can't go anywhere without him knowing it."

"But we can. We'll light a shuck come dark," O'Hara said.

Flintlock took a swig from the bottle and then said, "O'Hara, why are we sitting out here?"

"Because we don't like to be confined by four walls, I guess."

"Do you realize that right now a couple of the Old Man's riflemen could be drawing a bead on us?"

"Maybe we should go back inside," O'Hara said.

"Now that's a crackerjack suggestion." Flintlock rose to his feet. "Bring your chair and the bottle."

But he never made it to the door.

A horse headed toward them at a dead run and on its back was the slumped figure of a rider. It was Tom Smith, and even at a distance Flintlock saw by the scarlet stains on his shirt and the shoulders of his horse that the man had been shot all to pieces.

■ ■ ■ ■

O'Hara ran out and grabbed the reins of Smith's mount, and Flintlock gently lowered the wounded man to the ground. Tom Smith was dying, but by superhuman effort he clung to life, determined to make his last words matter.

"They took her . . . took Louise . . . left me for dead." Smith's words came embedded in pained gasps. He grabbed the sleeve of Flintlock's buckskin shirt. "Save her, Sam . . . save her from the monster . . . Pitchfork Pass . . ."

Tom Smith coughed up blood and then death drew a line under the narrative of the man's life.

CHAPTER TEN

He dreamed his opium dreams of China.

For a while at least, he returned to the Bund, where he'd learned much of his criminal trade. For hundreds of years the famous waterfront, teeming, noisy and rich, had been regarded as the very living symbol of Shanghai. Then and now the Bund stretched for a mile from along the west bank of the Huangpu River from the Wai-baidu Bridge to the Nanpu Bridge, crowded with the architecture of a dozen foreign nations, including tall buildings in the Gothic style, the baroque, the Roman, the classical, the Renaissance and latterly, sprawling mansions that were a combination of British colonial and Chinese traditional.

Jacob Hammer, as he was then, graduated with honors from Bund University, a hard school that taught the lessons of murder, extortion, rape, robbery and, above all else, the opium trade, a drug to which he'd become addicted.

Hammer, now known as the Old Man of the Mountain, dreamed of good old days, the fat merchants he'd blackmailed, the men he'd robbed and often killed and the shrieking women he'd ravished, and he woke up, smiling, to the sound of a silver bell.

The Old Man let the pipe fall from his mouth and slowly sat up from his pallet on the floor. He felt groggy as he always did and felt grief for his lost heaven. But he would smoke again soon and drift into paradise on a sapphire cloud.

The Chinese girl with the bell stood with her head bowed, very still, silent. She was one of a pair the Old Man had bought from a Barbary Coast brothel. He used and abused them, reckoning their worth at exactly what he'd paid for them, five hundred dollars and a bull mastiff puppy.

His gray head in his hands, the Old Man didn't look up as he said, "Get the hell out of here. Send in Maxwell St. John."

A few moments later St. John, still limping from a leg wound he claimed he'd taken when he and another man got jumped by a thirty-strong Flagstaff posse, stepped inside and said, "You sent for me, boss?"

"Has my bride arrived?"

St. John, disgusted by the piss and vomit

stink of the opium den, shook his head. "Not yet, boss."

"Tell me when she gets here. I wish to welcome her with all the pomp and ceremony due a princess."

"Sure thing, boss."

"You can go now. No, wait."

"Yeah, boss?"

"Have one of the men take ten thousand dollars from the revenues that just arrived from Philadelphia and tell him to give it to the Detroit pimp . . . what the hell is his name?"

"Crayton Hanlon." St. John grinned. "You have a way with words, boss. *Revenues,* no less. I'd say *protection money.*"

"Yeah, you would. That's why I'm giving the orders and you're taking them." The Old Man laid his opium pipe aside and rose unsteadily to his feet. "I want our man to warn Hanlon that I expect a five hundred percent return on my money. Tell him to hire more whores and work them to death if he must, so long as I show a profit."

St. John, a Texan and a named shootist, had killed eight men. He was tall, wiry, with a neatly trimmed goatee and reckless eyes. He smiled and said, "I'll send Ryker Klein. He has a way of making two-bit hoodlums like Hanlon toe the line."

"Hanlon has six months. Make him aware of that. Tell him if he doesn't pay up in time, Klein will visit him again."

St. John waited a respectful length of time then said, "Will there be anything else, boss?"

"Yeah, send in the Chinese girls. Drag them out from under a man if need be. I want to be washed and dressed in my finest robes before I greet my bride."

Louise Smith was sure her father was dead. She'd seen him reel in the saddle as he was shot multiple times and then he'd fallen to the ground. She had no chance to go to him. Rough men grabbed the reins of her horse and she was led away, surrounded by a grinning rider who pushed up her skirt and made vile remarks about her legs and breasts.

Louise was numb, horrified by the death of her father. She rode in a daze, as if she weren't there, as though all this were happening to someone else, a girl she watched in a nightmare.

Her way led across a tableland of flat limestone rock, much cracked, bunchgrass and a few wildflowers struggling to grow in the crevices. A flight of crows flapped overhead, quarreling, filling the air with their irritable *caw-caw*s. The day was still bright but massive thunderheads, black and ominous, piled high to the south and growled their presence.

The rock bench gradually sloped to a natural grassy amphitheater about ten acres in extent, studded around its perimeter with mixed stands of juniper and piñon. Beyond the clearing rose the vast bulk of Balakai Mesa. Among its foothills was what at first glance appeared to be a crack in the rock, but the man riding beside Louise pointed in that direction and said, "That there is Pitchfork Pass, little lady." Then, grinning, "Where your groom awaits you." He winked at her. "If the Old Man of the Mountain can't satisfy you, look me up."

Louise, more scared than she'd ever been in her life, stared straight ahead and said nothing.

The pass was no more than a narrow arroyo with a rocky, brush-covered floor. On one side of the entrance was a V-shaped talus slope, on the other a sheer cliff that soared to about fifty feet above the flat. Unlit torches in iron brackets had been driven into both walls of the pass and to Louise's horror, at regular intervals yellowed skulls grinned from rock niches, all of them painted in the style of the Mexican

Day of the Dead sugar skulls. But these were not made of sugar; they belonged to men and woman who'd once been alive and had been decapitated on the maniacal whim of a madman for his amusement.

"Halt. Who goes there?"

Three riflemen blocked the passage ahead of Louise and the gunmen.

"It's me, Simpson."

"Come on ahead, Bill." Then, "You got the bride?"

"She's right here, Cade, and she says she's looking forward to her wedding night. Can't wait to sleep with her handsome groom."

"Hell, you expect me to believe that?"

Bill Simpson laughed. "No, I don't."

Thunder boomed and lightning scrawled across the sky like the signature of a demented god. Simpson looked up at a rectangle of black sky as rain ticked around him and said, "Hope this doesn't spoil the boss's wedding plans."

The man called Cade slimed Louise with his gaze, grinned and said, "It wouldn't spoil mine."

"Mine, neither," Simpson said, and behind him men laughed.

CHAPTER ELEVEN

Sam Flintlock stared moodily out the cabin window as thunder crashed and sizzling lightning bolts spiked across a land as stark, rugged and remote as the mountains of the moon.

"What do we do, O'Hara?" he said.

"Do about what?"

Without turning, Flintlock said, "God, you can be a vexation by times. I mean what do we do about Louise Smith?"

O'Hara had found rags and oil in the cabin, and now his Colt lay on the table in front of him in gleaming pieces. He inserted the cylinder back into the frame, pinned it in place and tested the hammer a few times before he said, "Where the hell is Pitchfork Pass?"

"I don't know."

"North or south of the mesa?"

"I don't know."

"Want me to clean and oil your pistol?"

"Yeah, it's hanging there by the door."

O'Hara rose, slid Flintlock's Colt from the holster and sat down again. He proceeded to remove the cylinder for cleaning and said, "This gun is dirty."

"It works."

"Much dirtier and it won't work."

Thunder banged and for an instant the gloomy cabin was illuminated by a searing flash of white light.

"Is my ma out there in this storm?" Flintlock said.

"Probably so," O'Hara said. He held up the Colt and stared down the barrel. He shook his head and made a *tut-tut* sound. "Dirty as a saddle tramp's horse blanket."

"I hope she found shelter," Flintlock said.

"There might be caves around. She could be in a cave."

"Why doesn't she come here?"

"I don't know. Maybe she doesn't trust us."

"I'm her son, for God's sake."

"She doesn't know that."

"Hell, O'Hara, she saved my life."

"She killed one of the Old Man's gunmen to protect Tom Smith and his daughter. Sammy, all she knew was that you were on the right side and could've been anybody."

"Where's Barnabas when I need him? If

anybody knows where Pitchfork Pass is, it would be him." Flintlock turned from the window. "After all this rain, do you think you still could track Louise?"

"You need Dan'l Boone."

"No, I need an Apache who scouted for the army. Instead I got you."

"I scouted for General Crook. One time he gave me a cigar and said I'd done a good job."

"Can we go to the spot where the girl was captured and track her from there?"

"After a rain and across rock? It won't be easy."

"Can we do it? You're the scout that got a big cigar. Can you do it?"

"I'll give it a try. Sam, don't let your gun get this dirty and dry again. At least give it some oil every now and then."

"I'll try to remember your good advice," Flintlock said. "By the way, the harness mule is gone."

O'Hara nodded. "Seen that. Must have wandered off."

"A mule will do that."

"That's been my experience. I got kicked by an army mule once, never trusted one since." Thunder bellowed, accompanied by a blinding glare of lightning. "Hell, that was close."

"Right above the cabin," Flintlock said. He again stepped restlessly to the window and looked outside through hammering rain. "I thought it never rained in the Arizona Territory," he said, irritated. Then, "What the hell?"

O'Hara's head snapped up. "What do you see?"

"A feller."

"What kind of feller?"

"A feller walking through the storm. Hell, now he's shooting."

That last was followed by the rapid, flat reports of a Winchester rifle.

O'Hara jumped to his feet. "Is he shooting at us?"

"If he is, he's missing badly."

"It ain't a woman, is it?"

"I can't tell from here. No, he's a feller, wearing oilskins and one of them plug hats. Hell, he's coming this way at a run."

"Open the door, Sam."

"You sure? He might be shooting at my ma."

"More likely he met up with some of the Old Man's gunmen."

"If he is, he's putting a heap of git between him and them."

Flintlock swung the door open. A bullet immediately splintered wood from the jamb to his right, and a second and then a third zipped into the cabin like angry hornets. O'Hara picked himself off the floor and stood beside Flintlock. He yelled to the running man, "Move your ass!"

"Never heard an Apache say that," Flintlock said.

"That was the Irishman in me talking," O'Hara said.

The runner finally reached the door and stumbled inside, bringing with him a flurry of rainwater and a peal of thunder.

"Son of a bitch killed my mare."

A woman's voice.

O'Hara thumbed off a couple of shots, waited, and when there was no answering fire, closed the door. Then he turned and said, "We took you for a feller, maybe a sailorman."

"Who did?" the woman said.

"Him," O'Hara said, nodding at Flintlock.

The woman removed her plug hat, revealing a mane of pinned-up blond hair. "All right, Geronimo, tell him I'm a woman."

"She's a woman, Sam," O'Hara said. "And my name is O'Hara."

"Could've fooled me," the woman said. She pushed O'Hara aside, stepped to the door and opened it a crack, looked around, and then shoved it wider.

"He's gone," she said. "I'm good with a rifle, but I didn't even scratch the dirty, no-good louse."

The woman shut the door again and said, "Name's Bridie O'Toole. I'm a Pinkerton detective and new to these parts." She unbuttoned her oilskin and handed it, her Winchester and field glasses to O'Hara. "Here, Sitting Bull, put these away."

"O'Hara," O'Hara said. "I'm part Apache, part Irish."

"What part of you is Irish?"

O'Hara spread a palm at his waist and swept downward. "This part."

"It figures. That's an Irishman's favorite part as well."

Bridie O'Toole was a petite, slender woman who looked to be in her mid-twenties. She wore a high-collared blouse, a long, canvas skirt and high-heeled, lace-up boots and was armed with a Smith & Wesson .44 in a cross-draw holster. She was saved from plainness by beautiful brown eyes and a wide, expressive mouth that seemed used to smiling.

The woman looked around the cabin, then stepped to the shelf above the fireplace and picked up the rye bottle, sloshed it to gauge the contents, uncorked it and took a deep slug. She shuddered, recorked the bottle and said, "Thanks, I needed that."

"You're welcome," Flintlock said. "Now, tell us why are you in the Territory?"

"I could ask you the same question, tattoo man."

"I'm searching for my mother. She's a Pinkerton detective like you, and my name is Sam."

"Is her name Brown, Sally Brown?"

"Yeah. She calls herself Miss Brown."

"That's not her real name, you know. Sally likes to work under an alias."

"I figured that much."

"I don't know her real name, but I'm sure it isn't Flintlock, so she can't be your mother. No matter, I've been sent to find her. She hasn't dispatched a wire as to her whereabouts in a couple of months."

"Her whereabouts is right here," Flintlock said. "She saved my life yesterday, shot one of the Old Man's gunmen off me."

"The Old Man of the Mountain?"

"That's what he calls himself."

"He's the reason Sally is here, and me. President Arthur wants us to disrupt his business any way we can. The Old Man's real name is Jacob Hammer, and the president wants him destroyed, or weakened enough that he'll become desperate and make mistakes."

"Hell, why doesn't he send in the army?"

"He tried that before and it didn't work out very well. If Hammer's scouts see army troops they'll raise the alarm and he'll escape into this damned wilderness and conduct his business elsewhere. For him it will be a minor inconvenience, that's all, and another big embarrassment for the president. He's fond of saying that no duty is neglected by his administration and no adventurous project will ever alarm the nation. Invading Balakai Mesa to destroy Hammer is an adventurous project and one likely to fail. He trusts the Pinkertons to do what has to be done, and we will not disappoint him."

"So, they sent another woman to do the job? Don't the Pinks have any male detectives?" Flintlock said.

"Sure, they do, but they're spread pretty thin. I volunteered for this assignment." Bridie read the question on Flintlock's face and said, "There are a lot of men who say women shouldn't be in this profession and, like Sally, I volunteered to prove them wrong. I like to think we also took a step closer to getting the vote by proving that a woman can do any job a man can."

"A woman should stay home while her man hunts," O'Hara said. "That has always been the way."

"Is that a fact? Well, this lady does her own hunting." She turned to Flintlock. "I need to find Sally. Have you the slightest idea where she is?"

"The last place was up on a ridge" — Flintlock thumbed over his shoulder — "that way, shooting a man who badly wanted to kill me."

"And smoking a cheroot," O'Hara said.

Bridie looked crestfallen. "Not much to go on, is it?"

"Not much at all," Flintlock said.

"Well, for the moment we sit tight and see if Sally shows," the woman said. She opened the door of one of the two tiny bedrooms, glanced around and said, "No, too cramped." The second bedroom showed more promise. "This looks fine, a woman's quarters," she said. "I'll sleep in here."

"It was a girl's room," Flintlock said. "Her name is Louise Smith and yesterday her father was killed by the Old Man's gunmen. She was taken prisoner."

Bridie was shocked. "You mean a young girl is in the clutches of Jacob Hammer?"

"Yeah, that's what I mean," Flintlock said. "He wants her as his bride."

"Then God help her."

"Me and Sam mean to rescue her,"

O'Hara said.

"Don't be silly," Bridie said. "You'd both be killed and the girl would still be a prisoner. That is, if Hammer hasn't murdered her by now."

"Like I told you, the Old Man wants her as a bride," Flintlock said. "She's still alive."

"Then she faces a fate worse than death," Bridie said.

At that moment, O'Hara, scowling, was all Apache warrior. "All right, you're the damned detective," he said. "How do we save Louise?"

"I don't know," Bridie said. Then, without much conviction, "I'll think of something."

"Then think of something fast," O'Hara said.

"First things first. My horse is down the trail a ways. You two bring me my saddle and bedroll and there's a carpet bag, bring that, too."

"Hell, lady, it's raining and still thundering," Flintlock said.

"I know. But I need the female fixings in the bag."

"I thought you did your own hunting," O'Hara said.

"I do. But there are some jobs that need only a strong back, for which men are more

suited. Getting a saddle out from under a
dead horse is one of them."

CHAPTER TWELVE

"I tell you we shouldn't have done it, Sam," O'Hara said. "We should've said, *Go get your saddle and women's fixin's your ownself.*"

"That's what we should've told her, all right," Flintlock said. "Truer words you never spoke, O'Hara."

"Then why didn't we?"

"Because . . . well . . . just because."

"Because she's a woman?"

"And a right pretty one at that."

"So that's why we're out here in a damned storm? Because she's pretty?"

"That's part of it."

"Then what's the other part?"

"She's a bad woman to cross. That's the other part. She carries a big revolver and she isn't scared to shoot it."

"Well, she doesn't scare me. Right now, I'd like to have her scalp hanging from my bridle."

"You're just mad because she called you Geronimo."

"No, I'm mad because she's a nag. Nag, nag, nag, as hard on the ear as an out-of-tune banjo."

"Be sure to tell her that when we get back," Flintlock said, hiding his grin.

"Damn right I will, and I'll take a switch to her," O'Hara said.

Now Flintlock laughed out loud. "O'Hara, if you even pick up a switch in Miss O'Toole's presence she'll put a bullet in you for sure. I guarantee it."

O'Hara peered through the lashing rain and said, "I think I see her dead horse up ahead." Then he grinned and turned his head to look at Flintlock. "She would, wouldn't she?"

"Damn right she would," Flintlock said.

It took two hours and a lot of cussing to remove Bridie O'Toole's saddle from under her dead horse. By that time, Sam Flintlock and O'Hara were exhausted and soaked to the skin.

"Got the carpetbag?" Flintlock said.

"Yeah," O'Hara said. "It's heavy. What's she got in there?"

"Probably a brace of Colts."

"Wouldn't surprise me none." O'Hara

glanced at the sky. "It's clearing," he said.

"About time," Flintlock said. "I reckon it lasted —"

He stopped abruptly. A man leading a gray horse walked slowly toward him, his slicker pushed back from his holstered gun. The man was tall, granite-faced and clean-shaven, unusual at that time in the West. His mouth was hard, his blue eyes harder.

"What the hell are you doing?" he said.

"Retrieving this saddle for a lady," Flintlock said. "Her horse broke its leg and she had to shoot it."

"She should've stripped it first," the man said. "Pity. It was a good-looking sorrel." Then, "Who is the lady?"

"A friend," Flintlock said.

"There are no friendly women out this way," the man said.

"Well, you're right about that. When you come right down to it, she ain't too friendly."

"She pretty?"

"No."

The blue-eyed man said, "She a Pinkerton?"

"How did —" Flintlock bit his tongue, aware that he'd made a mistake.

The man's smile was neither neighborly nor pleasant. "Heard there's a couple of female Pinks hereabouts. Seems like the army and the regular law are scared to come anywhere near Balakai Mesa, so they send their womenfolk."

"You work for the Old Man?" Flintlock said.

"Mister, what do you think? And Injun, move your hand another half inch in the direction of that gun butt and I'll drop you right where you stand."

"O'Hara, do as he says," Flintlock said. He smiled at the gunman. "Well, it was right nice meeting you, but now we'll be on our way."

The man consulted his watch — gold, Flintlock noticed — then snapped the case shut. "I'm headed for Flagstaff, but I guess I can make a detour. Take me to the Pinkerton."

Flintlock shook his head. "I don't know where she is."

"Then show me to the place where you were taking the saddle."

"We were just going to leave it here, let her pick it up, like."

"You're a liar," the man said. "Name's Ryker Klein. Mean anything to you?"

Flintlock had heard of a South Texas hired gun by that name who was said to have run with King Fisher and that hard crowd, but irritated as he was at being called a liar he shook his head and said, "I don't ever recall hearing your name mentioned."

"Pity. Your deafness could be the death of you."

Flintlock knew what Klein saw: O'Hara, a bedraggled Indian who'd seen better days, and a tattooed man wearing a stained buckskin shirt, baggy pants, a battered, sweat- and smoke-stained hat and scuffed, down-at-heel boots. Nothing in that picture, even the Colt shoved into his waistband, suggested he was a man to be reckoned with. All in all, he looked more saddle tramp than shootist, and Klein badly underestimated him. Too many easy kills, too many terrified townsmen, ham-handed rubes and latterly toughs from the festering slums of New York and other cities who knew the ways of the knife, billy club and garrote but not the revolver, had given Ryker Klein an inflated opinion of his gun skills. A more careful man would have read Flintlock's eyes and realized that this man had been up the trail and back many times and was hardened to the violent, sudden ways of the West. He'd stand his ground, take his hits and still be upright when the shooting was done and the smoke cleared. Klein ignored the warning signs and would soon learn how dangerous a man like Sam Flintlock could be.

Klein's voice rang like a billet of hardened iron falling on a marble floor, his hand close to his gun. "I won't ask you again, mister. Take me to the Pinkerton or I'll shoot out both your eyes."

Every man who carries a gun knows there's a time for talking and a time for shooting. Klein had threatened Flintlock and there could be only one answer, spelled out in lead, not words.

Flintlock drew and fired.

Ryker Klein's jaw sagged and his eyes grew wide as he stared at Flintlock. His gaze dropped to the scarlet rose that bloomed across the middle of his chest. His own gun had not cleared leather, and now as he realized that the game was over he let it drop back into the holster.

"You shot me," he said. "Damn you."

"Seems like," Flintlock said, his smoking Colt still on the gunman.

Klein's face was ashen. "Nobody shades Ryker Klein."

"I just did," Flintlock said.

"Damn you, you did, and you've killed me."

Klein fell to his knees, stunned at the manner of his death, then fell on his face,

113

took a last, gasping breath and died.

O'Hara looked at the fallen man and said, "I reckon he thought there was nobody faster than him."

"Klein wasn't fast. He just thought he was and it's that kind of thinking that gets a man killed," Flintlock said. "The hell with him. Bring his gray for Bridie."

O'Hara had been rifling through the dead man's saddlebags, tossing out shirts and socks, but now he held up a wad of banknotes. "There's money in here, Sammy. A pile of money."

"Let me see that," Flintlock said. He poked through the saddlebags for a while and then said, "At least ten thousand." He glanced at Klein's body. "Where were you going with all that cash, huh?"

"Bridie O'Toole will know," O'Hara said.

"She'll tell us that this money belongs to the Old Man of the Mountain, and that we know already," Flintlock said.

"We can't keep it, Sam. Can we?"

"Who said anything about keeping it? We'll let the Pinkerton lady decide who keeps it . . . and it will probably be us."

CHAPTER THIRTEEN

Louise Smith reached a decision. She had not been searched and her .32 caliber revolver, a parting gift from Miss Brown, was still in her skirt pocket. She would use the pistol to shoot her abductor and then fire again to kill herself. She was determined to be no one's bride, especially of the man who was responsible for the murder of her father.

The girl was being held in a small bedroom in a strange house like one she'd seen in a picture book about the far-off and mysterious land of Cathay. Louise stepped to the small, rectangular window and looked into an open courtyard about two acres in extent. The house was flanked on both sides by what looked like barrack blocks, a row of partitioned units, each having its own door and single window. There was a large stable and a scattering of outbuildings, one with a smoking chimney that she took to be a kitchen and mess hall. The high sandstone walls surrounding the enclave were sharp and scarred and showed no sign of erosion, suggesting that gunpowder had blasted the clearing out of the heart of the mesa. Armed men patrolled constantly, including sentries placed on the rim of the surrounding heights, and in the center of the quadrangle a brass bell hung on an A-shaped stand, ready to sound the alarm. The entire compound smelled of a heady incense that drifted from several bronze burners in front of the house, as though the occupant preferred the odor of musky perfume to the tang of clean, mountain air.

Louise realized the place was a fortress and no escape was possible. She felt the reassuring weight of the revolver in her pocket and accepted her fate. It was a hard thing to die at sixteen, but preferable to years of a living death.

Then, the girl got a foretaste of the horror that was in store for her.

A hatless, barefooted man wearing only a long white robe emerged from a door to the left of Louise's window and stepped into the courtyard. He was boxed by four rifle-carrying gunmen and walking behind them strode a tall, stately and solemn Oriental man carrying a steel *jian,* the long, traditional straight-bladed executioner's sword of ancient China. With the older man were two Chinese youths, possibly his sons, dressed alike in black pants and a scarlet tunic. Both carried wooden buckets that seemed to be heavy and at a certain point they emptied the contents onto the ground. It was sand that they then spread into a circle with their sandaled feet.

Louise recognized the bound and robed man as Bill Simpson, the rider who'd pushed up her skirt and tried to fondle her breasts and made jests about her wedding night. The girl realized with dawning certainty that Simpson had been betrayed by another gunman and was now about to pay the ultimate penalty for his indiscretions.

Louise held her breath, alarmed. The man's behavior had been deplorable, certainly, but he'd done nothing to merit a beating with a sword. But then, as the two younger men forced Simpson to his knees, she fully understood what was about to take place . . .

There would be no beating — this was a beheading.

Simpson, ghastly pale, his thin hair sweat-plastered across his scalp, was not meeting his death well. Louise couldn't hear what he said, but his head was tilted upward and his mouth moved constantly as he desperately pleaded for his life, begging mercy from stone-faced executioners who had none.

The two young men — now the girl pegged them, correctly, as apprentices — each grabbed an arm and forced Simpson forward so that his heaving chest was parallel with the ground. The executioner took up a position on the condemned man's left, tapped the edge of the blade once on the back of Simpson's neck and then raised the sword, two-handed, high above his head. A moment later the blade descended in a gleaming arc and severed Bill Simpson's head neatly from his neck. The head hit the ground and rolled like a melon fallen from a farm wagon, and Louise gave a little gasp of horror and looked away. When she finally glanced out the window again the courtyard was empty and only a spreading scarlet stain on the sand remained.

A bronze key turned in the lock to the girl's room and two young Chinese women entered, both with colorful clothing draped over their arms. The women were followed by the two young men who'd assisted at the execution. They carried a brass bathtub and one of them got his ears boxed by the women after he let hot water slosh over the rim. The men were dismissed and despite Louise's struggles, the women, remarkably strong peasant girls, stripped her naked and forced her into the tub. She was bathed in perfumed water, and when she emerged she was forced to endure being waxed to remove all the hair from her body. Now the girls giggled and made a fuss as they dressed Louise in a *daxiushan,* the traditional floor-length dress of aristocratic Chinese women, its sleeves four feet long. The gown was of gold silk, embroidered with peacocks and flowers, and the bodice covered only the bottom half of Louise's breasts. Her long hair was left unbound, she guessed at the whim of her captor.

The Chinese women stood back to admire their handiwork and the younger of the two, after a struggle with the unfamiliar English word, clapped her hands and said, "Princess!"

Louise said nothing, but her mind raced . . . her .32 was still in the pocket of her skirt that had been carelessly tossed aside before her forced bath. Somehow, she must retrieve it.

In what had been an ill-omened day, Louise finally got lucky, if lucky can be applied to her recovery of the gun with which she planned to kill herself.

One of the Chinese girls left the room, and the other turned her back on Louise as she picked up towels, combs, perfume bottles and other detritus scattered around the floor. It took Louise only a moment to reach into the pocket of her skirt and grab the little revolver. She crossed her arms, her hands and the .32 hidden in the voluminous drapes of her sleeves. The two young men came in, carried out the tub, and then the remaining Chinese girl bowed to Louise . . . and left her alone amid a menacing, sinister silence.

After an hour, the key turned in the lock and the two young men entered, this time carrying a small table. The Chinese girls returned and laid out plates and several covered dishes on the table. Louise thought the smells were wonderful. The girls returned with wine and glasses and placed two thin sticks on top of each napkin. The girls then bowed and left. This time the door was left ajar and a moment later a man stepped inside.

He was very tall, muscular, with a wide mouth and pitiless eyes. His mane of gray hair was brushed back and tied at the nape of his neck and he had no beard or mustache. He wore a long black robe embroidered with silver dragons and there were black slippers on his feet.

"I am Jacob Hammer," the man said. He waved an elegant hand that had a gemstone ring on every finger and said, "Please be seated at the table."

Louise shook her head. "I will not eat with you. You're the Old Man of the Mountain and you murdered my father."

"Then I'll eat by myself," Hammer said.

The food smelled delicious, but the girl had no appetite. For ten minutes, she stood in silence and watched the man eat. He used the sticks to pick up morsels of sauced pork and chicken without spilling, as deft and delicate a diner as a cloistered nun. When he finished eating, Hammer laid down his chopsticks and looked at Louise. "Wine?"

The girl shook her head. "I want nothing from you except my freedom."

"You are my bride and this evening is our wedding night. That is the heart of the matter. After you give me a son" — Hammer waved a disdainful hand as though the rest of his sentence were unimportant — "you can go wherever you please."

"I will never agree to marry you," Louise said.

Hammer smiled. "Agree? There is no

agreeing, no preacher, no marriage vows. I will bed you and our union will be consummated. In other words, you little tramp, tonight we begin the process of making my baby."

"You sorry piece of murdering trash," Louise said. She rose to her feet, took a step back and her hand went for the .32 in her pocket. The girl thumbed back the stiff hammer of the little revolver but, moving with incredible quickness, Hammer tipped over the table, and dishes of food splattered over the bottom of her gown. Louise was distracted for a heartbeat, but it was time enough for the man to reach her. As his hands went for her throat she leveled the gun and fired.

The Old Man of the Mountain screamed, a shattering, nerve-shredding shriek, a combination of pain, surprise and spiking hatred. Louise backed away, trying to put space between herself and the raving man as she desperately tried to cock the recalcitrant revolver.

She never made it.

Driven by rage, Hammer's vicious backhand hit Louise too low and landed on her neck instead of her jaw. But the force of the blow was enough to send her staggering backward, and she crashed against the wall behind her and slid to a sitting position. Hammer, glistening blood staining the right side of his robe at the waist, was on her in a flash. He wrenched the gun from the girl's hand, threw it across the room and then hauled her to her feet.

This time Hammer's backhand did not miss.

Louise's head snapped back from the power of the blow, but she absorbed the pain and shock and turned defiant eyes to her assailant. "You better murder me now, because if I become pregnant by you I'll cut your madman's spawn from my body and kill us both."

As two of his gunmen burst into the room, Hammer snarled like an enraged animal and said to Louise, "You're done, slut. Finished. I would have given you riches, power, influence, in exchange for a son, but now all I'll give you is the sharp edge of the headman's sword."

Blood trickled from the corner of Louise's mouth. "Filth, better I have my head cut off than lie even a minute in your bed."

"Boss, you're wounded," one of the gunmen said.

Hammer ignored the man and pulled Louise's face closer to his. "You will die, depend on it. But it is not for you to know the day or the hour. One morning, it may be a week from now, or a month, or a year, I will wake from sleep and say to myself, *Yes, this is the day I cut off the head of the whore who betrayed me.* You will be dragged from your cell, taken out into the courtyard and your pretty head will roll." Hammer's smile was evil. "Something to look forward to, my dear, is it not?"

Louise did her best to look defiant, as though the man's threat had fallen on deaf ears. But she was scared, terrified, as she imagined how it would be to wait for her death, those days after days of not knowing.

Hammer dismissed the girl with his eyes, as though she now meant nothing to him, and said to his men, "Take her away. Put her in the rock dungeon with Viktor."

One of the gunmen seemed shocked. Then, as though he couldn't believe his ears, "With Viktor?"

"Yes, with Viktor."

"Boss, he'll kill her."

Hammer smiled. "No, he won't. Depend on it, Viktor will have a quite different plan for this young lady. Now, remove her from my presence and send in Dr. Chiang."

"You were lucky, the bullet just grazed your skin," Dr. Chiang said as he finished off ty-

124

ing the bandage around Hammer's waist. "It was a small-caliber bullet and did little damage."

"Little damage? It caused me pain and there was blood."

"The skin is broken here and there."

"Hardly a graze."

"Like a deep burn. I will give you something for pain."

"No, not morphine. I need a pipe."

Dr. Chiang nodded. "I will bring one to you. Perhaps it's best you dream for a while." His black eyes lifted to Hammer's face. "I heard the girl has been loosed to Viktor."

"Yes, he will take care of her."

"He will kill her."

"No. Viktor will play with her for a while and later I will kill her," Hammer said.

Somewhere in the deep recesses of the house a clock chimed, and a hawk soared over the mesa and cast a shadow on the courtyard that looked like it had been cut from black paper with a razor.

CHAPTER FOURTEEN

The thunderstorm had passed, the rain was gone and the parched land showed no sign that the tempest had ever been. Bridie O'Toole stepped out of the cabin and watched the two riders come on at a walk, leading a tall horse. Her hand dropped to the ivory handle of her Smith & Wesson and her eyes reached into the distance. After a while she made out Sam Flintlock, sitting his saddle like a sack of grain, and next to him O'Hara. Schooled in horsemanship by the Apache, who'd been mounted warriors as early as 1700, unlike Flintlock, O'Hara rode as though he and his mount were a single entity, a slightly bedraggled centaur.

When Flintlock reached the woman, he raised a hand in greeting and said, "Got your saddle and stuff and we brung you a horse, a good one, too."

"And ten thousand dollars," O'Hara said.

Bridie raised a skeptical eyebrow. "You

boys bushwhack somebody?"

"Nope," Flintlock said. "We met a ranny by the name of Ryker Klein who was very desirous of meeting you, so desirous he threatened to shoot out my eyes if I didn't lead him to you."

"And what happened?"

"Well, we talked around the thing and then when the talk ended we got into a gunfight."

O'Hara said, "Sam plugged him fair and square."

"We heard that Klein was working for Jacob Hammer," Bridie said.

"Who's we?" Flintlock said.

"The Pinkertons." She stared hard into Flintlock's eyes. "Ryker Klein had a reputation of being good with a gun, fast on the draw and shoot."

"He was fair to middlin'," Flintlock said. "Only he didn't know it. Any coffee in the pot?"

"Yes, it's on the boil. It took me forever to fill the pot from the spring. Someday soon the water is going to play out."

"Then let's hope it waits until we're long gone from here."

"Put up your horses, and thanks for bringing Klein's gray," Bridie said. She took her carpetbag from Flintlock. "You didn't paw through this, did you?"

"Hell, no."

"Good. A woman's intimate garments are her own concern."

"The bag is heavy," Flintlock said.

"That's because I have a brace of Peacemakers in there."

"Told you so, Sam," O'Hara said, rolling his eyes.

Sam Flintlock read somewhere that poets don't sleep much, always mooning around in the dark, writing verses about the moon and the pines. It seemed that the late Tom Smith was one of those because his room was small and hot and his bed was made to accommodate a small child. After an hour tossing and turning he gave up and spread his blankets on the cabin's uneven rock floor. As far as he knew, O'Hara had gone Injun and was sleeping like a baby under a tree someplace.

Flintlock had just drifted into uncomfortable sleep when a kick on the ribs woke him. He bolted upright, his hand groping for his holstered Colt, but he stopped in midreach when he looked up and saw Bridie O'Toole standing over him.

"Wish I could sleep that soundly," the woman said. "For a minute there I thought you were dead."

"Hell, I just got to sleep," Flintlock said, aggrieved. "Why did you wake me?"

He blinked Bridie into focus. She looked incredibly pretty, wore a light robe, had her hair tied back with a red ribbon and over one arm she carried several layers of white, frilly things. He wondered at how much stuff a woman could pack into a single carpetbag.

"I want to bathe at the spring," Bridie said. She had her holstered revolver over one shoulder. "Go move the horses and make sure there are no snakes or spiders around. And no other creepy-crawlies or lizards, either."

"Woman, I'm trying to get some shut-eye here," Flintlock said, irritated.

"And I want to bathe, so up and at 'em." She emphasized that statement with several more kicks to Flintlock's ribs.

"Damn it, lady, you got a big six-gun there to scare away critters and the like," he said.

"Scaring away snakes and spiders is not a job for a six-gun," Bridie said. And then with great emphasis on the last word of the sentence, "It's a task for a *gentleman*."

Grumbling, Flintlock got to his feet. "All right, I'll go look."

"I'll follow you," Bridie said. "After you

129

tell me it's safe you can leave."

"The Old Man of the Mountain's gunmen don't scare you worth a damn, but you're afraid of a bug?"

The woman shuddered. "Ooh, I just hate spiders."

How long does it take a woman to bathe in a spring? Flintlock didn't know, but he figured he could catch another forty winks before she came back. He lay on the floor, closed his eyes and was asleep almost immediately.

A kick in the ribs woke him.

What the hell?

Flintlock sat upright and saw O'Hara smiling like the cat that just ate the cream. "Sleeping like the dead is a damn easy way for a man to get himself shot," he said. "Coffee's on the bile. There ain't much left and even less firewood. The grub's holding out, though, at least for now."

"Any more good news?" Flintlock said, scowling his irritation.

"Yeah, I saw Bridie O'Toole bathing at the spring."

"You saw her?"

"I was passing that way and saw her with my own two eyes."

"What was she wearing?"

"Soap."

"Soap?"

"Well, soap bubbles. She waved to me as I walked by."

"She waved? That was bold."

"Yeah, I guess it was."

"Well, I'm not gonna ask you what she looked like," Flintlock said.

"Good, because I'm not gonna tell you."

"Pretty, I bet."

"Maybe. I didn't notice."

"You did notice. Any man would notice."

"Well, I didn't."

Flintlock shook his head. "O'Hara, the Irish half of you I can understand. The Apache half is a mystery."

"It was the Irish half that didn't notice. The Apache in me thought what a fine-looking squaw she'd make."

Flintlock got to his feet. "O'Hara," he said, "you are a very strange person." He thought for a moment and then said, "Maybe I should go make sure there are no spiders hanging around the spring."

"Bridie has her revolver handy," O'Hara said. "She waved to me because I was at a distance. She might gun a man with a tattoo on this throat who came too close. Coffee?"

"Sounds like a good idea," Flintlock said.

■ ■ ■ ■ ■

After a meager breakfast of a couple of mystery cans from the Smith larder that turned out to be baked beans and vile-tasting cod balls, Flintlock picked up his rifle and left on a scout. He didn't know if his mother was still close or had left the area, but he planned to spend a couple of hours searching.

Bridie O'Toole, who smelled of soap and lavender water, told him to be on the lookout for Jacob Hammer's men. "Don't take them on by yourself, Sam," she said. "Come back for me and I'll handle it."

"You think the Old Man's gunmen have found Ryker Klein's body yet?" Flintlock said. "And discovered that his ten thousand dollars is missing?"

The woman shook her head, damp ringlets of blond hair falling over her tanned brow. "I don't know, but if they have, there will be hell to pay, so don't scout far and stay away from Pitchfork Pass."

"Hell, I don't even know where Pitchfork Pass is," Flintlock said.

"I think you'll know very soon," Bridie said. "We're going to stop the illegal commerce in and out of there."

"Three of us?" Flintlock said.'

"Four, if you can find Detective Brown."

"I'll find her," Flintlock said. "She's my ma."

The vast land lay silent under the searing sun and Sam Flintlock's shirt turned black with sweat and his breathing was labored. After two hours he'd seen nothing, heard nothing and now the distances shimmered, distorting the shape of everything, and his burning, red-rimmed eyes refused to focus. A patch of shade at the base of a standing rock offered hope of relief from the heat and Flintlock made his way there. He sat, put his canteen to his parched mouth . . . and stopped in midgulp.

The ghost of old Barnabas sat on a nearby rock, watching him.

The wicked old sinner fluttered a large Chinese fan embroidered with dragons to cool himself and he wore a round Oriental hat with a tassel.

"Find your ma yet?" he said.

"You know I haven't," Flintlock said.

"Better find her before the Old Man of the Mountain does. I did some studying on him and he's a rum one, he is, has a kind of Chinese style about him and a violent streak that I like."

"Where is she, Barnabas? Where is my mother?"

"I don't know. Around here someplace, I reckon."

"Tell me."

"Sammy, I have nothing to tell. She's around, that's all I know." The old mountain man smiled. "Here, did I ever tell you about the Chinee man at the Horse Creek Rendezvous up Wyoming way in the summer o' '33?"

"No, that's one I missed," Flintlock said, thumping the stopper back into the neck of his canteen.

"Well, see, I was trapping for the American Fur Company with Bill Sublette and Joe Meek an' them and Joe had a heathen Chinaman with him. He'd picked him up somewhere but God knows where. Well, sir, we mountain men were about two hundred strong and there were ten times that many Indians, mostly Nez Perce an' Blackfeet camped with us. We was all drinking whiskey and carousing and having a grand ol' time, white men and red men alike, but our excesses was interrupted when there occurred one of them incidents of wilderness life that makes the blood curdle with horror. You listening, boy? I said, curdle with horror."

Flintlock nodded. "Yeah, I'm listening. At the moment, I'm so used up I don't feel like doing anything else."

"Good. Now attend, because you ain't very smart, Sammy, and you have to listen close. Well, this mad wolf had been hanging around the camp for two or three days and then came the night it snuck into camp and bit twelve white men and the Chinee. Two of them boys were seized by madness in camp and ran off into the mountains where they perished. One was attacked by a seizure on a hunt and that very same day the Chinaman himself had a fit. He threw himself off his horse, started to gnash his teeth and foam at the mouth and howl like a wolf. Well, me and Meek and Sublette hastened back to camp in search of assistance, but when we returned the damned Hindoo was nowhere to be found. It was thought that he was seen a day or two later, but no one could come up with him. Then Ben Harrison, he was the son of William H. Harrison, soon to be the president of these United States, said he'd spotted him clear as day. Ben had been brought west by his father to cure his drinking problem, but he was a real affable feller when he was sober and not much given to big windies. He told us he'd seen the Chinaman up in the mountains, running through the pines with a wolf pack. Ben fired a shot to bring the wild man down so he could take a closer look at him, but missed. So as far as anybody knows, that Chinee is still up in the forests hunting with the wolves."

"Barnabas, usually, if I look hard enough, your stories have a moral," Flintlock said. "Damned if I see a moral to that one."

"The moral is that the Old Man of the Mountain ain't a Chinee, though he looks like one, but he runs with wolves. Sammy, if you want to save your ma and yourself, you'd better leave this neck o' the woods mighty fast and take her with you."

"Good advice, Barnabas, but I can't find her."

"Keep looking, boy. Now I got to go. Oh, by the way, You-know-who" — Barnabas used his forefingers to make horns on his head — "says he's mighty disappointed in you."

"Oh yeah, why is that?"

"Because you didn't do that blond gal while she was naked at the spring. He said, 'That boy just ain't right.' "

"Well, you tell him . . ." But Flintlock was talking to thin air. Barnabas had vanished and only the smell of brimstone marked his passing.

CHAPTER FIFTEEN

"Barnabas was right about one thing," O'Hara said. "We can't do this alone, Sam. I say we go find some help."

"And by that time Louise Smith could be dead," Flintlock said. "And maybe my ma with her."

Bridie O'Toole stepped out of the bedroom and frowned. "Sam, are you still talking about the ghost you saw when you'd had too much sun and were imagining things?"

"Yeah, I guess I am. But Barnabas made sense when he said we can't take on the Old Man alone." He glared at the woman. "What do you suggest, huh? That the three of us storm Pitchfork Pass and force him to surrender?"

"You're being silly again," Bridie said. "You already hurt Jacob Hammer when you killed one of his operatives and took his money. All right, so it's a drop in the bucket, but if we can do it often enough eventually he'll come looking for us."

"With a hundred gunmen," Flintlock said.

"I need just one clean shot," Bridie said. "Kill Hammer and his organization will collapse. Cut off the snake's head and the whole snake dies."

"And what about Louise Smith?" O'Hara said.

"Forget Louise Smith. She's already dead."

"I don't think Hammer has any intention of killing his pretty young bride," Flintlock said.

"Then by now she wishes she was dead and there's not a thing we can do to save her," Bridie said. She read the stunned expressions on the faces of the two men and said, "I know that sounds harsh and unfeeling, but we must face the facts. I think you boys have the idea that we can wait for dark, sneak deep into the mesa and free the girl from Hammer's camp or compound or fortress or whatever it is he has in there. We'd survive a couple of minutes and that's if we're lucky."

Flintlock shook his head. "Bridie, Miss Pinkerton detective, ma'am, all you have to offer is to lure the Old Man of the Mountain outside, draw a bead and kill him. I'd say that's also thin, mighty thin."

"And somehow breaking into Hammer's quarters, hauling Louise Smith from his bed and then living to tell the tale is any better?"

"No, it isn't any better," Flintlock said. "We've already agreed on that. Now let me think."

Flintlock's face went blank, a brilliant or even mediocre idea eluding him.

O'Hara talked into the void. "The task here is too big for three people, four, if you count in Sam's mother."

"You're a master of the obvious, Crazy Horse," Bridie said. "So, what do you suggest?"

"There's a small town to the east of us called Dexter and we've met the local lawman there," O'Hara said, ignoring the dig.

"Doesn't surprise me," Bridie said. "Go on."

"The place is bound to have a wire, and I suggest you use it to get in touch with Pinkerton headquarters and ask for help. You can even get the Pinks to use their influence with the government and demand soldiers."

Bridie cocked her head and twisted a ringlet of hair between her fingers as she silently stared at O'Hara. Finally, she said,

"President Chester Arthur is the government. In the past, he was a man who'd been tossed out of political office for corruption and he made enemies along the way. But so far, he surprised everybody by a lack of scandals or controversies and he wants to keep it that way. He's not about to mount a major military operation against a common outlaw in the Arizona Territory that might fail and bring him disgrace."

The woman waited for a comment, and when none was forthcoming, she said, "Before I left Chicago, Allan Pinkerton told me that Jacob Hammer currently runs at least two hundred criminal enterprises across the country. In just about every major city he controls the opium trade, prostitution, gambling, protection rackets, murder for hire and God knows what else. Allan says that two hundred cities translates into at least a thousand crooked politicians and police chiefs currently on Hammer's payroll."

"Hell, there must be some honest lawmen in them big cities," Flintlock said.

Bridie nodded. "There are some honest coppers, but they're fighting a losing battle. If they close down an opium den or a brothel it reopens the following day in another block and no one is ever prosecuted.

The crooked town hall politicians see to that."

Flintlock said, "What did this Allan Pinkerton feller tell you to do?"

"He said to dig up Hammer's criminal empire by the roots — he's Scottish, you know, and says *rrroots* — and his various illegal enterprises will wither on the vine."

"In other words, gun the son of a bitch," Flintlock said.

"Mr. Pinkerton would not use those words, but yes, that's the general idea," Bridie said. "He also told me that none of his female operatives have ever failed him, and I don't intend to be the one who does. I'll kill Jacob Hammer, who styles himself the Old Man of the Mountain, if it's the last thing I ever do."

"It might well be," Flintlock said.

"The last thing any of us ever do," O'Hara said.

CHAPTER SIXTEEN

The dungeon was a natural cave in the side of the mesa wall with a door of latticed iron that clanged shut on Louise Smith after she was thrown inside. Her prison was dark and smelly, and was furnished with a couple of iron cots with filthy mattresses and a bucket. The cave seemed to tunnel into the rock for quite a distance, but after a few yards the daylight faded into pitch blackness and it was impossible to tell just how deep it was. It could be ten feet or a hundred. Still dressed in her Oriental finery, Louise sat on the edge of one of the cots, which squeaked under her weight, and looked through a diamond-shaped space between heavy iron straps into the courtyard.

After the earlier execution, the courtyard had been deserted, but now as the sun sank lower at least fifty men and several women took a promenade around the space, walking in a clockwise direction in complete silence. There was no banter, no laughter, none of the hum of conversation that Louise expected from such a gathering . . . just the shuffle of boots on bedrock and the occasional cough.

Then, in an instant, all that changed.

A cheer went up from the crowd as Jacob Hammer, dressed in the resplendent robes of a mandarin, stepped out of his house and walked into the courtyard, nodding and smiling as he greeted people and bowed over the hands of the curtsying females. Tables were set up that soon groaned under the weight of food and drink and the mood of the throng turned to noisy talk, laughter and merrymaking.

Watching from her cell, Louise marveled at the hold the Old Man of the Mountain had over his people. It seemed they ordered their lives around him and only his presence made them feel complete. He was their warlord, rich and mighty, and they were his obedient servants.

Louise lost all hope. She knew she could expect no mercy from these people. No one would speak up on her behalf and stay the headman's sword. The people in the mesa were Jacob Hammer's creatures and his will was theirs.

So engrossed was the girl at the gathering

in the courtyard that she jumped when a heavy hand landed on her shoulder. She turned . . . and saw . . . and bit back the scream that came unbidden to her lips.

The man, no, more animal than man, that loomed over her stood almost seven foot tall, his chest, arms and shoulders massive, his only garment a kind of breechcloth that covered his loins. His legs were hairy, as big as tree trunks, and his great bare feet with long, hairy toes, seemed to occupy a square yard of ground. His brow was low, almost to his eyebrows, and his bullet head was cropped close. He stared at Louise with quizzical gray eyes as small and round as dimes, as though he was trying to figure out who she was and why she was there. He smelled feral, like a caged circus beast.

He said, "I am Viktor."

The expression on the girl's face was one of sheer terror and this seemed to anger the giant. Viktor waved a hand, as though swatting a fly, and growled. He turned his whip-scarred back, hobbled to the other side of the cell, looked at Louise over his shoulder and said, "No!" Then he squatted on the ground, groaned, and his chin dropped onto his chest.

Nothing in her life had prepared her for a monster like Viktor, yet Louise's fear began to subside a little as she slowly saw him as a terribly wounded human being and not a living nightmare. But lingering fear made her keep her distance. She didn't trust a man who could pick her up in his huge hands and tear her apart like a rag doll. Or worse . . . much worse . . .

The noise of the crowd grew in volume as whiskey took partners for its merry dance, and the light changed as the bright sunlight slowly faded into the lilac of evening. Viktor did not move except once when he shoved his battered face into his hands. Louise, her back pressed against the wall, hardly dared to breathe, fearfully wondering what was to come.

She got part of her answer as torches were lit around the compound.

A key clanked in the lock and the iron door swung open. Two armed men stepped inside and Viktor looked up and seemed to shrink within himself.

"All right, my Russkie bear," one of the gunmen said. "Time to dance for the crowd."

Louise expected the giant to fight, but to her surprise he got to his feet and, helped along by blows from a riding crop, walked docilely out of the cave.

"Where are you taking him?" the girl said,

wondering why she cared.

"Don't worry, little missy, your boyfriend will be back," one of the gunmen said. "Missing him already, huh?"

The door slammed shut behind him and the key turned in the lock again.

The girl caught only fleeting glimpses of what happened next since the laughing, jeering crowd closed in around Viktor as soon as a concertina struck up with a lively hornpipe. Louise saw enough to determine that the giant danced like a monkey for a demented organ grinder, cuts from the whip landing on his back and head every time he faltered or missed a step.

"Stop it! Stop it!" the girl yelled, but no one heard her or cared to listen.

Viktor danced hornpipes and reels for thirty minutes before the crowd grew bored with him and he was returned to his cell. The giant was covered in sweat, and blood ran from a cut across his left ear. He threw himself onto a cot that shrieked under his weight and stared at the ceiling, holding a blood-stained hand to his split ear.

Outside as darkness fell and though the torches still burned, the crowd dispersed, the tables were taken down and a silence fell on the mesa.

Louise had spent her childhood nursing

little wounded animals back to health and the pity and concern she felt for them, she felt for Viktor. Drawing on a deep well of courage she didn't know she possessed, she crossed the cell and placed her cool hand on the man's forehead. The giant opened his eyes, stared at her in the gloom and then, to Louise's surprise, he gently removed her hand and kissed her palm. It took all of the girl's will not to jerk away from him, but she did not and she only stepped back when Viktor rolled out of the cot and walked back into the cave. He returned with a round loaf of bread, a piece of white cheese and a canteen. The man broke the loaf in half and did the same with the cheese and handed them to Louise. "We eat now," he said. He nodded in the direction of the courtyard. "Bad mens . . . all of them. Hurt Viktor. Make me dance and hurt me."

Despite everything, the girl found she was hungry. She ate the bread and cheese and washed the frugal meal down with water. Only then did she say, "Why are you here? What did you do?"

The giant shook his head and said, "Viktor once live" — he waved a hand — "out there, far, far away from people. Then bad mens come and steal Viktor's silver and gold." He spread his hands as though he were strangling someone. "Viktor kill one of them but the others beat me and bring me here." He grinned, revealing yellow teeth, bent his head and made a blade of his hand. He chopped at the back of his neck. "They cut off Viktor's head very soon now when they tire of his dances."

"And mine," Louise said. "I am to die, but I don't know when."

"No," the giant said. "Viktor will not let that happen. Pretty girl is kind to Viktor and he will protect you."

"I'm trying to be kind. But I'm still a little afraid of you."

"Viktor will not hurt you. Viktor is good man."

Louise said, "They said you would attack me, that you'd . . ."

"No! You wait here. I have something to show you that they did not find to take from me."

The giant went back into the cave again and this time when he returned he dropped something small into the girl's hand. "She would not like Viktor to do such an evil thing. Viktor say his prayers every night to the lady."

Louise looked at the object in her hand. It was a small, copper, Russian icon bearing a likeness of the Virgin Mary.

That night Louise slept soundly with her head on Viktor's chest, his huge, muscular arm wrapped protectively around her . . . beauty and the beast bonded by their common misery.

CHAPTER SEVENTEEN

The three-person war on the Old Man of the Mountain began with the realization that a fourth had taken a hand in the game.

"It's your ma's work, Sam," O'Hara said. "It has to be."

Flintlock looked down at the dead man sprawled at his feet. "Three shots to the chest killed him," he said. "I could cover the bullet holes with the palm of my hand."

"Good shooting, for sure," O'Hara said. "Seems like your ma is handy with a rifle."

Flintlock shook his head. "No, not my mother. It can't be. Ma isn't a Pinkerton. My ma sits in a rocking chair and embroiders stuff or knits and she drinks gin from a teacup. She doesn't put three bullets into the brisket of an outlaw in the middle of a godforsaken wilderness."

"Maybe your ma did all that knitting before she became a Pinkerton," O'Hara said. He opened his hand and revealed three

.44 cartridge cases. "She met this man face-to-face and outshot him. That took sand." O'Hara pointed to his left. "Mule tracks over there, probably a pack animal. Your ma took the dead man's horse, guns and his mule."

"If she really is my ma," Flintlock said. He looked around him, his face troubled. "What the hell went on here, O'Hara?"

"Near as I can piece it together, the dead man was riding toward the mesa, not away from it. Judging by the tracks the mule was carrying a fairly heavy load. My guess would be money, a good part of it coin, the small change spent by poor city folks playing the numbers." O'Hara saw a skeptical look on Flintlock's face and said, "Sam, multiply those nickels and dimes tens of thousands of times and you come up with some real dinero."

"If the Old Man of the Mountain is so rich, why would he bother to bring in a muleload of pissant coins?" Flintlock said.

"He's probably got a vault where he keeps the small change and then he sends it out again by the sackload to help finance his various businesses around the country," O'Hara said.

"Got it all figured, huh?" Flintlock said. "Well, I reckon it's more likely the mules carried gold. I bet the Old Man owns a few banks that convert all those nickels and dimes into double eagles."

O'Hara shrugged. "Money is money. Small coins or twenty-dollar gold pieces, it spends the same."

Flintlock kneeled beside the dead man. "Look at the boots on this ranny, Texas made on a narrow last with all them butterfly inserts. It would cost a puncher three months' wages to buy a pair like this."

"Sam, it would cost a puncher three months' wages just to walk into the store that sold those boots," O'Hara said.

"He was one of Jacob Hammer's high-priced gunmen, all right," Flintlock said.

"Yup, bringing home the loot until your ma plugged him."

"As I said already, if it was my ma."

"It probably was . . . unless she's somewhere with knitting on her knees drinking gin out of a teacup," O'Hara said.

"Your mother or not, Sam, she's a Pinkerton carrying out her assignment, to disrupt Jacob Hammer's illegal commerce in and out of Balakai Mesa," Bridie O'Toole said, laying her cup back in the saucer. She was much addicted to tea and the late Tom Smith had laid in an adequate supply.

Neither Flintlock nor O'Hara would touch the stuff. "But I don't understand why she hasn't contacted us."

"Some people prefer to work alone," O'Hara said. "Among the Apache there were always warriors who were lone wolves."

"Well, you would know, wouldn't you?" Bridie said.

"I've met a few," O'Hara said.

"This is the second time in the past few days that Hammer's had one of his men killed and money stolen," Bridie said. "He won't let that stand. Time to take to the hills."

"What does that mean?" Flintlock said.

"We move out of this cabin and find another place to hole up, somewhere where we can see him coming," Bridie said.

"Somewhere we can defend," Flintlock said. "We need a good, open line of fire."

"No, somewhere we can hide, Sam. Between the three of us we don't have enough ammunition to withstand a siege. Or didn't you think about that?"

"Any suggestions?" Flintlock said, irritated. God, Bridie O'Toole was a bossy woman.

"No. But we leave now, take what food we can and go looking for new lodgings."

"Now?" Flintlock said.

"Would you rather wait until Hammer and his gunmen are on our doorstep?"

"We can always wait until we see him coming and then make a run for it," Flintlock said.

"It's too late for that. By now Hammer is good and mad and out in the open he'd track us down real quick. Sam, we have to be gone from here and the more we talk about it the less time we have left to find a hiding place."

"Then let's quit arguing and light a shuck the hell out of this death-trap cabin," O'Hara said.

The great northern plateau of the Arizona Territory was once an inland sea, and Sam Flintlock and the others rode into a land torn and riven by immense gorges, deep canyons and soaring mesas, a mysterious wilderness of strange, unworldly beauty and spectacular grandeur.

After an hour, O'Hara, scouting ahead, rode into a narrow arroyo that narrowed further for several hundred yards before opening up into a natural amphitheater of about ten acres in extent. Its flat floor was covered with patches of shaggy grass, here and there Gambel oak and juniper, and growing among them stands of sage, manzanita and serviceberry. The high, surrounding walls of the enclosure were of rustred sandstone, much eroded, but, like cupped hands, they held the secret basin in their grasp away from prying eyes. The last thing O'Hara expected to see was a source of groundwater, but to his surprise and joy a small rock pool, not extensive but a couple of feet deep, lay in the shadow of the eastern wall. Whether it was caused by infrequent rains or fed by an underground source he had no way of telling, but there was enough of it to last three people and three horses a month at least.

O'Hara dismounted and let his horse plunge its muzzle into the pool before he too drank. The water was cool and clear and tasted good. Remounting, he headed back the way he'd come.

O'Hara rode out of the arroyo and swung east where he planned to meet up with Flintlock and the Pinkerton woman and tell them of his find.

But a flurry of gunshots in the distance upset his plan.

O'Hara drew rein and listened into the day. He fixed the fight at a mile ahead and a little to the north, five or six rifles firing, and he arrived at the obvious conclusion that Flintlock and Bridie O'Toole were under siege. He slid his Winchester from the boot and kneed his paint into a wary canter.

A high bluff that angled to the southeast blocked his passage and O'Hara slowed to a walk as he rode along its base, seeking a way around. After a couple of hundred yards the ridge abruptly broke off, ending in a jumble of fallen boulders where a few stunted spruce trees struggled to make a living.

Now the firing was very close, more intermittent but steady as riflemen took time to mark their targets.

O'Hara stepped out of the saddle and left his horse under the thin shade of the trees and, crouching low, he advanced toward the gunfight. The sun was scorching, the air thick and hot and hard to breathe, and sweat stained the back of his shirt. He made his way through the rocks and then stopped in his tracks.

Fifty yards ahead of him five men fired rifles from cover, shooting upward at a low, rock-covered rise where a cloud of gray gunsmoke hung in the still air. O'Hara caught a quick glimpse of Flintlock rising up to shoot only to duck down again when a bullet *spaaanged!* off the rock inches from his head. Flintlock, or more likely Bridie, had chosen their defensive position well, but they were pinned in place by accurate fire and their supply of ammunition was limited. It was only a matter of time before Flintlock, as was his way, said, "The hell with it!" and gave up on an empty rifle and came out of the hiding place with his blazing Colt bucking in his hand. When O'Hara saw Flintlock rise to fire again and heard the *BOOM!* of the Hawken he knew that time was close at hand. The old rifle was a gun a man fought with when he'd nothing better.

O'Hara was behind the gunmen, and the Apaches had taught him none of the niceties about not shooting a man in the back. He drew a bead on a big fellow wearing a black-and-white cowhide vest and cut loose. The man had been lying on his belly and when the bullet hit he simply dropped his head and died. For a moment, his companions stared at the dead man, trying to figure out where the hell the bullet had come from that killed him. O'Hara didn't give them time to ponder the question. He fired and another man, who wore a bandolier of rifle ammunition across his chest, jerked and fell kicking, the rowels of his spurs scarring the rock.

But the three surviving gunmen were

professionals and they kept their heads. They returned fire and bullets ricocheted around O'Hara . . . then one slammed into the left side plate of his Winchester's receiver, bounced away, its lead nose deformed, and plowed into his shoulder. O'Hara staggered, dropped his jammed rifle and went for his revolver, determined to sell his life dearly.

BOOM!

Barely hanging on to consciousness, O'Hara's vision narrowed into fleeting images . . . Flintlock running, shooting the Hawken from the hip, dropping one of the gunmen . . . Bridie O'Toole on one knee, working her rifle . . . the two surviving gunmen snapping off a few shots before taking to their heels, suddenly wanting no part of what was happening . . . Bridie chasing after them, shooting as she ran, but scoring no hits . . . the woman cursing a blue streak as she watched the gunmen vanish among the rocks.

Then came a sound of steel-shod hooves on stone and the fight was over.

At least for now.

Flintlock moved warily toward O'Hara, the old Hawken in his right hand, hanging by his side. His eyes widened when he saw the blood on O'Hara's shirt. "You've been hit," he said.

"Seems like," O'Hara said. He sat on a rock. "Bullet's still in there. I can feel it." He shook his head. "Hell no, I don't. Right now, I don't feel anything."

Bridie stepped to O'Hara's side. "Let me take a look at that wound." Then, to Flintlock, "Collect their guns and ammunition." She raised an eyebrow at the Hawken. "Dan'l Boone, if we get into another shooting scrape I don't want you using that thing. Are you out of your mind?"

With a woman's gentleness, but with firm, strong hands, Bridie removed O'Hara's bloodstained shirt and examined the wound. After a while she said, "It's bad. I have to get the bullet out of there."

"Listen up," O'Hara said. "Those boys will be back with their friends, a lot of friends. I found a place where we can hole up." He grimaced as Bridie put his shirt around his shoulders. "There's water and grass. Not much but enough."

The woman nodded. "You're right, the sooner we leave the better. Where's your horse? Can you ride?"

O'Hara thumbed over his shoulder. "Back a ways. When there's gunmen coming after my hide, I can ride."

"Just sit there while I help Sam," Bridie said.

"I'm not going anywhere," O'Hara said.

Flintlock and Bridie stacked up the rifles and gunbelts and then led their horses down from the rise. When Flintlock returned with O'Hara's mount he said, "O'Hara, can you hear me?"

"Of course I can hear you," O'Hara said, opening his eyes, his face gray and drawn. "I'm not dead yet."

"You won't believe this."

"Try me."

"One of those boys we killed was Benny Lake. Remember him? Short little feller, did a lot of talking, shacked up for a spell with a redheaded whore by the name of Rusty Something-or-other."

"Sure, I remember. Rusty Rawlins was the gal's name, or so she said. Benny plugged two men that time, a United States Marshal and a Methodist preacher."

"Yeah, back in '79 up on the Platte. Me and you went after him for the thousand-dollar reward. We had us a time, chased him halfway across Nebraska."

"And we never did get him," O'Hara said. His voice was weak, strained.

"No, but we got him now. Maybe once I find my ma, we can go claim the reward."

"Bet it's grown some over the years," O'Hara said. "But we'd need proof. You could take his head, Sam, but it won't keep, not in this heat."

"I know. Damned shame," Flintlock said.

"You boys are having such an interesting conversation I hate to interrupt," Bridie said. "But it's time we got out of here."

After O'Hara was helped into the saddle and Flintlock and Bridie mounted and settled their load of guns and belts, the woman said, "I don't know why I'm even asking this, but why did Benny Lake shoot the Methodist preacher?"

"Benny's shooting was a little off that day," Flintlock said. "He was aiming for a Baptist preacher."

"Oh, that explains it, then," Bridie said.

CHAPTER EIGHTEEN

Darkness and a rising moon found Flintlock and the others in the basin at the end of the arroyo. Postponing what she had to do, Bridie ate the thin slices of bacon Flintlock had broiled over a small fire that he'd started with banknotes from the ten thousand dollars they'd taken from Ryker Klein. She'd tried to get O'Hara to eat, but he'd refused, though he drank a little water and then slept for an hour.

"Sam," she said, "the bullet has to come out."

Flintlock nodded. "I've never done that before, but I've seen it done. I'll have to use my Barlow and dig deep enough." Flintlock, his face creased with worry, looked at the sleeping O'Hara. "It will hurt him."

"I'll do it," Bridie said.

"Have you dug out a bullet before?"

"No. I don't make a habit of digging bullets out of men's shoulders."

Then, at a loss for words, deciding to state the obvious, Flintlock said, "It has to be done."

"Yes, it has to be done. Give me a canteen and your knife."

Flintlock did as he was told and said when he opened the folding knife, "I can use the sole of my boot to give it an edge, like barbers do to razors. Of course, they use a special kind of leather strop for that."

"If we'd whiskey we could wash the blade, to rid it of impurities," Bridie said. "But I remember being told that fire does just as well."

"I never heard that," Flintlock said.

"Well, you've heard it now."

Bridie held the blade in the flames for a minute or so, and then said, "I'm ready. Sam, hold O'Hara down. I don't want him to move when I begin cutting. And keep the canteen handy."

"Why?"

"Because my hand will get bloody and the knife could slip. When I ask, pour water over both my hands. Now hold him down and whatever you do don't let him move. Ready?"

"He's half Apache warrior," Flintlock said. "He won't move."

O'Hara roared and bucked like a wild stallion when the knife blade entered his wound, digging, probing, as Bridie tried to pry out a mangled bullet that was in deep and had caused considerable damage.

"Hold him, damn you!" Bridie O'Toole yelled, sweat already beading on her forehead.

"Hell, I'm trying," Flintlock said, his whole weight pressing on O'Hara's chest. Then, "He's in tolerable pain."

"We're all in pain," Bridie said. "Throw wood on the fire. I need more light."

"Can't you feel the bullet yet?"

"No. I can't. I don't know where it is." She shook her head. "I can't find it. It's deep, very deep."

Flintlock, a man strong in the arms and shoulders, held O'Hara down with his forearm and stretched out enough to toss some twigs on the fire.

"My hand, Sam!" Bridie said, her voice cracking under strain. "Use the water."

O'Hara was also a strong man and pinning him down was like wrestling an angry Irish railroad track layer who didn't want a tooth pulled. "I can't let him go," he yelled.

"Oh my God, look at that! He's bleeding bad."

Bridie stuck the knife blade in the fire, used the canteen to wash the blood and sweat from her hands, dried them on her shirt and picked up the Barlow again. "Hold him," she said. "Don't let him go. Do you pray?"

"Not as a rule."

"Then pray now. We need all the help we can get. Are you ready?"

Flintlock didn't answer, but to O'Hara he said, "You lay still, damn it. You're the poorest excuse for an Apache warrior I ever did meet."

Through gritted teeth O'Hara said, "Sam, when this is over I'm taking your scalp."

"And welcome to it if it stops your caterwauling," Flintlock said.

"O'Hara, this is going to hurt," Bridie said. "I have to go deeper."

Flintlock lay almost on top of O'Hara, holding him down.

"Here goes," Bridie said. "I'm so sorry, O'Hara."

Her face was spotted with blood and when she pushed her hair from her eyes she left a scarlet smear on her forehead.

Bridie pushed the blade deep into the wound and this time O'Hara, at the limit of his endurance and on the ragged end of consciousness, had only the strength to groan.

Then, after a couple of hellish, blood-soaked minutes of probing . . . cutting . . .

"I feel it!" Bridie said. "I scraped the bullet. O'Hara, stay with me for a just few moments longer. I'll have the bullet out in a moment."

But she spoke to an unconscious man.

"Got it!" the woman yelled. She laid the knife aside and picked out the bullet with her fingers. It looked like a small, gray mushroom. "For a moment there, I thought I'd never find it."

"So did I," Flintlock said. "Now what do we do?"

"Sam, I'm not a doctor," Bridie said. "All I can do is wash the wound and then cauterize it."

"Cauterize it? What does that mean?"

"Burn the wound to kill the poisons."

"A doctor would do that?"

"I don't know."

"Are you sure you want to burn it?"

"I heard or read somewhere that it's been done."

Bridie washed the Barlow and then lifted the hem of her skirt and used the knife to cut off a length of white petticoat. She poured water into O'Hara's gaping wound and dabbed it dry with the cloth.

"Sam, use two sticks and pick me a coal from the fire," Bridie said. She pointed into the flames. "There, that one seems big enough."

"I don't like this," Flintlock said. "I don't think we should do this."

"You'd like gangrene even less. Now do what I told you to do."

Reluctantly, Flintlock, after a few fumbling tries, used sticks to pick up a cherry-red coal about the side of a walnut.

"Drop it into the wound," Bridie said. She read the hesitation in Flintlock's face and said, "Now! Before it cools."

Flintlock let out with a great, shuddering sigh and then placed the glowing coal on the open wound. Flesh sizzled. A smell like burning bacon and then Bridie used the knife again to remove the now-dark ember. She folded her piece of petticoat into a pad and placed it on O'Hara's shoulder. "I'm glad he didn't feel that," she said.

"I felt it," Flintlock said.

Bridie nodded. "So did I. Hopefully he'll sleep now and gather his strength."

"I'll make sure there are no guns near him," Flintlock said. "If the Apache part of O'Hara wakes up before the Irish does, he

167

could play hob."

Bridie looked at Flintlock, her eyes shadowed in the darkness.

"I pray that's the case," she said. "I hope he wakes up."

Her face was empty, betraying none of her thoughts.

CHAPTER NINETEEN

In the teeming rain, the hansom cab stood outside a rundown, clapboard tenement building in one of Washington's poorest black neighborhoods, the iron clash of the horse's pawing hoof on the wet cobbles loud in the hissing quiet. The top-hatted driver sat huddled in an oversized oilskin coat, miserably waiting the return of Major General Claude Elliot, who had grimly promised him that his visit to this dismal, poverty-stricken place would not be of an extended duration. So far, the soldier had been gone for only ten minutes, but to the driver, who feared for his life and worried that his horse might be stolen from the shafts, it seemed like an eternity.

"My dear Senator Flood, the excellence of your port almost makes up for the dreariness of our surroundings, but is such secrecy really necessary?"

Adam Flood, a short, stout man in his

early sixties with a network of red spider veins across his nose and cheekbones, wore sober black broadcloth in contrast to the general's blue and gold finery. He smiled and said, "Alas, the president insists that our negotiations with Colonel Janowski on what he calls the Arizona Affair be conducted in the utmost secrecy. I brought the port from the president's own cellar, knowing how dreadfully melancholy these proceedings might be."

General Elliot reached into his surtout coat and produced a gold watch the size of a soup plate. "The bounder is already ten minutes late," he said.

"I'm sure he will be here shortly," Flood said. "Colonel Janowski is quite infirm from his many war wounds and that does slow him, especially in inclement weather."

Elliot was a tall, well-built fifty-year-old with a gallant war record, his wide face with its broad, lower-class nose saved from mediocrity by a pair of magnificent mutton-chop whiskers and an equally magnificent mustache.

He waved a hand. "Why here in such a depressing slum?" He looked around him at a small room, peeling paint on the walls, furnished with three wooden chairs and iron cot jammed against a wall, and an oil lamp.

There was no rug on the stone floor and the room smelled of its previous occupants, probably an entire family. "Who owns this place?"

"The Senate and people of the United States," Flood said. He smiled. "We keep this place for, shall we say, clandestine meetings like this one and it's occasionally used to house someone the government wishes to keep well away from the public eye."

"Spies, do you mean?"

"Yes, spies and others, and sometimes professional assassins."

"I didn't know our government employed such men, assassins, I mean."

"When the security of the nation is at stake, we employ many unsavory characters. Alfons Janowski is one of them."

"The deuce you say! An assassin? I was led to believe the colonel is a soldier of fortune."

"My dear general, and what is a soldier of fortune but a paid killer? Ah, I think I hear his carriage now."

At first meeting, Colonel Alfons Janowski was a disappointment. And General Elliot could not hide his dismay. Could this small, thin man hobbling with a cane, missing his left eye and right arm, really be a hero of the Crimean War, the French conquest of Senegal, the Russo-Turkish War, the Anglo-Zulu War and latterly a hired warrior in Arizona's Pleasant Valley War? Add to those a dozen other foreign and domestic conflicts in which he distinguished himself by his bravery and daring and Elliot expected the man to be ten foot tall, not a stunted . . . cripple.

Senator Flood made the necessary introductions and Janowski gratefully sat on a chair, accepted a cigar and refused a glass of port. He turned a black eye that was as bright as a bird's to General Elliot and said, a faint smile playing on his lips, "Please excuse my present infirmity, General. I have been wounded in battle seventeen times and this damp weather reminds me of every one of them."

"Not at all, Colonel," Elliot said. "You look" — he could not bring himself to tell an outright lie and finished lamely — "just fine."

Janowski's smile widened. "You are too kind," he said. His accent was tinged by a trace of his native Poland.

Elliot poured himself another glass of port that he seemed to need urgently, took a swig and then said, "Colonel, did Senator Flood make you aware of the, ah, Arizona Affair, and our dilemma?"

"Yes, he did, and by *dilemma* you mean the president's need for secrecy?"

The general nodded. "We can do nothing that might embarrass President Arthur and empower his enemies in government. You understand?"

"Perfectly," Janowski said. He leaned forward in his chair, his thin, sallow face alight, and for the first time that evening Elliot became aware of the little man's hidden well of vitality. "The president wants this common criminal who calls himself the Old Man of the Mountain crushed and his lawless empire destroyed. Am I correct?"

"Destroyed, yes, but discreetly, Colonel, discreetly," Senator Flood said. "Not to belabor the point, if you succeed no one will ever hear of it. There will be no medals."

"And if I fail?"

"Then, my dear colonel, if you are unfortunate enough to survive the encounter you will be erased. That unhappy task will fall to General Elliot and his security agents."

Janowski took the threat in stride, revealing no change of expression. He said, "The British gave me similar terms back in '68 when I was charged with the liquidation of a troublesome native princeling in the

Indian province of Uttar Pradesh. That expedition became somewhat onerous because in addition to an eight-hundred-man private army Prince Raamiz had two hundred servants and a harem of fifty beautiful Eurasian women. My seventy mercenary stalwarts defeated the prince's army, stormed the palace and I personally shot Raamiz in the head. There was ancillary damage of course, some eighty servants dead and most of the women. The harem took up arms and wanted to die with their lord, and naturally we obliged."

"By God, sir, that was an efficient operation," Elliot said. "Tip-top." He pounded a fist into his knee. "How many of your own force did you lose?"

"Eight. Seven died from battle wounds and one succumbed to dysentery. The British were very happy with the outcome and paid me ten thousand pounds and eight shillings. Then they warned that if I or my mercenaries ever spoke of the Uttar Pradesh incident we'd be hunted down and hanged."

"Damned unsporting of them if you ask me," General Elliot said.

Janowski nodded and said, "Indeed, sir. The British can be quite ruthless when it suits them."

"Can you still raise a mercenary force,

Colonel?" Senator Flood said.

"Even as we speak, I have fifty fighting men right here in Washington," Janowski said. He noted the surprise on Flood's face and said, "There's been talk of an excursion into Mexico on behalf of President Porfirio Díaz and I wanted my men close."

"Will they agree to join you for the Arizona Affair?" Flood said.

"Of course, if the money is right."

"Good men?" General Elliot said, looking like a stern soldier.

"None better. Americans mostly, but there are a few Poles, Germans, British and French among them."

"Will they stand?" Elliot said.

"They won't break, General, if that's what you mean. Mercenaries fight to the last man, that's why they are paid so well."

"You and your men will be well rewarded, Colonel Janowski," Flood said. "You have my word of honor on that."

It didn't enter into Janowski's thinking to doubt the senator. A gentleman had given his word of honor and he needed no more assurance than that.

General Elliot flicked cigar ash from the front of his surtout and said, "I must ask a question of you, Colonel, by your leave?"

"Please, ask away," Janowski said.

175

"An expedition into the Arizona Territory's mountainous region could prove exceedingly arduous, even for a young army officer," Elliot said. "Somewhat infirm as you appear to be, are you sure you are up to the task?"

Janowski smiled. "Fear not, General, I still have a few more wars left in me."

"I had to ask," Elliot said. "You understand, I trust?"

"Of course, you had to ask. This expedition will cost the United States government a considerable amount of money and it's your duty to make sure it is well spent."

Elliot didn't know it then, but within a short period of time he would witness firsthand how durable was Colonel Janowski's bullet-shattered body.

Flood spoke again. "Within reason, General Elliot will supply you and your men with what you need. I mean horses, munitions and the like, but no regular troops."

"I understand. What am I attacking, Senator?" Janowski said.

"A mesa," Flood said. "An outlaw encampment within a mesa. Carved out of the heart of a mesa, I'm told."

"Mesa?"

Elliot smiled. "A flat-topped hill with steep sides, Colonel. How high it is or how steep the slopes I do not know."

Janowski pondered that last for a silent few moments and then said, "General Elliot, I'll need a map of the area, two twelve-pound mountain howitzers, a supply of explosive ammunition and a dozen pack mules to carry the dismantled pieces of the cannon, ammunition and the food and water. Elephants would be better than mules, but I don't suppose you have any of those."

"No elephants," Elliot said. "But I can supply the rest."

"And for artillery spotting I'll need an observation balloon, one of the tethered type used in your Civil War," Janowski said. "And a gas generator, of course."

"I think that can be arranged," Elliot said. "Given time to pull it all together."

"Speed is of the essence, General," Flood said. "The president is most anxious that this affair be settled quickly."

"I'll need a couple of weeks," Elliot said. "The observation balloon —"

"General, you have a couple of days," Flood interrupted. "There's a large arsenal here in the capitol where I'm sure you can find the cannon and munitions you need."

"But, Senator —"

"No buts, General Elliot," Flood said.

"You will commandeer a train to take Colonel Janowski and his men to Flagstaff in the Arizona Territory. He can load his mules and make his way north from there. The president wants this sorry business concluded and in a very short time."

"Yes, sir," Elliot said. He looked worried and miserable at the same moment.

Flood got to his feet. "Colonel Janowski, you can contact General Elliot if you have any further needs. Now, it's me to my bed. This has been a wearisome day."

Elliot doused the oil lamp and trailed Flood and Janowski to the door. The senator was about to open it, but the colonel stopped him.

"Allow me to exit first," he said. Flood looked mildly surprised and Janowski said, "On my way here I was followed by another cab. Then, about a block away, two men got out and proceeded on foot, but in this direction. A man in my line of work makes many enemies, and that pair might be two of them."

"It's late," Elliot said. "Surely you saw revelers making their way home, Colonel. Drunks abound in this blighted neighborhood."

Janowski nodded. "That might well be the

case, but better safe than sorry." He reached inside his coat and drew a beautiful French Modele 1874 Chamelot-Delvigne 11 mm revolver, then popular with several European militaries. "Push the door open and then stay behind me, gentlemen," he said, holding the gun up alongside his head. "I'm more used to this kind of cloak-and-dagger work."

"I'm armed," General Elliot said.

"Then if I'm killed, use your weapon to defend yourself," Janowski said.

He turned the handle of the door, kicked it open and stepped into the gaslit street.

For a moment, there was only the sound of the sweeping rain on the cobbles, falling like steel needles in the bluish-white light of the gas lamps. A stray dog limped along the opposite sidewalk and then vanished into darkness. A cab horse tossed its head and snorted.

A few tense moments passed and then a high, shrieking scream of rage splintered the night silence. Out of the murk two men ran at Janowski, firing Colt revolvers as they came. The distance between the colonel and his assailants was twenty yards and closing fast. Deliberate, unhurried, deceptively slow, the mercenary took up the duelist's stance. He placed the inside of his right foot behind the heel of his left, turned his body sideways to the enemy, his left arm extended in a straight line from the shoulder, the French revolver steady in his fist.

He fired at a distance of five yards. Like a circle of red sealing wax, a bullet hole appeared between the eyes of one of the gunmen and he fell flat on his face onto the wet cobbles. The second man, tall and gangly, stopped, raised his gun and fired. The round tugged at Janowski's empty right sleeve and at that moment the shooter knew he was a dead man. An experienced gunman can thumb back the hammer and fire in less than a second, but the tall man was not experienced. He was an Indian peasant of the untouchable caste and unused to the practice of arms. He died with Colonel Janowski's bullet in his brain.

As the cab drivers fought to control their frightened horses, Janowski stood in the rain, his revolver hanging loose in his hand, gunsmoke drifting around him. In the distance, he heard a police whistle's tinny shriek of alarm.

Elliot stepped beside the colonel, glanced at the bodies of the two young men sprawled on the cobbles and said, "My God, Colonel, who were they?"

"Indians, by the look of them," Janowski

said. "Maybe brothers of one of the harem women we killed at Uttar Pradesh. But who knows? I make so many enemies."

"Quick, there's no time to be lost," Flood said. "Colonel, into a cab with you. General Elliot and I will handle things here."

Janowski was bundled into a cab that drove away at a canter and a few moments later the police arrived.

"A street fight between foreign thugs," Flood told the caped police sergeant who was first on the scene. "They killed each other."

"Yes, indeed," Major General Claude Elliot said. "The senator and myself witnessed the whole sorry affair."

CHAPTER TWENTY

Sam Flintlock and Bridie O'Toole stayed awake the entire night to keep vigil over O'Hara, who had developed a high fever and tossed and turned, muttering to himself, sometimes talking with Apache warriors who had died in battles many years before.

By sunup, O'Hara's fever had not broken and his forehead was hot to the touch.

"He's very sick," Bridie said, fear squeezing her hard. "Sam, I'm worried about him."

Flintlock nodded, said nothing. He'd seen strong men die of fever before and he knew exactly how sick O'Hara was.

"Strip him, Sam," the woman said finally. She saw Flintlock's face and said, "We must get the fever down."

"How?"

"Take his clothes off, everything."

"You mean, let O'Hara lie there naked?"

"No, not lie there. We'll take him over

there and put him in the water."

"In the pool?"

"Such as it is, yes. The water cooled in the night. It may be cold enough."

"Hell, we could kill him."

"If we don't break the fever he'll die anyway."

Then Flintlock said, "That's our only drinking water."

Bridie gave him a long, steady look, one eyebrow raised.

"I'll get him ready," Flintlock said.

He was surprised. O'Hara's face and hands were sunburned a deep mahogany color, but his body, protected by his clothes, was white, Irish white. If Bridie noticed she didn't say anything.

Flintlock carried O'Hara to the rock pool and gently lowered him into water that was cool, much cooler than his fevered, sweating body. Bridie used a canteen to constantly pour water over O'Hara, frowning in concentration.

"Will this work?" Flintlock said.

"I don't know. His wound looks very bad. Did O'Hara live with Apaches long?"

"His entire boyhood, but an Apache boy is a man at twelve. He needed to be if the tribe was to survive."

"Did he ride with the Apaches and kill

white men?"

"Before I met him? I have no idea. He was an army scout for a spell. Being half white, they didn't send him to Florida with Geronimo and the rest of them. I heard the Apaches are dying in Florida, but I don't know if that's true or not. I suspect it is."

"You like him a lot, don't you?"

"O'Hara is my friend. The only one I have. We've gone through some hard times, me and him." Flintlock smiled. "And some good times. Once we found a golden bell that the old Spanish men made."

Bridie spilled water over O'Hara's head. "Keep splashing him, Sam," she said. "The pool is shallow. What about you, Sam? What will you do after you find your mother?"

"I haven't thought about it much. The West is changing and the day of the bounty hunter is just about over. Now the telegraph catches more bad men than bounty hunters ever did. Well, I did have one thought about my future. There's talk that a Frenchman by the name of Lesseps is building a ship canal down in South America that will join the Pacific and Atlantic coasts. They say he's paying big money to laborers, enough that a man can work for a couple of years and then retire. I figure I can talk O'Hara into joining me, though by nature he normally shies clear of pick and shovel work or any kind of manual labor."

"It sounds like an adventure," Bridie said. "Building a ship canal in South America."

"Like I said, big money. I could retire and buy a hardware store. A man can prosper in hardware. O'Hara could come work for me. He'd be good with customers because he can be right personable by times."

"And the liquor trade is a lucrative business, or so they say," Bridie said.

Flintlock shook his head. "No, if I owned a saloon I could be forced to use my gun again. Nobody gets shot in a hardware store. He feels cooler. Doesn't he feel cooler to you?"

Bridie made no answer, but her stricken expression spoke volumes.

Shadows had gathered on O'Hara's face. His eye sockets and cheek hollows were dark and his lips were very pale and his chest no longer rose and fell with his labored breathing.

"He's starting to feel better," Flintlock said. "I mean, look at him. He's asleep. That's a good sign, isn't it?"

Bridie's face paled under her tan, her eyes wounded. Quickly she placed her ear against O'Hara's chest and listened. She straightened, pulled her hair back and tried again.

This time she listened for long moments and when she sat up all color had drained from her cheeks.

"Sam, oh God, Sam," she said, then slowly, emphasizing each toneless word, "O'Hara is dead."

Flintlock stared at the woman. "No, he's not dead. He's asleep."

"He's dead, Sam."

Flintlock lifted O'Hara by the shoulders and held him close. "O'Hara, wake up! Wake up, damn you!"

Bridie reached out and laid her hand on Flintlock's shoulder. "He's gone, Sam. The bullet must have done more damage than we thought."

As though he hadn't heard, Flintlock shook O'Hara hard and cried out, "Damn you for a stubborn Apache Irishman! On pain of death, don't you dare die on me."

O'Hara's head rolled loosely on his shoulders and then fell forward on his chest.

All the life that was in him had gone. It was obvious to Bridie O'Toole and now, despite his refusal to accept it, it became obvious to Flintlock. He'd seen enough dead men to know death when it came calling.

Bridie said, "Sam, I'm so sorry. I just don't have the words . . ."

Flintlock made no answer. He held O'Hara's lifeless body in his arms, silent in his grief, his face carved from white marble.

"I didn't want him to die," Bridie said. "I did what I could to make him live."

Cocooned by his terrible grief, Flintlock neither heard nor saw.

"O'Hara was brave, Sam. Brave to the end."

Flintlock rocked back and forth and made a strange, keening sound. Bridie sat beside him, her hand on his broad back . . . and so a moonlit hour passed . . . and then another.

After a while Bridie got to her feet, picked up her rifle and explored the perimeter of the clearing. Within minutes she found what she was looking for, a talus slope to the right of the arroyo that had brought down the rocks that covered the ground at its base. The woman cleared away brush and rubble from a flat spot nearby, the work of an hour that left her with a sore back and a broken fingernail. When she returned to the pool Flintlock had not moved, O'Hara still in his arms.

"Sam," she said.

No answer.

"Sam. We've got a burying to do."

Flintlock didn't respond. Silent. Lost in

some dark place.

"Sam, we must lay O'Hara to rest."

This time Flintlock's eyelids flickered and he looked up at Bridie and said, "Then help me dress him. I will not let O'Hara stand before his Maker naked."

After he and Bridie clothed O'Hara, Flintlock said, "Bring his rifle and his pistol and his knife. An Apache warrior should be buried with the arms he used in life."

Flintlock carried O'Hara to the spot by the talus slope and laid him on the patch of ground Bridie had cleared. He placed the dead man's weapons beside him and then used the fallen rocks to cover his body and when it was done he said, "I wish I could sing his death song, but I don't know how."

"Nor do I," Bridie said. "But I will sing for the Irish warrior in him and help him find peace." Then, in a fine, clear voice she sang for O'Hara.

The Minstrel-Boy to the wars is gone
In the ranks of death you'll find him;
His father's sword he has girded on,
And his wild harp slung behind him.
"Land of song!" said the warrior-bard,
"Though all the world betrays thee,
One sword, at least, thy rights shall guard,
One faithful harp shall praise thee!"

Then, as though the song had become too much for her to bear, she said, speaking in her normal voice, "The Minstrel fell, but the foeman's chain could not bring that proud soul under. The harp he loved ne'er spoke again for he tore its chords asunder; and said, 'No chains shall sully thee, thou soul of love and bravery . . .' Bridie faltered, swallowed hard and continued, " 'Thy songs were made for the pure and free, they shall never sound in slavery.' "

Slow seconds ticked by before Flintlock said, "That was a warrior's song, all right. O'Hara would have loved it."

A wind rose and swirled around the clearing and stirred the trees and Bridie said, "I'm sure he heard it."

When the dawn came, Bridie made coffee, thin and watery, using the last few beans, and they shared some pan bread fried in bacon grease.

If the coffee was thin, Flintlock's cigarette was thinner. He lit it with a brand from the fire and said behind a drift of blue smoke, "Did we kill O'Hara? Did we cause the fever that caused his death?"

Bridie looked as though she'd been half expecting the question. "No, we didn't. We didn't cause his death, Sam."

"Getting the bullet out, I mean. You dug deep."

"But I didn't kill him, nor did you."

Flintlock's face was cut through with deep lines, as though he'd aged a decade in a single night, and the thunderbird on his throat stood out in stark relief, as though it was about to take wing and flutter skyward and proclaim the death of a warrior.

"Do you want to know who killed O'Hara?" Bridie said.

"Yes, tell me."

"Jacob Hammer killed him."

Flintlock thought about that for a few moments and then he said, "Then I'll bring hell to Pitchfork Pass. That I swear to God and to O'Hara's spirit."

Chapter Twenty-One

Louise Smith made her way from the cave behind her cell, a place she visited for some privacy and its relative coolness. When she returned to the cell, Viktor beckoned her to the iron door.

"Man leaving this place, riding somewhere."

Louise looked outside, where a rider who'd just been handed a pair of bulging saddlebags took up the lead rope of his pack mule. Jacob Hammer had forgone Chinese dress and wore a frilled white shirt, tight riding breeches tucked into English boots and, unusual for him when he was within the compound, crossed gunbelts carrying a pair of ivory-handled Colts.

In the early-morning light Hammer looked up at the rider and talked.

"What's he saying?" Louise said. "I can't hear."

"Viktor can hear. Viktor can hear grass

grow." He turned an ear to the door and after a while said, "He talks of the dream smoke."

"Opium?"

"Opium, yes. He tells the man on the horse to buy opium."

"What else does he say?"

"I don't know. Old Man of the Mountain angry. He sees us. Viktor not listen anymore."

The giant quickly stepped away from the door and sat on his cot.

After the rider waved to some onlookers standing around the courtyard and left, Hammer watched him go and then crossed to the dungeon. He stood, legs apart, and stared fixedly at Louise for long moments. Then he said one word, just one syllable that oozed menace and hate like pus from a rotten wound.

"Soon."

Hammer smiled his cold smile, turned on his heel and walked away.

Louise was very afraid. She turned to Viktor, seeking to draw assurance from his great strength, but to her horror the giant's face was a mask of terror.

It was possible that Sam Flintlock would have kept vigil in his sun-seared hiding place among the rocks for days, perhaps many days, and after sipping his canteen dry would have been forced to leave. But fate, the arbiter of a man's destiny, had other plans.

Bridie O'Toole had been against the scheme from the start.

"Sam, I think it's best, at least until we meet up with Detective Brown —"

"My ma, you mean?"

Bridie ignored that. "We use the arroyo as our headquarters and ride out every day in search of Jacob Hammer's couriers. There may be food we overlooked at the Smith cabin and that will be our first stop."

"There's no grub left in the cabin — we took it all," Flintlock said. "Hammer's men carry grub, coming and going, and we'll step over their dead bodies and take it from them."

"Sam, without food and plenty of water you can't maintain a surveillance of Pitchfork Pass. You'd very soon become too weak to raise your rifle."

Flintlock managed a thin smile. "I think the Hawken is lighter."

"You're being silly again, Sam."

"Will you show me the way to Pitchfork Pass?"

"You're dead set on the idea?"

"Yeah. Dead set."

"Then I'll take you there."

"What will you do?"

"First I'll go to the cabin. There just might be some cans left."

"And then?"

"I'll scout around for signs of Detective Brown."

"Hammer's men will still be out hunting us."

"I'll take my chances. That's what the Pinkerton Agency pays me for, after all."

Flintlock and the woman mounted and then stopped briefly by O'Hara's grave to pay their respects. They rode through the arroyo into the dawn light, but after a few minutes, Bridie drew rein.

"Sam, are we both being foolish?" she said.

"In what way?"

"I'm still here because I can't bear the thought of a woman failing as a Pinkerton. And you are here because you want to avenge O'Hara's death. The destruction of Jacob Hammer's criminal empire has become secondary and that's not why I was sent here."

"Bridie, look around, look how vast is this landscape and how insignificant we are.

We're two people whose lives don't matter a damn. If you're killed, you'll become a one-line entry in a Pinkerton ledger. And me? Nobody gives a damn whether I live or die."

"What are you telling me, Sam?"

"Just this . . . we can't beat the Old Man of the Mountain. He's way too powerful. All we can do is make the cost of him doing business too high, force him to move on and set up in some other place."

"So we stay?"

"Yeah, we stay."

"I must keep telling myself not to turn tail, Sam, not to give up and ride away."

"Me, neither. That's why you're taking me to Pitchfork Pass."

"You never answered me — are we being foolish?"

"Of course, we're being foolish, sort of like David was when he tried to outdraw Goliath."

"David slew Goliath," Bridie said.

"I know, shot him with a rock." It was good to see Flintlock grin again. "See, we're not being foolish."

"Yes, we are," Bridie said.

"Damn right we are," Flintlock said. "But if we light a shuck then O'Hara died for nothing, and I won't let that happen."

He kneed his horse forward.

■ ■ ■ ■

Flintlock had been in his rocky perch above the entrance to Pitchfork Pass for only an hour when fate dealt him all the aces in the pack.

As the sky brightened to blue and a whip-tail lizard did push-ups on a rock at his elbow, a solitary rider leading a pack mule left the pass and three armed men walked out of the entrance and watched him go.

Flintlock waited, eyes narrowed against the rising sun. The rider headed northeast for fifty yards and disappeared into a gully. Flintlock watched until the three men turned and walked back into the pass. He rose to his feet and scrambled down the steep incline behind him to his waiting horse. He mounted and headed through a flat brushy area among some sturdy piñon and juniper trees and headed northeast, riding between high, red sandstone walls where night shadows still lingered. His trail led upward, the height of the walls gradually decreasing until he found himself on a dome-shaped plateau that overlooked the broken landscape to the east.

He dismounted and saw below him and a little north the rider with the pack mule, his hat brim pulled low against the sun glare, eyes fixed on the trail ahead. The distance between Flintlock and his prey was at least 150 yards and he did not have enough faith in his skill with a rifle to chance a shot at that range.

He raised his canteen to his lips, drank and then, his face grim and set, stepped into the saddle and looked for a way off the bench. To his left was a point where the rock had broken away, leaving a drop of about three feet onto a brush-covered slope that fell away gradually to the flat. His mount balked at the jump, but Flintlock thumped the buckskin in the ribs with his heels and after some hesitation the horse decided enough was enough and hopped down onto the slope.

Flintlock leaned from the saddle and whispered into the big horse's ear. "Pain in the ass."

He took the slope and swung after the rider, closing the distance at a canter. A man in hostile country who doesn't check his back trail is either stupid or overconfident, and Flintlock decided that in this case it was both. This was no-man's-land, a savagely hot, waterless waste slashed by deep arroyos and uplifted ridges of sandstone rock. It was a desolate and dangerous country to travel over, and the Pitchfork rider should have been wary.

When the man heard hoofbeats behind him he finally turned his head and his eyes popped when he saw Flintlock bearing down on him. He slid his rifle out of the boot.

Too late . . . way too late.

Flintlock came on at a gallop, trailing dust, firing his Winchester from the shoulder. The buckskin had a smooth gait and at a range of thirty yards Flintlock's aim was deadly. He shot the rider out of the saddle, covered the remaining distance between him and the downed man and levered two shots into him as the Pitchfork rider clawed for his belt gun as he struggled to rise to his feet.

Flintlock jumped from the saddle and advanced on the wounded man, levering and firing his rifle as he came, scoring shattering hits. "This is for O'Hara!" he yelled. "And this! And this! And this!"

The Pitchfork gunman died with a look of bafflement on his face, unaware of the reason for his death.

Then Flintlock's terrible anger fled him. His eyes burned and there was a taste of green bile in his mouth and he felt exhausted. Then he looked at the bloodstained corpse at his feet and, in a small voice, said, as though explaining his wrath to the dead man, "That was for O'Hara."

The Pitchfork's gunman's horse had fled the gunfire but the pack mule stood a few yards away, head down, its guide rope trailing. Flintlock led the mule back to his own mount and stepped into the saddle. In this silent land, he had no doubt the sound of the firing had been heard and a hue and cry would soon follow. Time was of the essence and he had to light a shuck. Searching the contents of the mule's pack would have to come later.

CHAPTER TWENTY-TWO

"Yeah, I saw a party of Hammer's gunmen in the distance, but they didn't see me," Flintlock said.

Bridie O'Toole's hair was damp from her wash at the pool, a waste of precious water, Flintlock thought. "I didn't find any food at the cabin," she said. "I didn't find any trace of Detective Brown, either."

"My ma is out there somewhere. And there's bound to be grub on the mule. The feller I killed was traveling northeast and there are no railroad depots in that direction so he must have been carrying grub."

"Tracks are being laid all over the Colorado Territory," Bridie said. "Plenty of new rail depots up that way."

"That might be the answer," Flintlock said. "I reckon Jacob Hammer is thinking ahead. He's breaking new ground, worried about Pinkertons and government agents in Flagstaff and other places in the Arizona

Territory."

"Do you think it's possible that we're crowding him?" Bridie said.

"Yeah, we're crowding him. Why else would he send a rider north into Colorado to break new ground?"

"Help me strip the mule," Bridie said. "Let's see what the man was carrying."

The results of the search through the pack stunned Flintlock and Bridie into silence. There was grub, enough for a couple of weeks, but what amazed them was the sum of money the Pitchfork gunman had been transporting, fifty thousand dollars in bundled banknotes, a fortune that could support a man in reasonable comfort for a hundred years.

Bridie looked into Flintlock's eyes and said, "Sam, we've hurt him. Even Jacob Hammer can't take such a loss."

Flintlock nodded. "It's going to make him mad as a red-eyed steer, all right."

The woman looked around her. "This place isn't going to remain safe. Hammer will comb the whole territory to get this much money back."

Flintlock made a swift mental calculation. "Except for the notes I used to start a fire, we now have just under sixty thousand dollars of Hammer's money. Is that enough to put him out of business?"

"I doubt it," Bridie said. "But it's a start."

Flintlock shook his head. "No, it's a start and an end. We'll load the money onto the mule and then get the hell out of here for a spell."

"And go where?"

"Anyplace where there's law."

Bridie thought that over for a few moments and said, "Wait. I have an idea."

She rose to her feet, rummaged through her carpetbag and triumphantly waved a piece of folded paper at Flintlock. "It's a map, Sam."

"Hell, woman, we don't need a map."

"Yes, we do."

Bridie opened the map and laid it on the ground. She perused it for a few moments and then jabbed a spot. "Yes, there it is, right there," she said. "Fort Defiance. Where there's a fort, there's soldiers and a telegraph."

"We'll be safe there," Flintlock said. "Hammer won't attack a fort."

"He'd be a fool if he did. I can telegraph my superiors, tell them about the money and await further instructions."

Flintlock picked up the map and peered closer. "How far away is this Fort Defiance?"

"A three days' ride, four if the mule doesn't behave."

"And if the Old Man of the Mountain doesn't slow us up permanently. All this map shows between here and the fort is open space. Suppose we come up on a mountain range or a river?"

"I don't think there's a mountain or a river between here and Fort Defiance. If there was, it would be marked on the map."

"Bridie, there's nothing on this map but a few scattered towns and badlands. Look, right there and there, it says *badlands.*"

"I see it, but I'm sure a man in your line of work has crossed badlands before," Bridie said. "Men with a price on their heads and badlands go together."

"Seems like I always had O'Hara to scout for me in that kind of country."

"And now you have me, Sam. I'll ride scout."

Flintlock smiled. "You're not O'Hara, Bridie, but I guess you'll do."

"Then it's settled. We ride for Fort Defiance."

"And hope we don't run into Jacob Hammer's gunmen."

"I don't even want to think about that, not now," Bridie said.

"Me, neither," Flintlock said. "Not now, not ever."

That evening Flintlock and Bridie O'Toole dined on fried salt pork, fresh sourdough bread and sweet little rice balls that Bridie said were Chinese and a big restaurant favorite in San Francisco and other places.

"The Old Man feeds his gunmen well," Flintlock said, a grain of rice sticking to his unshaven chin.

Bridie removed the rice and said, "And now he's feeding us."

"Real nice of him, huh?" Flintlock said.

"Mmm . . ." Bridie said. She looked beyond Flintlock. "Rider!" she said in sudden alarm. She picked up her gunbelt and slid the Smith & Wesson .44 from the leather. She and Flintlock rose at the same time.

"State your intentions or you're a dead man," Flintlock called out into the gloom and the rider, a black silhouette against the backdrop of darkness, drew rein.

"Don't shoot. I'm coming in."

A woman's voice.

"Are you Detective Brown?" Bridie said.

"Who the hell else would I be? Seems like there's only two women in the whole Arizona Territory. I'm one and, honey, you're

204

the other."

"Ride forward and be identified," Flint-lock said. "And don't make any fancy moves. I'm not a trusting man."

"Mister, I'm too tired to make any kind of move," the woman said. She urged her horse into a shambling walk and when she was a few yards from the fire she stopped.

"Light and set," Bridie said. "I'm Detective O'Toole."

"Saw you once or twice," Detective Brown said. "I took you for somebody's wife." She nodded at Flintlock. "Maybe his."

"I'm a Pinkerton," Bridie said. "They sent me to find you."

"Well, you've found me, or I've found you. It wasn't difficult."

Letting out a little groan, the woman stepped stiffly out of the saddle. "I could use a cup of that coffee," she said, walking to the fire.

"Coming right up," Bridie said. "I'm very glad to meet you at last, Miss Brown."

Flintlock could contain himself no longer. His eyes shining in the firelight he grinned and yelled, "Ma!" He threw himself at the woman and took her in a bear hug, only to jump back as though he'd been burned as something hard rammed into his belly.

"Back off, mister," the detective said. She

held a Smith & Wesson in her hand. "Or I'll blow your navel clean through your backbone."

"But . . . but . . . Ma, it's me. I'm your son."

"His name's Sam Flintlock and he claims you're his mother," Bridie said. "He says he's been searching for you for years. Here's your coffee, Detective Brown. Watch out, it's hot."

The woman stared hard at Flintlock as she holstered her revolver. "Don't ever do that again," she said. "Next time I'll gun you for sure."

"But it's true, I am your son and you're my ma," Flintlock said.

"Mister, if you're my son, you're a sore disappointment to me. My son's back East somewhere and he's a doctor or a lawyer or maybe an army officer, not a thug dressed in buckskin with a big bird on his throat."

Flintlock displayed his irritation on his frowning face. "After you left me with old Barnabas he had an Assiniboine woman put the bird on my throat. If you'd been there, you could've stopped him."

Detective Brown was suddenly interested. "Did you say Barnabas? Would that be Barnabas McIntyre, the mountain man?"

"Yes, it would, and a wicked old stick he

was. One time he pinned me down as grizzly bait."

"My father's name was Barnabas McIntyre and he was a mountain man."

"And he didn't approve of your choice of men and you ran away with a gambler and left me behind," Flintlock said. "Now, I want you to give me that man's name, since he was my pa."

"What's wrong with the name you got?"

"For God's sake, woman, are you crazy? I was named for a rifle, not my father."

"That's no way to talk to your mother."

"So, you admit that you're my ma?"

"It seems that's the case. My name is Jane McIntyre, but you can call me Ma if you like. But don't ever try to hug me again without warning."

"What was my pa's name, Ma?"

"I'll tell you that when I think you're ready."

"I'm ready."

"No, you're not."

"You're not what I thought you'd be," Flintlock said.

"What did you think I'd be?"

"Well, not as tall. I mean, smaller and . . ."

"Prettier?" She nodded in Bridie's direction. "That I'd look like her?"

Flintlock couldn't come up with an answer, and Jane said, "I'm not pretty, and I'm not small, Sam. I'm tall and bony, all angles and flat planes, and I've got big hands and feet and men tell me I look like one of them."

"You've got nice hair, Ma," Flintlock said.

"Yes, Barnabas once said that I got the chestnut hair from my mother and my scarecrow body from him." She smiled and her teeth were good. "I think, Sam, we're a sore disappointment to one another."

"You're my ma, and I plan to love you," Flintlock said, betraying a softer side that Bridie O'Toole didn't think he possessed.

Jane shook her head. "No, Sam, don't plan on loving me. One day I'll move on and leave you again. Just be glad we finally met and let it go at that."

"My pa's name?"

"The day I leave, I'll tell you, but not until then."

"Why not now?" Flintlock said.

"Because I need Sam Flintlock the bounty hunter and sometimes outlaw for what has to be done. No one else." Jane smiled. "Don't look so surprised, Sam. I've heard about you. In Pinkerton circles, you're quite famous. They say just the mention of your name makes fugitives from justice quake."

"Quack?" Flintlock said.

"Quake. It means 'to shake, tremble all over.' "

"I do that?"

"So I heard. But then people say all kinds of things about outlaws."

"I'm not an outlaw," Flintlock said. "Well, most of the time, I'm not."

Jane sat by the fire and held out her cup to Bridie. "Enough of family matters. Refill that, Detective O'Toole, and what are those white things?"

"Chinese rice balls. They're sweet. Would you like to try one?"

"I sure would, and while I'm eating tell me what's going on with you."

"What do I call you now?" Bridie said. "Still Miss Brown?"

"Call me Jane. I have a strong feeling the time for an alias is over."

CHAPTER TWENTY-THREE

Sam Flintlock's mother, now Pinkerton Detective Jane McIntyre, listened in silence as Bridie O'Toole recounted the private war she and Flintlock had waged on Jacob Hammer and the money they'd taken. She then told of the death of O'Hara and their plan to head for the safety of Fort Defiance.

Before she said anything else, Jane surprised Flintlock. "O'Hara was half Apache. Did he sing his death song?"

"No, he didn't," Flintlock said.

"Pity," Jane said. "You can be sure he had one. Every Apache composes his own death song and keeps it secret until his time comes."

"O'Hara just closed his eyes and died," Bridie said. "I sang 'The Minstrel Boy' at his grave."

"A fine song for a dead warrior, but it is not Indian and O'Hara's spirit is not at peace," Jane said. "That is one situation we can remedy before we do anything else. Take me to his grave."

Flintlock seemed uneasy. "Ma, I don't think —"

"Take me to the Apache's grave, Sam."

Jane carried the lantern to the pile of rocks that marked O'Hara's resting place and said to Flintlock, "We will sing his death song to set his soul free to enter the spirit world."

"We don't know what it is, Ma," Flintlock said. "Maybe we can just say a prayer."

"I have another song that will suffice," Jane said. She laid the lantern on the grave. "It's a death song of the Shoshone that a shaman taught to your grandfather and your grandfather taught it to me. It tells of the battles the warrior fought, the scalps he took, the horses he stole, the women he loved and the tall sons he fathered. He says he will now go to the land where his father has gone and the old man's ghost will rejoice at his prowess. He says death comes as a friend and relieves him of pain and he ends by saying that he will never complain that his time to die has come."

Before Flintlock could say a word, in a strong, clear voice his mother sang the Shoshone death song, not a song the white man sings of grief and loss, but one that

211

celebrated the dead warrior's life and rejoiced in his journey to the spirit world.

When Jane finished, the lantern flame guttered in a rising wind and, suddenly appearing out of the darkness, an owl swept over the grave on silent wings and then vanished into the night.

Jane smiled. "All is well. The owl is a creature of the night and it speaks with the dead. It has told us that O'Hara's spirit is now free."

Flintlock's eyes were fixed on a spot beyond the flickering lantern and he nodded and said in a strange, hollow voice, "Yes, I know, Barnabas. O'Hara is now following the buffalo."

The two women stared at him, but neither spoke.

"I've given it some thought, Bridie, and I think your plan is the right one," Jane said. "We'll take the money to Fort Defiance and wire for further instructions."

"It's going to be a dangerous trip, Ma," Flintlock said.

"No more dangerous than staying here," Jane said. "I found your camp easily enough and Jacob Hammer's thugs can do the same. In a wilderness of stone, the smell of a wood fire and boiling coffee carries far."

"Then we'll ride out at first light," Flintlock said. "Since we've added the smell of salt pork and —"

"Rice balls," Bridie said, smiling.

"I was going to say fried bread," Flintlock said. He helped himself to coffee and said, "Ma, you shot a man off of me at the Smith cabin. Where have you been since?"

"Not a mile from here on a rock shelf banking a dry creek bed," Jane said. "I found the place after I got into a shooting scrape with one of Hammer's gunmen and decided to lay low for a spell."

"We saw the aftermath of that, me and O'Hara," Flintlock said.

"I didn't count it, but as near as I can guess I took twelve thousand dollars in gold and silver coin from the man, and his horse and pack mule. We'll pick up the money tomorrow before we ride east." She raised an eyebrow. "There's a hot spring on the ledge, Samuel. It isn't much, but maybe you could take a few minutes to use it before we leave for the fort."

"Use it for what?"

"For bathing."

"Well, I'll study on it," Flintlock said.

"Please do. I have soap in my saddlebags."

CHAPTER TWENTY-FOUR

As he swung into the saddle in the gray light of dawn, Jacob Hammer seethed with rage. He'd lost men and more important he'd lost money. Somebody, probably some two-bit lawmen leading a posse of hayseeds, was trying to put him out of business. And at the rate his losses were piling up, that might not be long.

The two men who'd fled the fight with the posse said a woman was with them and one of the rubes used a muzzle-loading squirrel rifle. They were sure of that. The cowards looked a lot less sure when Hammer ordered them executed and soon their heads joined the others in Pitchfork Pass.

"If you can, take them alive, especially the woman," Hammer told the thirty mounted gunmen who surrounded him. "We'll bring them back here and have us some fun."

This brought a cheer and after the noise subsided, Hammer said, "A five-hundred-dollar bonus to the man who brings me the head of the leader of the rabble." He waited until another cheer died down. "We've enough grub and water to last a week, but I want this matter over before then." He waved a hand and yelled, "Scouts forward!"

Two bearded men in buckskins detached themselves from the rest and rode into the pass. Dave Coombs and Pete Fox had scouted for the army and had murdered, raped and scalped their way through the Sioux and Cheyenne nations. Both badly wanted that five-hundred-dollar bonus.

When the scouts were out of sight, Jacob Hammer led his men forward.

The Old Man of the Mountain was on the hunt . . . a conscienceless killer who was as dangerous and merciless as a wounded cougar.

Jane's hot spring was not a spring, it was a seep, and Flintlock, soaped up and irritated, tried to bathe in a basinful of water. Bridie O'Toole had the good manners to avert her eyes as she busied herself loading the mule, but Jane considered her son with a critical eye.

"Wash all of your parts, Samuel, and then your hair and don't forget behind your ears," she said.

"It ain't easy," Flintlock said, scowling. "There's hardly any water."

"There's enough, so do the best you can. Remember, cleanliness is next to godliness."

Bridie had loaded both pack mules and Jane asked her to switch her saddle to the horse she'd taken from the Pitchfork rider, a better mount than her own. When that was done, Bridie took up her rifle and said, "Jane, I'm going to look around."

The older woman's eyes searched Bridie's strained face and she said, "We're safe here, at least for a short while."

Bridie shook her head. "I feel something. My grandma always said I had the Irish gift of second sight, and right now I feel uneasy, as though a goose flew over my grave."

Jane nodded. "Allan Pinkerton always told me to go with my gut. By that he meant follow my instinct. Yes, Bridie, take a look around and come hotfooting back here if you see any sign of Pitchfork riders."

Bridie smiled. "You can depend on that."

Except for the buckskin shirt, Sam Flintlock dressed in his duds that his mother had washed for him. Every item was damp and only served to increase his early-morning irritability. "Damn it, Ma, what kind of soap was that? I smell like a Denver brothel."

"Have you ever been in a Denver brothel, Samuel?" Jane said, looking stern. "Or any other kind of brothel, for that matter?"

"No, Ma," Flintlock said, blinking.

"Well, I have, when your father was traveling the gambling circuit, and they smelled nothing like Pears soap, I assure you."

Flintlock saw a way out and took it. "Well, I'll get used to it. It doesn't smell so bad, I guess."

"I should think not, since Sarah Bernhardt swears by Pears soap and I imagine she knows a thing or two about bathing." Jane looked stern again. "Besides, in another three or four months you'll smell like your old self again."

Flintlock was spared a further discussion of his personal hygiene by the timely return of Bridie O'Toole, who had news . . . all of it bad.

"A big dust cloud to the southeast, a lot of riders," Bridie said. "And they have a pair of scouts out. Those two I saw clear."

"The army?" Flintlock said.

"I doubt it," Jane said. "Someone would have told the Pinkertons if there was a plan to send soldiers into this area."

"If it's not the army, then it's Jacob Hammer and his men," Flintlock said.

"They're out hunting for us," Bridie said.

Flintlock thought about that and said, "Forget riding for Fort Defiance this morning. Hammer's men are bound to spot our dust and head us off."

"Then what do you suggest, Samuel?" Jane said.

"You and Bridie take the pack mules and ride north into the rough country up there. I'll do what I can to hold Hammer here for a while and buy you some time."

Jane was alarmed. "Samuel, you could be killed."

"I'll be careful. What we don't want is the Old Man of the Mountain to recover his money. He has to get those ill-gotten gains back or his businesses will suffer and that's why he's out in force after us."

"But Samuel —"

"Ma, you and Bridie head due north, away from Hammer. Keep the money safe and I'll find you later and then we'll make another plan."

"I don't like this, Samuel," Jane said. "It's very thin."

"Can you think of a better plan?"

"Well, we could all head north and lose ourselves in the mesa country," Jane said.

"Hammer is using scouts and you can bet the farm they know their business," Flintlock said. "They'd catch up with us before noon."

Another protest died on Jane's lips as she faced the harsh facts. If they got caught in the open they couldn't buck the odds. They'd all die and Hammer would have his money back and his evil empire would be saved. It was unthinkable. After a while she said, "Samuel, come back to us."

"Sure, I will. I'm not about to let a two-bit scoundrel like Jacob Hammer cut my suspenders. Now go, both of you."

Bridie O'Toole rose on tiptoe and kissed Flintlock on the cheek. "Good luck and be careful, Sam." She smiled. "You smell real nice."

Flintlock puffed up a little. "It's Pears soap. Sarah Bernhardt swears by it and she knows a thing or two about bathing," he said.

"Good luck, Samuel," Jane said.

"You, too, Ma. Good luck."

Chapter Twenty-Five

Flintlock rode out of a dry creek bed as a rising wind talked around the rocks and despite the early-morning hour a heat haze shimmered to the south and a silence lay heavy on the land. After a while he drew rein and looked around, his every sense attuned to the dry, lonely country that surrounded him. He saw and heard nothing. But he knew that somewhere out there were two of Jacob Hammer's scouts and behind those, and not too distant, a dust cloud marked the main force. Flintlock calculated at least forty riders, and maybe more, coming on at a trot.

From where he sat his buckskin a shelf of deeply split rock, bookended by dramatically high bluffs, sloped downward for several hundred yards to a flat, grassy canyon with heavy growths of piñon and mesquite. Finding the scouts was Flintlock's first order of business. Put out Hammer's eyes and he'd be riding blind, at least for a while . . . perhaps long enough for Flintlock to carry out the second part of his newly formulated plan.

He rode down the slope onto the flat and drew rein again as, unbidden, the thought came to him: What would O'Hara do? The answer came back quickly, as though O'Hara were here by his side . . . *Dismount, hide among the trees and let the scouts come to you.* It made sense. The canyon was a natural thoroughfare that cut through a copper-colored wasteland of dizzying heights and plunging gorges. The scouts were bound to ride this way — if they hadn't done so already.

Flintlock stepped from the saddle and led his horse into a thick stand of juniper and piñon where he was concealed but still had a good view of the canyon. The sun rose, the heat became intense and Flintlock smelled his own sweat mixed with the lingering fragrance of Miss Bernhardt's favorite soap. To the southeast the blue arch of the sky showed no sign of a dust cloud. Had Hammer and his gunmen stopped, waiting on a report from the scouts? It was possible. Hunting a few people in that immense, lost land was like looking for a needle in a haystack.

The best part of an hour passed and Flintlock's eyes burned from the strain of searching the canyon through the sun glare. Above his head, visible through the tree canopy, a flock of quarreling crows flapped across the sky and insects droned their small music in the brush.

Then suddenly, the scouts appeared, but not in the canyon as he'd expected, but riding down the sloping rock shelf that he'd taken earlier. One of the men led the horse that Jane had left at her hideout. If the scouts were good, and Flintlock had no reason to believe they were not, they already knew that two women with pack mules had headed north and a man had ridden south. Based on that information Hammer would probably split his command, most of them following the tracks of the women, the rest hunting the fugitive male.

There was a bottom line to all this and it was starkly defined — the scouts had to die.

When you're forced to kill a man who needs killing, there are no niceties involved, no chivalrous code of triggerometry, you do whatever it takes to get the job done. And that was Flintlock's philosophy as he slid his Winchester from the boot and then lay flat on the ground, the rifle at his shoulder.

The scouts, big, bearded men wearing bowler hats, both with army-issue field glasses hanging on their chests, navigated the slope, talking, grinning to each other, the possibility of getting bushwhacked the last thing on their minds. Hammer had told them they were hunting rubes, and a rube doesn't scare men who'd killed more than their share.

Sweat broke out on Flintlock's forehead as he took up the slack on the Winchester's trigger, his sights laid on the man to his left, the one doing most of the talking, his head continually turning to his companion.

Flintlock smiled.

Mister, you should be watching the trail ahead of you. Big mistake.

Flintlock held his breath, let a little of it out, and then squeezed the trigger. The butt plate slammed against his shoulder as the rifle roared its flat statement and the scout jolted in the saddle as the bullet slammed into his chest. For a second he sat tall and erect, like a soldier on parade, and then slowly . . . slowly . . . he toppled over the side of his horse.

The surviving scout was stunned, but only for a moment. He shucked his rifle and charged. Down the slope and onto the flat he came on at a gallop, riding for the drift of smoke lacing among the trees.

Flintlock fired, missed, then jumped to his feet, levering the Winchester. He and the scout fired at the same time. The man's bullet burned Flintlock across his right thigh, drawing blood; his own round went nowhere. Never a great hand with a long gun, Flintlock dropped the rifle and drew his Colt. The range was now short, twenty yards separating the two men. The scout levered his Winchester from the shoulder and fired. It was a hurried shot that splintered bark from the tree at Flintlock's side. Flintlock worked the Colt, shooting very fast. His first bullet missed the mark, but the remaining two took effect, one plowing into the scout's left shoulder and the second raked across the man's neck. But now the rider was right on top of him. The horse reared and shied away from Flintlock as the man on its back tried to work his rifle. Unbalanced, he was thrown from the saddle, landed on his back and lost his grip on the Winchester. He sprang to his feet, his hand going for his belt gun that was butt forward and unhandy in an army flap holster. The scout looked into the muzzle of Flintlock's revolver and right there and then gave up the fight.

"All right, I'm done," he said.

"I'm not," Flintlock said.

He triggered his remaining two shots. At a range of five feet, both bullets slammed into the scout's chest and dropped him dead as yesterday's mutton when he hit the ground.

Flintlock looked down at the man and said, "That's two more for O'Hara." Then, to force home his message, "I hope you hear that in hell, you son of a bitch."

Chapter Twenty-Six

According to Sam Flintlock's mother and Bridie O'Toole the pass that led to the Hammer compound lay due south, but the entrance was difficult to see unless you were real close and Flintlock intended to do just that . . . get real close.

He rode out of the gulch as the Hammer riders' dust cloud again stained the sky. The mesa country was a land of echoes and it was difficult to pinpoint the source of gunshots that racketed relentlessly around the rocks. But his pursuers were coming on steadily, beating the bushes for him, and Flintlock had to put a heap of git between himself and them or his scalp would decorate the Old Man of the Mountain's parlor wall.

Once again he found himself among a lofty maze of sandstone rock that took on all kinds of fantastic shapes and cast strange shadows the farther south he rode. He depended on the big buckskin to pick its own way among the labyrinth and the horse did not fail him. After thirty minutes Flintlock found himself in yet another gulch, this one narrow and treeless, the looming bulk of Balakai Mesa forming a massive backdrop. Hammer's horsemen had come from the southeast and he turned his horse in that direction.

His ma had been right, the entrance to Pitchfork Pass was well hidden, recessed into the mesa slope. But it was there. He'd found it.

Flintlock didn't take time to consider how foolhardy his plan was. Uppermost in his mind was that he was about to take the war to Hammer's doorstep and that pleased him . . . and he was sure it would've delighted the Apache in O'Hara.

He retrieved his Winchester, dried sweaty palms on his pants, took a deep breath, steadying himself, and then touched spurs to the buckskin's flanks.

The big horse took off at a gallop. The mouth of the pass was fifty yards away . . . forty . . . thirty . . . twenty . . . then he was right on top of it. He yanked the buckskin to a skidding halt, threw the rifle to his shoulder and cranked off three fast shots, sending bullets into the gloom of the arroyo, heedless of where they hit. He cantered the buckskin for a short distance and then swung around. Flintlock's blood was up and he grinned, ferocious as a lobo wolf. Now the fun was about to start.

He was not disappointed.

Like angry ants leaving a trampled nest, three men spilled out of the arroyo and he heard them cuss a blue streak, one of them with a flesh wound to his forehead that trickled blood.

Flintlock roared a war cry that was savage from his pent-up anger and charged, firing the Winchester from the shoulder. The range was short, the encounter brief, but he dropped two of the Hammer gunmen, one of them chawing up the ground with his kicking feet. Taken by surprise at the suddenness of Flintlock's attack the bloodied man snapped off a shot from his Colt, missed and ran back into the arroyo.

Flintlock thought about another run but the sound of angry voices within the arroyo convinced him not to push his luck. He'd brought the fight to Hammer, killed one, possibly two of his gunmen, and the Old Man would never again sleep quite as easy in his bed.

Flintlock swung the buckskin north and lit a shuck, bullets cracking past his head as a dozen outraged gunmen wished him a fond farewell of flying lead.

In the late afternoon as the sun began its descent, Sam Flintlock cut his mother's trail north, the passage of two horses and a pair of pack mules leaving enough scars on the land that even a fair-to-middling scout like himself could follow.

He had not seen any sign of Jacob Hammer and his men and that troubled him. Where were they? There were a couple of possibilities. After losing his scouts Hammer had called off the hunt. But that was unlikely. The second was he'd heard the gunfire at Pitchfork Pass and returned to investigate. Of the two options, the second made the most sense. Maybe the Old Man had feared that his fortress was under assault by lawmen or the army.

Flintlock was thankful that Hammer was nowhere in sight, yet he felt uneasy, as though something bad, something disastrous, had happened outside of his seeing. He told himself he was being foolish, an old maiden aunt who hears a rustle in every bush, but could still not shake the feeling that his ma and Bridie were in danger.

As the day shaded into evening, he rode through a gap between two towering crags and then picked his way across a boulder-strewn ridge before riding into a meadow bright with late-blooming wildflowers. Flintlock was halfway across the meadow when something at the far end caught his eye. Even in the growing darkness he made out the roofs of a couple of buildings and what was possibly a windmill. The tracks of the two women had led Flintlock in this direction. Maybe they'd decided to stay the night at an isolated ranch. There was one way to find out. He kneed his tired horse into a walk and headed for the ranch . . . or whatever it was.

Sam Flintlock rode into a ghost town.

That is, if a ruined hotel with an adjoining saloon, a blacksmith's forge and a general store with a windmill could be called a town. But someone had given the place had a name. The fading words DEAD HORSE were painted on a sign nailed to a post that had tipped over years before.

Were the women here?

Flintlock slipped his rifle out of the boot and walked the buckskin to the hotel. He drew rein, stood in the stirrups and yelled, "Ma!"

The answering silence mocked him.

A hitching rail still stood outside the

saloon. Flintlock tethered his mount and walked back to the hotel. He pushed the creaking door open and stood in what had been the lobby. "Anybody here?"

His voice echoed hollow in the quiet darkness and somewhere in a corner a rat rustled.

"Ma, are you here? Bridie?"

A solemn hush, as though the building were holding its breath, waiting for something to happen.

There was a rickety staircase to Flintlock's left that gave access to the upper-floor rooms. He thumbed a match into flame and climbed steps that creaked and groaned, protesting his weight. There were three bedrooms and all were empty of furniture. But Flintlock's exploration had not been entirely in vain. On the windowsill of one of the rooms stood a brass candelabra, still holding two of its original three candles. He lit the candles, made his way downstairs and walked into the saloon. Holding the candelabra high Flintlock's eyes roamed over the place. There were no tables or chairs or a bar. But a battered, upright piano still stood against the far wall and above it, draped in black crepe, hung a portrait of an elderly, serious-looking gent with a gray beard down to his watch chain. Flintlock guessed he was either a former mayor of Dead Horse or the proprietor of this modest drinking establishment. Whoever he was, like the town, he was long gone.

Flintlock's next stop was the general store . . . where he found the body of a dead man. It was a good-looking corpse. The man was a young towhead, well dressed, wearing an expensively tooled gunbelt, the revolver gone from the holster. Wear on the boots revealed that the youngster had worn spurs, but those, too, were missing. Even in the guttering candlelight, the cause of death was obvious, a neat, round bullet hole smack in the middle of the man's forehead. The body had cooled, but was not yet stiff and Flintlock decided the man hadn't been dead for long, maybe since late afternoon. Suspicious now, Flintlock examined the corpse more closely. As he'd half expected, the man's hands were smooth, free of calluses, not the horny mitts of a laboring man, but, coupled with the pricey revolver rig and fine duds, obviously those of a man who made his living with a gun.

And the only hired guns in this neck of the woods worked for Jacob Hammer.

Flintlock stepped outside again, concern spiking at him. It had been dark when he'd ridden into the ghost town and he hadn't examined the ground for tracks, but now in the light from the candelabra he kneeled and saw that the dusty street bore the hoof-prints of many horses. And booted men had been here, and faint, barely discernible among the rest, were the smaller prints of women's feet.

Flintlock rose, his face stricken. The signs were obvious and had a story to tell. Jacob Hammer and his gunmen had been here and his ma and Bridie O'Toole had been taken. But not without a fight, as the body in the general store testified.

Were the women dead or alive?

Flintlock dreaded the answer to that question.

Sam Flintlock stepped into the general store and, holding the candelabra high, studied the floor for obvious signs of a struggle. There were none. His ma and Bridie had been there, all right, and one of them had shot down an attacker before they were overwhelmed and dragged outside. It had happened quickly. Killing the scouts had solved nothing. Hammer had no difficulty tracking the women, he'd had other scouts out, cut their trail and arrived in Dead Horse just after Ma and Bridie rode in. He'd taken a different route, probably coming in from the east, and that's why Flintlock had not seen his dust.

The Old Man of the Mountain had outfoxed him.

Despondent, an aching hollowness inside him, Flintlock decided to spend the night at the hotel for no other reason than that was what it was for, to accommodate travelers like himself.

He unsaddled his buckskin, staked him out on a patch of grass that had grown up around the windmill and carried his bedroll back to the hotel. He spread his blankets in the lobby and suddenly bone weary lay down on his back, the candelabra casting its fitful light over him.

But before he could drift off to sleep, the familiar odor of brimstone filled his nostrils and, without opening his eyes, he said, "Go away, Barnabas, I don't want to talk to you."

"Boy, you're an idiot," the old mountain man said.

"You've told me that before."

"Yeah, and I'm telling you again. You found your ma and then lost her again. Only an idiot does that."

Flintlock sat up. Barnabas squatted cross-legged on the floor, burnishing with a bright yellow cloth some kind of metal mask.

"I'll find her again," Flintlock said.

"No, you won't."

"Yes, I will."

"She's my daughter," Barnabas said.

"I know."

"There's a one-eyed man that might help you, Sammy."

"Who is he?"

"I'm not telling you. That's for you to find out. But there's also a chance that he'll kill you. Hey, boy, do you like this mask?"

Barnabas positioned the mask over his face, a brass effigy of an evil, smiling demon. "What do you think?"

"It doesn't become you, old man."

"Well, I have to wear it since I've been promoted."

"Promoted? To what?"

"Gatekeeper. I have to terrify the damned, you understand. It's my line of work." Barnabas took the mask away. "Sammy, in hell there is only one emotion I'm allowed to feel, no happiness, no joy, no hope . . . only sorrow."

"Why are you telling me this?"

"Because I felt sorrow over O'Hara's death. As breeds go, he was one of the best." Barnabas shook his head. "I never thought I'd have to say this again, but go find your ma."

"I know where she is. I'll find her."

"I hope so."

"Tell me about the one-eyed man," Flintlock said.

"No, I can't. He might help you, or he might kill you, that's all I know."

Barnabas got to his feet. "The gatekeeper of hell is a full-time job, so you won't see me again."

"Well, that's a sore disappointment."

"Afore I go, did your ma tell you your real name?"

"Not yet."

"Pity. Now you may never know."

"I'll know, Barnabas. The one-eyed man won't kill me and neither will Jacob Hammer."

"It's good to be confident, boy. Well, it's against the rules for me to wish you good luck, so I'll be on my way. If you're ever in my neck of the woods, I'll open the fiery gate for you."

"Go to hell, Barnabas," Flintlock said.

At dawn, Sam Flintlock saddled up and rode to the arroyo where he and Bridie O'Toole had found safety. He spent several hours standing silently beside O'Hara's grave and only when his vigil was done did he finally talk.

"Why did you have to go and die on me,

Injun?" he said. "Without your guidance, your support, I'm lost. What do I do, O'Hara? Where do I go?"

There was no answer, only the indifferent wind that whispered in Flintlock's ear and offered no advice at all.

Chapter Twenty-Seven

The Old Man of the Mountain sat at the head of a U-shaped table. Four hard-bitten gunmen sat to his left, four to his right, ready to pass judgment on the accused, the Pinkerton detectives Jane McIntyre and Bridie O'Toole.

Jacob Hammer wore the traditional red judicial robe of China and a stern expression, the face of a man about to impose a harsh sentence.

"You, the guilty, have admitted that you are Pinkertons, that you murdered a number of my men and that you robbed me of monies that were rightfully mine," Hammer said. "Have you anything to say in your defense before sentence is passed?"

"Yes," Jane said. "Only this, Hammer . . . you're a piece of low-life trash and I'll see you in hell before I plead for my life with the likes of you, a common criminal."

"Bridie O'Toole, have you anything to say

to this court?" Hammer said, his face expressionless.

"Miss McIntyre took the words out of my mouth," Bridie said. She'd battled her captors and the left side of her face was bruised.

Hammer smiled his thin smile and said, "It is the inclination of this court to extend to the guilty parties a measure of mercy. Answer my question and I will give you both a swift and honorable death by the sword. Refuse to answer and you will burn."

Neither Jane nor Bridie spoke, but their angry eyes blazed their defiance.

"Very well, you choose to be obstinate," Hammer said. "But I will put you to the question nonetheless: A vile murderer with a bird on his throat attacked my home today and killed several of my men. Where is he and where is the Indian that sometimes rides with him?"

"I don't know where he is," Jane said.

"And I don't know, either," Bridie said.

"Is that your final word?" Hammer said. He waited, then, "I have no choice, that is, if the rest of the judges concur, to sentence you, Pinkerton McIntyre and you, Pinkerton O'Toole, to burn at the stake. Judges?"

There was a muttering among the gunmen and then one of them spoke for the rest. "Death at the stake," he said.

Hammer nodded. "A wise decision." He looked at the two women and said, "Sentence to be carried out this seventeenth of August during the Hungry Ghost Festival when the Chinese and all here present honor our ancestors." Hammer waved a negligent hand. "Now I grow weary of their treacherous faces. Take them away."

"Miss Brown!" Louise Smith helped Jane stay on her feet after she and Bridie were thrown roughly into the cell and the iron door clashed shut behind them. Then, the obvious question, "What are you doing here?"

"I was captured by Hammer's men," Jane said. "This is Pinkerton Detective Bridie O'Toole. We were both taken at the same time."

"Are you hurt?" Louise said.

"Bruised," Bridie said. "We were roughly handled."

Louise said, "Miss Brown —"

"Jane McIntyre, Louise. The time for aliases is over."

"Are you to be . . . harmed?" the girl said.

"Burned at the stake," Jane said. "On the seventeenth of August."

"And I'm to be beheaded," Louise said. "I refused to be Hammer's bride and one day he'll take his revenge."

Bridie managed a smile. "Then all three of us are in a pickle, aren't we?"

"Four of us," Louise said. She called out, "Viktor!"

The girl heard Bridie's sharp intake of breath and saw the fright in her eyes when the giant stepped from the cave and into the cell. "This is Viktor," Louise said. "He's my friend."

"Viktor frighten everybody," the man said. "But he means no one harm." His face hardened. "Except Jacob Hammer. Him, Viktor will kill one day."

"Viktor, you surprised us," Jane said.

"Yes," Bridie said, swallowing hard. "I was very surprised."

"Surprise, frighten, is all the same," Viktor said. "Hammer say I am more animal than man. He makes me perform like a dancing bear." The giant smiled. "Like a Russian dancing bear."

"Hammer is the animal, Viktor," Jane said. "Not you."

"Tell us what happened to you, Jane," Louise said. "How were you captured?"

Using as few words as possible, Jane told of the events of the past few days and the death of O'Hara.

"And now we're also condemned to

241

death," Bridie said.

"But there is still hope," Jane said. "My son is still out there and he'll move heaven and earth to save us."

"Your son?" Louise said.

"Yes, I'm Samuel Flintlock's mother," Jane said. She smiled. "I'll tell you the story of that one day." She swayed on her feet. "Suddenly I'm very tired."

With amazing gentleness Viktor helped Jane to his cot. "Lady, you the oldest of us," he said. "Get tired quicker."

"Thank you, I think," Jane said.

"We have bread and beans, Jane," Louise said. "Perhaps if you ate you'd feel better."

"No. Once I rest awhile, I'll be fine," Jane said.

Bridie looked around her. "Four of us crammed into this little cell with no bath. It's going to get ripe in here."

"Bridie, it's ripe in here already," Louise said.

Darkness fell and torches flickered around the compound.

Jane lay on Viktor's cot, Bridie on the other while Louise and the giant stretched out on the floor.

A horned moon rose and cast a beam of light into the cell and on top of the mesa prowling coyotes yipped their hunting song. Louise whispered into the darkness. "Jane?"

"Yes, what is it?"

"Do you really believe that your son can save us?"

A long, drawn-out pause, and then, "If anyone can, it would be Samuel."

"Jane, I'll say a prayer for him."

"When you're at it, say a prayer for all of us."

"Jane?"

"Yes?"

"I'm very scared. I'm only sixteen and I don't want to die."

"I'm scared, too, Louise."

"Sam will save us," the girl said. "I just know he will."

"Yes, Louise, go to sleep with that thought uppermost in your mind," Jane said. "Sam will save us."

CHAPTER TWENTY-EIGHT

Lieutenant Colonel Benjamin Brand gazed out on the dusty Fort Defiance parade ground, where fifty men had formed up in a single, shambling rank. Under his great dragoon mustache, the soldier's lips were curled in contempt. "Damn my eyes, Senator, but I hate mercenaries," he said. "I hate seed, breed and generation of them."

"Better Janowski's rabble get killed than your own men," Senator Adam Flood said. "The colonel says he expects to lose half his force in the assault on Balakai Mesa." Flood smiled. "Win or lose."

"Damned impertinence, if you ask me," Colonel Brand said. "If I'd been asked, I would've told General Elliot that I could take the mesa with a single infantry company." He glared at Flood. "But I wasn't asked."

"With his enemies looking for any excuse to attack him, what the president doesn't need right now are casualty lists of dead American soldiers appearing on the front pages of the newspapers," the senator said. "Let the mercenaries do the job. They're expendable."

"Damned impertinence," Colonel Brand said again.

"You have the mountain howitzers?" Flood said.

"Yes, and the mules and the damned observation balloon. I said it during the war and I say it again, battles are won on the ground, not by madmen in balloons. Now what the deuce is that Polish lunatic doing? He's got my Gatling gun, the scoundrel."

"Colonel Janowski is to be given whatever he wants, that's our agreement with him," Flood said. "And that's why I'm here, to make damn sure that his demands are met."

The Gatling opened up, a distinctive, rattling fire that sounded like a brass bedstead being dragged across a knotty wooden floor.

"Damn him, he's trying to shoot his own men," Colonel Brand said, louder to be heard above the din.

Flood stepped to the window. Janowski's mercenaries were on their bellies, crawling toward him as he fired over their prone bodies. The senator smiled. Shouting, he said, "The colonel's training methods are quite unorthodox. Rather, shall we say, dramatic."

"A true soldier doesn't fight on his belly, sir," Brand said. "He stands tall and proud in —" The firing had abruptly ceased and the colonel realized he was still shouting. He dropped his voice and said in a quieter tone, "He stands tall and proud in the ranks and exchanges volleys with the enemy. That's how it was done in the war and that's how it will be done a hundred years from now."

Flood said, "For regular armies, perhaps, but not for guerilla fighters."

"Guerilla, you say," Colonel Brand said. "The very sound of the word makes my skin crawl."

Flood stepped to the office door and opened it wide. "Colonel Janowski, a word, if you please."

A moment later, leaning heavily on his cane, the mercenary walked inside. "What can I do for you, Senator?" he said.

"Please be seated," Flood said. "You seem quite out of breath."

Colonel Brand didn't try to conceal his disdain as he procured a chair for Janowski and then, good manners overcoming his dislike, he said, "A whiskey with you . . . ah . . . Colonel?"

"Please, Colonel Brand," Janowski said. "You are very kind."

After he saw the Pole settled with a whiskey and a cigar, Flood said, "When can you move your assets west, Colonel?"

"Tomorrow morning, we join the train at Cooper's Junction and from there to Flagstaff. I expect to have my force in position at Balakai Mesa by the sixteenth of the month."

"Let's see, that's four days from now," Flood said. "You can do it that quickly?"

"Yes, sir, but it all depends on the reliability of the train."

"The train will get you to Flagstaff on time," Brand said. "You have my assurance on that."

"Then my mind is set at rest," Janowski said, instantly going up several points in Colonel Brand's estimation. Only a gentleman accepts the word of another gentleman without question.

"Colonel Brand, I beg your pardon, but could you leave us for a while?" Flood said. "We have some matters to discuss of a private nature."

"Of course," the soldier said. "I have inspections to carry out." He bowed to the senator and said, "Your obedient servant, sir."

After Brand left, Flood leaned forward in his chair and said, "Colonel, this must be a clean operation, no residuals left behind. Jacob Hammer must be eradicated and his assets expunged. I mean to the last man. At your fancy, you may choose to spare the lives of women, if any, and children, if any, but every male bearing arms will be expunged. Understand? Clean, Colonel, make it clean. There must be no prisoners."

Janowski nodded. "That can be accomplished quite easily."

"Now then, and I only mention this because the Army Corps of Engineers asked me to . . . try and keep artillery damage to the mesa to a minimum, since after this action it will be secretly restored to its original condition so that no questions are asked."

"That very much depends on the whereabouts of this man Jacob Hammer," Janowski said. "If he lives on top of the mesa then extensive shell damage to the plateau will be an unfortunate reality. However, if he and his band of rogues live within the mesa, harm to the outward structure can be kept to a minimum."

"Very well, splendid. I'm sure the engineers will work it out," Flood said. "The main thing is that you succeed, Colonel. The president will brook no failure."

"Senator, you may inform the president that my men and I will not fail. I will remove the Hammer albatross from around his neck."

"Then, a word of advice, Colonel," Flood said. "Should you, God forbid, not succeed in this endeavor it would be better for you that you save the last bullet for yourself. You have your mercenaries and your cannons but be not proud, Colonel Janowski. Remember that men of action are but the unconscious instruments of men of thought and are thus expendable."

CHAPTER TWENTY-NINE

Sam Flintlock knew that he'd lost, lost badly, but now wasn't the time to throw in the towel, not with his mother in Jacob Hammer's clutches. He had to do something, anything, to strike back against the man's evil empire.

The question was *how.*

Flintlock had spent a wakeful night beside O'Hara's grave, but he could not look to the dead for help. There was only himself. He had it to do. He drank water from the pond, filled his canteen and then saddled the buckskin. Flintlock had no plan. His hope was that as he rode toward Balakai Mesa inspiration would come to him.

He avoided Pitchfork Pass and approached the mesa from the west and dismounted in a stand of mixed piñon and juniper where he could not be seen from the summit. Flintlock rubbed the rough stubble on his jaw and bleakly stared up at the vast bulk of the plateau that soared seven thousand feet above the flat. The wind that rustled in the trees felt cool on his neck and streamed the buckskin's mane. His hoped-for inspiration had not come to him but for one treacherous thought . . . maybe there was nothing he could do . . . not a damned thing . . . David against Goliath, only this time the Philistine had won.

Flintlock loosened the buckskin's girth and then fetched his back against a tree. The wakeful vigil beside O'Hara's grave finally caught up with him and he closed his eyes and slept . . .

The sun rose to its highest point in the sky and then dropped toward the west and Flintlock dreamed of fern-shadowed ponds where O'Hara lay surrounded by green frogs that jumped from his naked body and plopped headfirst into dark water.

He woke with a start and rose quickly to his feet. His horse grazed on bunchgrass and the wind still stirred the trees. Nothing had changed but the fading light.

Acting more on instinct than inspiration, Flintlock took up his Winchester and prowled the base of the mesa. About a hundred yards from where his horse stood he found a point where there was a bowed drop in the caprock, and the shingled slope swept gradually upward. Flintlock studied the incline for several minutes, scratching his chin, thinking. Then his inward voice prodded him . . .

Damn it, man, you've no chance of rescuing your ma . . . but at least do something.

Shaking his head at his own foolishness, he began to climb.

The slope was steeper than it had appeared from the ground, and Sam Flintlock's progress was slow. His rifle hindered him but he resisted the temptation to ditch it in order to use both hands to dig into the shingle and haul himself upward. Something told him he may have need of the Winchester once he gained the crest.

In that, as events would show, he was correct.

It was almost full dark when Flintlock reached the top. His hands were scraped bloody and the knees of his pants were torn, the skin underneath grazed. In the distance, maybe two hundred yards away, a fire winked in the darkness. Sentries. He should have anticipated such, but had not. The question was *how many*. And what would be gained by confronting them?

Flintlock got down on one smarting knee and considered the situation. He answered the questions in his mind. It didn't matter how many because once again he had a chance to hurt the Old Man of the Mountain. Besides, what did he have to lose except his life? Right now, defeated as he was, that counted for little.

Flintlock rose and on cat feet walked closer to the blaze. At one point, he bent low and crossed a rough wooden bridge that spanned a narrow point of Pitchfork Pass. Then, stopping frequently to merge with the night, he listened, trying to gauge how many of Hammer's gunmen were around the fire. Judging by the voices, he thought three, but there could be a few more that were not talking men. He moved forward again. The night was cool and soon the moon would rise. The sky was bright with stars, stretching to the horizons like diamonds strewn on purple velvet, and the air smelled of drifting woodsmoke. Flintlock heard a small *clink,* a metal ring on the side of a bottle. Good. The gunmen were drinking and that would slow them and give him an edge, a small edge to be sure, but if he hoped to get the drop that night, he needed all the help he could get.

Flintlock closed the distance. The three men by the fire were intent on their conversation and the whiskey bottle. Closer still.

Moving a little faster now. Damn it, he was close enough. He racked the Winchester and said, "Howdy, boys, fine night, ain't it?"

The three gunmen scrambled to their feet, panic in each face.

"How the hell did you get here?" one of the men, a burly, bearded fellow said.

"I walked," Flintlock said. "You with the wart on your nose, I wouldn't."

The wart man let his hand ease away from his gun.

"You one of the boss's new hires?" the bearded man said. "Did Mr. Hammer send you up here?"

"Nope," Flintlock said. "Right about now I'm his worst enemy."

Firelight flickered on the face of the third gunman, younger, tougher, with reckless eyes. "What do you want with us?" the youthful gunman said. "Speak up now. State your intentions."

The shabby man with the tattoo on his throat had come out of the darkness and well and truly had the drop . . . and three gunmen didn't like that one bit.

Then Flintlock had a moment of inspiration. "You boys came up this mesa, so you know the easy way down. You're coming with me."

"What the hell for?" the bearded man said.

"I'm going to do some swapping with Jacob Hammer, you three for the prisoners he's holding."

"The boss ain't gonna dicker with you, saddle tramp," the youngster said. "Be on your way and we'll let you live."

The bearded man said, "Hey, I know you. You're the ranny with the big bird on his throat. There's a reward on your head."

"And you aim to claim it, huh?" Flintlock said.

The man's eyes glittered in the firelight. "That is my intention."

His hand dropped for the draw, fast and practiced, a shootist for hire out of El Paso who was acknowledged to be among the very elite of his profession.

But Sam Flintlock's trigger finger was faster by a heartbeat.

His bullet hit the bearded man's chest dead center. It shattered through the breastbone, destroyed his heart and exited just below his left shoulder blade. It had been the work of a moment . . . and now Flintlock was in a gunfight.

The kid with the reckless eyes drew as Flintlock racked the Winchester and both men fired at the same time. The kid had hurried the draw and his first shot missed badly, whining off the caprock between

Flintlock's boots. He didn't get a chance to thumb off a second. Flintlock shot him in the belly, knew it was a killing wound and didn't wait to see the youngster fall. He swung on the third gunman, who was obviously not in the same class as the other two. The man had two-handed a Colt to eye level and now he shoved the revolver out in front of him and cut loose, working the hammer with his left thumb. *BLAM! BLAM! BLAM!* Three shots very fast, all of them misses. An icy coldness in him, Flintlock closed on the man, cranking and shooting the Winchester as he advanced. The gunman staggered, blood in his mouth, dropped his gun and fell on his back.

From somewhere down below men's voices yelled questions into the night. Flintlock looked behind him into darkness and saw no one. Then the realization hit him that the shouts came from his right. Holding the Winchester ready, he stepped in that direction. Ahead of him was a circular patch of darkness that he took for a depression in the caprock, but as he drew closer he saw that it was a cavity about twenty feet across. Flintlock walked to the edge and peered into the hole, expecting to see only blackness, but to his surprise he saw below him the glimmer of burning torches and yelling men scurrying around like ants. For a few seconds Flintlock took time to study the pit. Pitchfork Pass carved across the mesa from north to south and its floor rose gradually as it followed the contours of the limestone substrata. At its widest spot the pass had been enlarged with dynamite that had blown a hole in the caprock and created a large hollow. Flintlock couldn't see, but he guessed that beyond the clearing the pass had been blocked with rubble to prevent access from that direction. It was a considerable feat of engineering and it must have cost Jacob Hammer a small fortune.

But Flintlock did not have time to dwell on Hammer's finances. In the distance, he heard men calling out to one another and one overly excited rooster cut loose a couple of shots. It was Flintlock's cue to leave, but the devil was in him and he wouldn't let it go. He shouldered his rifle, levered off a few rounds down into the chasm, and then, his voice echoing in the stone shaft, he called out, "Hey, Hammer, I got presents for you, three of them!"

One by one Flintlock dragged the bodies of three gunmen to the rim of the crater and tossed them over and one by one they hit the courtyard with a terrible, crunching splat.

The angry voices were closer now and Flintlock feared he'd left his escape too late. He sprinted for the bridge, crossed, his boot heels thudding on the timbers, and then, visible in the dim starlight, he ran for the place where he'd climbed the slope. As bullets split the air around him, Flintlock didn't hesitate. He reached the rim of the caprock and launched himself into space.

CHAPTER THIRTY

After what seemed an eternity hurtling through thin air, Sam Flintlock hit the mesa slope hard, feet-first, and then tumbled forward onto his chest and shoulders . . . and began to cartwheel. He rolled down the incline head over heels, heels over head, grunting in pain every time a rock gouged into him or gravel raked across his back and shoulders. He slammed onto the flat so violently that it knocked the breath out of him, and then a shower of shingle cascaded over his head and added to his misery.

For a moment Flintlock lay stunned, gasping for air. Bullets kicked up Vs of dirt around him, unaimed probing shots fired from the top of the mesa into darkness, but rounds were nonetheless dangerous and could score a lucky hit. But of more immediate concern to Flintlock was the sound of pounding boots as gunmen spilled out of the pass and ran alongside the mesa, hunting him.

Flintlock staggered to his feet and made his way back to his horse, stumbling through malevolent trees that seemed to reach out to snag him in their branches. The firing had made the buckskin jumpy and it took Flintlock several tries before he tightened the girth. He swung into the saddle and was surprised that his Colt was still in his waistband, but the Winchester was still somewhere on the slope and it was a grievous loss. But the Hammer gunmen were closer now and he'd no time to go back for it. He slapped spurs to his horse and rode away at a gallop, allowing his mount to pick its own route to safety. Flintlock's concern now was to put distance between himself and his pursuers and the direction of his flight was of little concern. For a few moments bullets followed him, but they were wild shots and none came close. Suddenly the buckskin's hooves drummed on flat, treeless rock, running between a pair of parallel sandstone bluffs, and Flintlock was in the clear.

At least for now.

Jacob Hammer was beyond anger, his blind rage burning like scalding acid in his belly. He stood beside the three broken bodies of his gunmen, tilted back his head and screamed his terrible wrath. Men rushed to him, some of them buckling on gunbelts as they ran. Hammer turned on them, his face devilish with hate.

"Out! All of you out! Find him!" he roared. "I want the tattooed man alive. Bring him back alive! You hear? Alive!" Hammer laid about him with a riding crop, cutting furious blows at his startled gunmen. "What are you waiting for? Damn you, bring me the tattooed man!"

Hammer watched his gunmen make a hurried departure, called out, "A thousand dollars to the man who brings me the tattooed man," and then, without a glance, he stepped around the bodies of his men and stalked toward the dungeon.

The three women were awake and stood at the door looking into the torch-lit courtyard, wondering at Hammer's scream. The man did not keep them in suspense for long.

"Your fellow murderer killed three of my men tonight," he said. "I will find him and" — he pointed at Jane and Bridie with his crop — "you two will die with him."

"You'll never find him," Bridie said. "Sam Flintlock has outsmarted you and your thugs before and he'll do it again."

"Is that his name?" Hammer said. "A name for a scoundrel if ever there was one."

"No, you are the scoundrel," Jane said. "And one day I hope to see you hang."

As though he hadn't heard, Hammer said, "I will have this Flintlock skinned alive, right there in your cell while you watch and hear him scream, and then you will burn." The man's grin was demonic, Satan in the flesh.

Jane felt a chill of fear. The monster was talking about her son, and suddenly she was a she-wolf protecting her cub.

"Hammer, you sorry piece of trash, my son will kill you," she said.

"Your son?" Hammer said.

"Yes, my son, and he's more of a man than you will ever be."

"Wait . . . how exquisite," Hammer said, his mood suddenly shifting. Almost dreamily he said, "How flawlessly charming. My Chinese headsman long ago perfected the death of a thousand cuts and to have it done to the tattooed man while his mother watches . . . oh, that will be so . . . divine." He slapped the door with his crop and said, to Jane, "Dear lady, when the cutting starts there will be blood, much blood. Best you hike your petticoats when you watch."

Hammer walked away from the cell, laughing.

Jane watched him go and her face was ashen.

CHAPTER THIRTY-ONE

The distant red rock country shimmered with heat, and under his buckskin shirt sweat trickled down Sam Flintlock's back. He hurt everywhere. There was not a part of his body that did not hurt, especially his hands, which were stiff and painful from his climb to the top of the mesa. His rifle was gone, and holding on to his Colt in a gunfight with a shredded hand would be a mighty uncertain thing. He poured precious water from his canteen over his hands in an effort to ease the pain, but his palms and fingers were rubbed raw in places and the water did little to help.

Flintlock had taken refuge in a shallow drainage basin close to a slender, thirty-foot hoodoo that offered at least an illusion of shade. Around him grew patches of prickly pear and ball cactus and a few thin patches of wild rye grass that the buckskin gratefully tore up and munched. The sun was at its highest point in the sky but Flintlock was exhausted and, his back against the base of the hoodoo, he closed his eyes and surrendered to the day's warm embrace.

Two hours passed, then Flintlock woke to the sound of a birdcall. Or was it? A long, low whistle of the sort a man sometimes uses when he wishes to attract the attention of another on a hunt. And Flintlock was the hunted . . . were the huntsmen close? A fly brushed his face and he waved it away and stood. He flexed his stiff, painful gun hand and wondered if it would hold up to the draw and shoot. Likely not. Then, to his left, from the corner of his eye he saw a flash. Not one caused by nature, the sun on rock, but the gleam of a gun barrel. A moment later he saw the man, the bright red bandanna he wore around his neck and the fancy buckle of his gunbelt, and then the black muzzle of the man's rifle.

Flintlock had often wondered how his death would come and now with stark certainty he knew. It would come from the barrel of a Winchester in the hands of a man with a fancy belt buckle.

But the rifleman did not shoot.

"Stay right where you're at or you're a dead man," the gunman said. "Now ease that pistol out of your pants and lay it at your feet. I see a fancy move and I'll shoot you in the belly."

Flintlock, aware that his fingers were so stiff he would have fumbled the draw, did as he was told.

"Now get your hands up," the man said. He motioned with the rifle. "Higher."

Flintlock raised his arms and said, "Hell, they don't go any higher."

"That there big bird on your throat rings a bell with me," the man said. "What's your name? Would it be Flintlock?"

"Yeah, Sam Flintlock."

"Then my memory serves me right." Without taking his eyes off Flintlock, the gunman turned his head and yelled, "Hey, Loss, I got the son of a bitch dead to rights."

The other man appeared from between rocks about twenty yards from the rim of the basin. He was short with piggy eyes and he wore a brown leather vest and carried a brass-framed Henry. "Fifty-fifty, Brandt, that's how it goes, huh? Friends, huh?"

"Sure, Loss, sure," the man called Brandt said. "A thousand dollars split right down the middle between friends for bringing in the tattooed man alive. That's how it's gonna go down."

"Brandt, you're true-blue," Loss said.

"Ain't I, though," Brandt said.

He grinned at Flintlock and fired.

The bullet hit Loss high in the chest and dropped him where he stood.

Brandt watched the man fall and said, grinning, "Sorry, Loss. These days a thousand dollars ain't near enough money to split two ways."

Flintlock shook his head. "I got to hand it to you, you're some kind of friend."

"I don't have no friends," Brandt said. "Loss was a business associate and I cut him out of the partnership." He levered his rifle. "I'm thinking about you, boy."

"What are you thinking?" Flintlock said.

"Thinking that I heard about you, way back. Yeah, I recollect now, Sam Flintlock. You're a Texas bounty hunter, ran with Apaches for a spell, or so they say."

"Only one Apache."

"One is enough." Brandt smiled. "I don't trust you, Flintlock, you're too slick by half and you know how to make fancy Apache moves. I'm supposed to take you in alive but a lot can happen between here and Pitchfork Pass and that means you got a choice to make, tattooed man."

"Choice about what? Man, you talk in riddles."

"Then I'll spell it out for you. I'm going

to shoot you in a knee to slow you down some." He shouldered the Winchester. "Left or right, the choice is your'n."

Lady Luck wears many disguises when she comes to a man, and sometimes he's aware of her visit only when it's all over and he finds his fortunes have changed. But the lady didn't wear a mask that day and Flintlock was aware of her instantly.

Brandt said, "All righty then, I'll choose. Left it is."

But before he had time to trigger his shot, a bullet crashed into his temple and a fan of blood, brain and bone erupted over his head. As Brandt dropped, his rifle clattering onto the rock, Flintlock turned and saw Loss on his belly, a smoking revolver pushed out in front of him.

"Now nobody gets a share, Brandt," the man said.

Then he was dead . . . grinning his way into hell.

Flintlock shoved his Colt into his waistband, stripped the two dead men of their cartridge belts, canteens and the beef jerky and pint of whiskey he discovered in their saddlebags. Brandt's Winchester was damaged, and Flintlock picked up Loss's Henry and then slapped the rumps of the two horses and they took off at a trot. They would find their own way back to Pitchfork Pass and deliver a message to the Old Man of the Mountain that all was not well.

CHAPTER THIRTY-TWO

The Pitchfork riders returned at sunset and rode through the pass two and three at a time, all of them fearful of Jacob Hammer's wrath. They were not disappointed. And an hour later when two horses wandered into the pass and were brought to Hammer, his anger exploded.

Loss Secombe and Brandt Armstrong were a team of draw fighters out of the Texas Pecos River country. They'd fought and killed together in the Colfax County War in the New Mexico Territory, where they'd put the crawl on Clay Allison. Intensely loyal to each other, they were tough, dependable and took orders, and their deaths were a grievous blow. Hammer knew that the Sam Flintlock creature, damn his eyes, did not have the sand or the shooting savvy to kill two named gunfighters, so he must have had help, a lot of help. That thought troubled Hammer deeply. Who the hell was out there and how many? He was about to take a major step forward in his business and the last thing he needed now were more enemies on his doorstep.

For a while Hammer ranted and raved at his gunmen and cursed the name Sam Flintlock, but he didn't go too far because he planned to send four of the gunmen out on a new quest that was of the utmost importance and now was not the time to raise the alarm.

Ten years before these events a German chemist had invented a new opium derivative, a potent and highly addictive drug he named heroin. Now it was making its way into United States cities and Hammer quickly saw there were vast profits to be made by shipping it west. He already controlled a large portion of the opium trade and now he wanted a piece of the heroin pie that promised to be a big moneymaker.

At first his assembled gunmen were a cowed, chastened group but Hammer, to prove there were no hard feelings, had invited them into his house and supplied bourbon and cigars that considerably lightened the mood. He gave them an hour and then rose to his feet at the head of the table, getting instant silence as conversations were abruptly terminated.

"I have news to impart," Hammer said. "First, you know what has been happening around the mesa of late. A criminal element has been murdering and robbing my couriers and threatening our business interests."

This brought a growl of outrage from the assembled gunmen and the few women who had followed their men to the Territory.

Hammer waited until the uproar died away and then said, "The good news is that two of the scoundrels, both Pinkerton agents, are now in custody and will pay the ultimate penalty for their crimes."

Cries of "Hear! Hear!" and "Serves them right!" followed this announcement.

Again, Hammer waited for silence and then said, "Fortunately my latest courier from New York successfully ran the gauntlet and had exciting news to impart that will benefit all of us."

Hammer went on to talk about the fortunes already being made from heroin in major eastern cities and as far south as the port of New Orleans, and he laid out his plan to move in on the new and lucrative drug trade.

"Our contact in New Orleans is a Sicilian gentleman called Giuseppe Morello, who was extradited for his criminal activities in 1881 and returned to his native Italy. He's now back in the country and will advise me on how to proceed in the heroin business." Hammer took a sip of bourbon and over the rim of his glass studied his gunmen and then said, "In light of recent happenings I will choose four of you married men to make the journey to New Orleans. You will leave tomorrow and carry a hundred thousand dollars seed money that you will pass on to Mr. Morello. Do I trust you with that large amount of money? No, I don't, not you, not anybody, and that is why your women will remain here as . . . not hostages . . . but my guests." Hammer flashed his demonic smile. "But that will change quite rapidly if the money is not delivered."

"You can trust me, boss," a man said.

"Thank you, Mr. Dawson. I'm sure your young wife is glad to hear that."

The woman sitting beside Dawson, a pretty brunette, blushed.

"We won't let you down, boss," another married man said. "We know you'll take care of us."

"And I will, Mr. Sherry. Every man jack of you who joins in this great endeavor will retire from business as a rich man."

This brought a cheer and Hammer raised his hands for silence.

"Now my last piece of news that I'm sure

will please most, if not all, of you," he said. "Our sojourn in the middle of this mesa is soon coming to an end." Hammer expected a cheer and got one, then, "The Pinkertons are already nosing around and it's only a matter of time before the army moves against us in force. For that reason, and many others, I am moving our place of business to the great city of New Orleans, where we can take advantage of its port and rail services."

More cheering.

"This facility will be burned before we leave, and with it the Pinkertons," Hammer said. "I've reserved the headman's sword for my faithless bride. She will be executed during our farewell feast, a piquant sauce to enliven our repast."

"Boss, when will that be?" a gunman asked.

"Are you so impatient, Mr. Malone?" Hammer said. "Anxious to witness the spectacle?" Then, after the laughter died away, "The Pinkertons will be burned at the stake on the seventeenth of August, the day of the Chinese Hungry Ghost Festival when we honor our ancestors. My treacherous bride will meet her fate the following day during our banquet."

"And then we burn this place," the man

named Malone said.

"Yes. That will be two weeks from now and afterward we leave the accursed Arizona Territory forever and return to civilization. Now, eat, drink and be merry and look forward to better times to come."

CHAPTER THIRTY-THREE

Sam Flintlock was holed up, fully conscious of the fact that hard times had come down and it was useless trying to buck a stacked deck any longer. By rights he should be dead. The Brandt feller had gotten the drop on him too easily and his life had been saved by a man who was already half dead himself.

It was not a comforting thought.

Like a wandered horse that will return to the barn because it's the only home he's ever known, Flintlock had made his way back to the arroyo and O'Hara's grave. He told himself it was because of the grass and water, but he knew that was a lie. He was there because he was beaten, whipped, and he'd nowhere else to go. Another attack on the mesa was out of the question. This time they'd be waiting for him. He had no chance of rescuing his mother and Bridie and the Smith girl, no chance at all. The only course open to him was to continue waging war on the Old Man of the Mountain by attacking, killing and robbing all those coming and going through Pitchfork Pass. Well . . . he'd already tried that and the only result was a lot of dead men, including O'Hara. Jacob Hammer had all his money back, his criminal activities had been barely damaged, and now his ma was the madman's prisoner.

Good going, Sam. You're doing great.

Unshaven, unkempt, Flintlock angrily tossed the empty whiskey bottle away. For a short while it had helped, helped him sleep anyway, a temporary crutch to support a mentally paralyzed man.

He faced the truth. It was finished. He was all used up. Done.

For the third time since he entered the arroyo Sam Flintlock curled up in his blankets at sundown and slept.

He dreamed of white, ghost horses ridden by dead men and woke with the cold edge of a bowie knife pressed against his throat.

"Easy there, feller," a man's voice said. "Wake up nice and slow."

Flintlock saw a bearded face above him and a pair of bright blue eyes. "Damn you for a bushwhacker," he said. "Did Jacob Hammer send you?"

"Never heard of the gent," the man said. "But I'm sure he's a fine gentleman."

"What are you doing here?" Flintlock said, remaining on his back, still with the knife edge against his throat. His Colt lay beside him, but he'd be cut bad before he got to it.

"My mule brung me here," the man said. "He's what you might call a water mule."

"What's a water mule?"

"A mean, ornery son of a bitch that can scent a spring from a mile away."

"Handy in this country," Flintlock said.

"Handy in any country."

The bearded man took his knife away. "Sorry about the blade, but it's never a good idea to wake up a man who sleeps with his gun. No telling what he'll do when he wakes up an' sees another feller looking at him. Name's Lon Stringer and I'm new to these parts. Oh hell, lookee there. My mule pushed your hoss out of the way so he can drink. He's a mean one, that water mule. I hope you don't mind."

"I don't mind." Flintlock sat upright and held out his hand. "But you'd better ask my horse. Name's Sam Flintlock."

"That's a grand name," Stringer said.

"Well, it will do until I find one better. You on the scout, Mr. Stringer?"

"Call me Lon. No, Sam, I'm an explorer.

Been exploring the wild country since . . . oh, I don't know . . . close on twenty years."

Stringer's beard and hair under his pith helmet were bleached from too much time spent in sun, sleet and snow, and a network of deep lines were etched on his face. Only the bright eyes gave the lie to his features. The man was probably years younger than he appeared.

Apparently feeling that some kind of explanation was necessary, Stringer said, "I was a tinpan for a spell, oh, a ways back, but then I realized I loved the land more than I did gold, not that I found much. Well, anyhoo, I quit prospecting and I been exploring ever since. Had a woman once, but she didn't like my way of life and left me. Married a drummer, I was told, but he dumped her in Deadwood and I don't know what happened to her after that. She was a fine woman though, was Clare, but the love of exploring just didn't enter into her thinking."

"What have you explored?" Flintlock said, prepared to be sociable.

"I'd like to say the Dark Continent and Cathay and maybe the Amazon River down South America way, but I didn't explore any of them. Mostly I just explore our very own deserts and mountains and such. I explored

Old Mexico a while back and then Texas, where I bought the water mule, and now the Arizona Territory. Later I figure to make my way north and study the wild Canadians in their natural habitat."

"You get around, Lon," Flintlock said.

"Well, since you're a stranger, I can tell you that I do have an exploration problem. I mean, a big problem."

"And what's that?"

"I keep getting lost. I take a right instead of a left and end up in places I didn't really want to explore. Somebody, a fellow explorer, once told me that I've no sense of direction, but I do. At least, I think I do." He pointed. "That's south, ain't it, Sam?"

"No, That's west."

"See, it's a worry."

"When you head for Canada, just follow the North Star," Flintlock said.

Springer brightened. "That's splendid. Um . . . what star is that, Sam?"

Flintlock pointed at the night sky. "That one there. See how bright it is? Just keep following it."

Springer clapped his hands. "Crackerjack!" But then his face fell. "But what do I do in the daytime when there are no stars?"

"Well, get yourself a big straight stick and sharpen one end. At night point the sharp end to the North Star and come morning, head in that direction."

"That's a wonderful plan," Springer said. "I'll find Canada real easy with a pointy stick."

"That's what I figure," Flintlock said.

"Huzzah! I'll never get lost again. And now, if you don't mind me saying so, Sam, you look like something the cat dragged in. When did them cheeks last see a razor and that there mustache scissors? Been a spell, I reckon."

"Seems like," Flintlock said.

"I'd say you're a man on a high lonesome, maybe grieving for somebody, huh?"

"Yeah, he's buried over there."

"Sorry to hear that."

"Well, by now I guess he's exploring, just like you, following the buffalo."

"Good way to think on things."

Flintlock yawned. "What time is it?"

"Breakfast time."

"I got none of that."

"I do," Stringer said. "Now I'll get coffee and bacon ready and give you time to shave and clean up."

"Don't much feel like doing that."

"I seen many things in my travels, and I recognize a man who's losing all respect for himself, and I'm looking right at you, Sam

Flintlock."

"Seems like I'm a man born to troubles."

"Self-pity never helps a man, and no troubles are worth sacrificing your dignity and self-respect for, Sam."

Flintlock smiled. "Maybe so, but then you never heard of Jacob Hammer, who calls himself the Old Man of the Mountain. Now he's trouble, pure pizen." He rose to his feet. "All right, put the coffee on. I have a razor stashed in my possibles bag and Pears soap. Sarah Bernhardt swears by it and she knows a thing or two about bathing."

Stringer nodded. "Well, good for her. I'll get a fire going."

"You clean up real nice, Sam," Lon Stringer said. "I think your nose doesn't look so big now you trimmed your mustache. My eyes were drawn to it afore."

"Thanks. I think," Flintlock said.

"Now tell me about this Old Man of the Mountain feller that's causing you all your problems."

Stringer listened in silence as Flintlock drank coffee as he sketchily outlined what had happened to him since he rode into Arizona, spending a little more time on the death of O'Hara, the half Apache, and the capture of his mother and the other women.

When Flintlock was done talking, Stringer shook his head and said, "You have a fearful task ahead of you, Sam, and no mistake."

"And I can't do it alone," Flintlock said.

"Can me and the water mule help?" Stringer said. "I got me a British Bulldog revolver that I got to shoot snakes and critters. But I've never shot a snake or a critter since I bought it, and if I tried I'd probably miss."

Flintlock smiled. "It's not a job for an explorer, Lon. I need a gunhand. Fact is, I need about fifty gunhands. But thanks for the offer."

"Wish I could do more to help."

"Lon, you've helped more than you know. I was feeling pretty low and used up before you and the water mule showed up. Maybe I needed another human being to tell me just how low I'd sunk. You made me face up to it, look at myself in the mirror and see what I'd become . . . a beaten man."

"A feller with a big bird on his throat who handles a gun like it's part of his hand has been places, done things. I don't think you've ever been beat yet."

"There's always a first time."

"And this ain't it."

"I'll keep that in mind."

"What are you going to do?"

283

"Free my ma. See Jacob Hammer in hell. Stuff like that. My dance card is full, but for a spell there I sure thought I'd run out of space on the floor."

Stringer was silent for a while, the firelight playing on his weathered face. Finally, he said, "Sam, I've thought it through and no matter how hard I try I can't come up with any advice."

"Like I said, Lon, right now I need gun-fighters, not advice."

Stringer nodded. "Yeah, I guess advice comes cheap. Wise men don't need it and fools won't take it."

"And what am I?" Flintlock said.

"A wise man who happens to have more trouble than he can handle."

"That about sums it up, except if I was really wise I wouldn't be here."

"Where you be, Sam?"

"Kansas maybe, in the hardware business, me and O'Hara."

"You miss him, don't you?"

"I was raised rough and he was the only friend I ever had."

"Sounds like he was a good man."

"He was a man like any other, neither all good nor all bad. O'Hara led a full life and was prepared to die at any time. It is the Apache way."

"I would like to have met him," Stringer said.

Flintlock smiled. "O'Hara would have made a good explorer. He wasn't a one for being cooped up in towns."

"And neither am I, when you come to mention it. I enjoyed breakfast and talking with you, Sam, but now I'm getting a mite restless," Stringer said. "Me and the water mule must be on our way."

"There's water here. You can set a spell."

The man shook his head. "Nope, I got to be moving on, Sam. Canada is a long ways from the Arizona Territory and I best be making tracks. I heard they got forests and mountains that haven't been explored yet, home to grizzly bears as tall as a tree an' wolves the size of yearling steers. Of course, folks exaggerate and that's why I want to go see for my ownself."

"Be careful, Lon," Flintlock said. "And never trust a wolf until it's been skun."

"Sound advice. I'll remember that."

Flintlock walked Stringer and the water mule to the arroyo and there the man said, "Well, so long, Sam. Good luck and you take care, you hear?"

"You, too, Lon, and thanks again."

"Nothing to thank me for, you would have

come around to a right way of thinking without my help." Stringer waved a hand and walked into the arroyo. "Good luck, Sam."

"And you, Lon. Good luck."

Then the explorer and the water mule were gone and Flintlock felt a surprising sense of loss at their leaving.

CHAPTER THIRTY-FOUR

A gray fog drifted among the junipers as six men dismounted in the shadow of the looming peaks of Balakai Point and stood in a circle to talk treachery.

"Listen up," Luke Dawson said. He was big, broad and bad to the bone. "In them saddlebags are a hundred thousand dollars in scrip, that's over sixteen thousand a man. Tom Sherry, what would you do with that amount of money?"

The man called Sherry grinned. "Keep me in whiskey and whores for a long time, that's for sure."

"For damn sure," Dawson said. "Jack Blair, what about you?"

"Oh, I dunno. Maybe I'd buy me a ranch and settle down with the little woman and raise some kids," Blair said.

"Except you won't have the little woman. She'll be dead."

This from Milt Stevens, a young Texan

who'd made a gun reputation when he outdrew and killed three gamblers in a Nacogdoches saloon, one of them Billy Joe Sand, a badman out of Kansas who'd killed seven men.

Dawson grinned and said, "So who the hell cares? Jack can go down into Old Mexico and buy any woman he wants for a hundred dollars."

"That's a fact," Blair said. "I need something younger, getting mighty tired of ol' Kate and her constant whining and complaining."

"There you go, Jack. That's mighty informed thinking," Dawson said. He turned to the remaining two men. "George, Harry, how would you like sixteen thousand to spend?"

George Divers and Harry Parker were shotgun men, a pair of ambush killers for hire who, for fifty dollars, would cut any man or woman in half with a load of double-ought buckshot. Divers's common-law wife, Lucy, a reformed whore, was four months pregnant and Parker cohabited with the six-foot-tall Mary "High Timber" Goodrich, a whore who had no intention of reforming. The two men exchanged glances but said nothing.

"Think about it," Dawson said. "Are them

two floozies back at the compound worth sixteen thousand dollars apiece?"

Parker, a bearded man with black, reptilian eyes, seemed to make up his mind. "Mine ain't. Hell, she ain't worth sixteen thousand when any man can buy her for two dollars and get change back."

"That goes double for me," Divers said. "Lucy is gonna whelp soon and what do I want with a woman and wailing brat?"

Parker's voice suddenly had an urgent edge. "Luke, if I catch your drift, you're asking us if we want to take the hundred thousand for our ownselves. Am I right or am I wrong?"

"You're as right as ever was, Harry," Dawson said. "There are some things a man can't walk away from, and a pile of money is one of them."

Parker nodded and said, "Well, the way I see it, if we're gonna split the money, we'd better make tracks out of here. I don't want Jacob Hammer coming after us. I heard tell he's got one o' them crystal balls that Chinamen use and it shows him everything."

Dawson thought about that, then said, "I reckon us six can handle anything he can throw at us, but you're right, Harry, best we light a shuck for Flagstaff and split the money there."

Parker said, "Good. Then after the dividing is done, I'll jump a train headed north with sixteen thousand dollars in my pocket. Man . . . I'm going places."

"You're not going anywhere, Harry, except to New Orleans like the Old Man told us," Milt Stevens said. "I'm not leaving Clara to be killed just to fill my pockets with cash. Besides, it's Jacob Hammer's money and it's not ours to steal."

"Went to West Point, did you, Milt? You sure sound like it. Hammer stole the money himself, and we're just stealing it back," Parker said.

"What's good for the goose is good for the gander," Divers said.

"Yeah, that's right," Parker agreed. "Whatever the hell what you said means."

"It means we're five for, one against," Dawson said.

"The majority rules," Divers said.

"Yeah, you're right again, George," Parker said. "The majority rules. It's the American way."

"Not in this case," Stevens said. His hand dropped close to his gun. "We ain't taking Mr. Hammer's money."

Dawson's eyes narrowed. "Milt, draw iron and we'll kill you."

Stevens hesitated, not liking the odds, and

said, "Luke, I say we go on to New Orleans and talk about it then. Maybe you boys will think things over and change your minds by then."

Dawson shook his head. "There's no changing minds in this outfit. But all right, we'll wait until New Orleans for the split."

"Yes, and we'll talk more about it then, Luke," Stevens said. "But the money still goes to the Giuseppe Morello feller, like the Old Man told us."

Parker, looking tense and mean, said, "My talking is done, here or anywhere else. I want my sixteen thousand and it ain't going to a damned furriner with a name I can't pronounce."

Tom Sherry, sudden and dangerous on the draw and shoot, had been silent, listening, and now he said, "I got a plan."

"Let's hear it," Dawson said, peering at him through the mist.

"Milt is all-fired set on us not stealing the Old Man's money, right?"

"Right," Dawson said.

"So, he takes his own share, sixteen thousand, and gives it back," Sherry said. He fixed Stevens with a stare. "That way, Jacob Hammer doesn't take a complete loss and your conscience is clear, Milt."

"What's good for the goose is good for

the gander," Parker said.

"What the hell does that mean?" Dawson said.

"Nothing," Parker said. "I just like saying that thing about gooses."

Dawson shook his head and said, "Well, don't say it again. Milt, we'll give you your share in New Orleans and you can do whatever the hell you want with it. Give it back if stealing it troubles you."

"No, I'll have no part of this," Stevens said. "I'm riding."

"Right to the Old Man," Dawson said. "You aim to spill the beans, huh?"

"That is my intention, Luke. I want no part of this."

"He'll send thirty men after us," Dawson said.

Stevens said, "Luke, it's not too late to change your mind, and that goes for all of you. Once the money is safely delivered to Morello, Mr. Hammer will reward us. You know he will."

"He won't reward us sixteen thousand dollars," Parker said. "Or anywhere close."

"Make that twenty thousand, Harry," Dawson said.

He drew and fired.

Milt Stevens saw the draw coming and even as he took the bullet he shucked iron and got a shot off, but it missed Dawson by a yard and the young gunman knew it . . . then he hit the ground and knew nothing at all.

Dawson grinned as he holstered his smoking Colt. "Five shares, boys," he said.

"And I want them fancy boots of his," Parker said. One by one he lifted Stevens's legs, pulled off the dead man's boots, whooped and brandished them in the air. "This is my lucky day," he yelled.

It wasn't . . . as the four bullets that crashed into his head and chest duly informed him.

Chapter Thirty-Five

Sam Flintlock drew rein when he heard the gunshot . . . followed a few moments later by a racketing fusillade that roared around the rocks like thunder and then suddenly stopped. A minute or two passed, and then there were several more revolver shots, but these were spaced out, deliberate, as though someone was taking his time to deliver a coup de grâce to wounded men.

In a thick fog, rare in that part of the Arizona Territory, Flintlock had just navigated a dry wash bordered by cottonwoods on the east side of Balakai Mesa, riding farther south than he ever had before. He had water in his canteens, some grub that Lon Stringer had left him, and he was looking for a fight, so far without success. It seemed that Jacob Hammer's men were staying close to home, guarding Pitchfork Pass.

But the firing had changed all that.

Glimpsed through breaks in the mist, ahead of him a flat, sandy valley heavily covered in saltbush, sagebrush, juniper and bunchgrass, and after scouting around Flintlock picked up horse tracks, six riders heading south. There was no doubt in his mind that they were Hammer's riders, perhaps headed for the railroad depot in Flagstaff. He didn't like the odds, but he leaned over in the saddle and followed the tracks anyway. Perhaps he could shake those gunmen up a little and send them scuttling back to Hammer's bosom. Flintlock liked that last so much he grinned as he said it aloud: "Hammer's bosom."

After an hour, more dry washes cut across his trail as did stands of cedar, greasewood and rabbitbrush and the sand became gravelly, holding large rocks in places. The fog lingered, but the morning was unusually hot and humid, the rising sun a dull orange ball obscured by mist. In an unnatural silence, the only sounds were the buckskin's hooves on the coarse sand and the creak of saddle leather. The air smelled of sage and then, as he lifted his nose and sniffed . . . a faint tang of gunsmoke.

Wary now, Flintlock drew rein. Ahead of him, and much closer, lay the location of the gunfight. Had the Hammer riders casually murdered people on the trail, soldiers or lawmen perhaps? Or had they themselves been ambushed? There was one way to find out. He slid the Henry from the boot and then patted the old Hawken for luck. He had a feeling that before this day was done, if he got into a shooting scrape he'd need all the good fortune he could get.

Sam Flintlock rode up on a peaked rampart of rock that formed a jutting point in the southeast corner of Balakai Mesa. A stand of juniper grew at the base of the precipice and it was there, among the trees, he found the bodies of six men.

Flintlock swung out of the saddle and approached the dead men. They'd been shot to pieces and three of them showed an additional neat bullet hole in the middle of their foreheads, surrounded by a powder burn. Those three had been shot at close range, either to put them out of their misery or to make sure they were dead. The bodies had been laid out in a neat line and one of them was missing his boots that had been dropped nearby. The dead had been stripped of weapons and their horses were gone. But to Flintlock's joy, as a tobacco-hungry man, two of the dead men carried the makings. One of the tobacco sacks was soggy, covered in blood, but the late owner of the other had been plugged in a more convenient spot and both sack and papers were unspoiled.

As the sun rose higher and the fog thinned, Flintlock smoked a third cigarette and then made a scout around the area. He found dozens of empty rifle and revolver cartridge cases and the tracks of at least a dozen booted men.

The six men had been bushwhacked in the fog and shot down without mercy. Flintlock doubted that it was the work of Pinkertons in force, but rather a number of professional killers who knew what they were doing.

He inspected the hands of the corpses and as he expected all were soft and well cared for with clean fingernails, not the calloused hands of miners or laboring men — and they each had the same tattoo of three red triangles on a blue line he'd seen before. Whoever they were, these men had been an elite, and this close to the mesa it meant they were hired guns . . . Jacob Hammer's hired guns, and they'd fallen foul of men as skilled and dangerous as themselves.

But who were they?

The spent rifle cartridges were all from Winchesters, not the Springfield .45-70, and that ruled out the army. A posse of lawmen was plausible, but unlikely. Deputizing enough civilians to ride into the red rock country and take on a feared enemy would be difficult, well-nigh impossible.

The whole affair was a mystery and Flintlock had no answers.

Deciding to wait until the fog lifted completely, Flintlock ate a meal of pan bread and a couple of slices of cold bacon. After an hour, in clear air, he mounted the buckskin and followed the tracks of the ambushers. They'd headed due north and had probably passed him, invisible in the murk. Another mile brought him up on a column of slanted rock that rose above the flat like the yellowed rib of a gigantic animal. Windblown sand and rain had polished the surface of the rock to a sheen that reflected the sunlight. But what caught Flintlock's attention was that here the tracks of the men he followed merged with others, many mounted men riding north followed by the smaller prints of mules, heavily loaded, judging by the depth their hooves had sunk into the sand. The horse droppings were still fresh, so the riders and their pack animals were not far ahead of him.

But Flintlock had reason to be cautious.

It seemed that he was tracking a small army and seeing what they'd done to the six men back at Balakai Point, they were not inclined to be friendly.

But whose army?

Flintlock refused to speculate . . . whatever answer he came up with was bound to be wrong.

His curiosity roused, wondering how this turn of events would affect his mother and the other Hammer prisoners, for the rest of the day he shadowed the column, and when they camped at dusk he found a deep dry wash where he could spread his blankets and keep out of sight. Like himself, the mystery riders made a cold camp, and the thought came to Flintlock that they planned an attack on Jacob Hammer. He had no reason to believe that, but why else would a small army of men be in this country? But there was also the chance that they were allies, men hired by the Old Man of the Mountain for one of his villainous schemes. Flintlock decided to keep his distance and see what happened.

Pretty soon, Flintlock got into his blankets and, surprised by his tiredness, he fell asleep instantly.

Sam Flintlock woke with the dawn, saddled

the buckskin and tied down his bedroll. Breakfast was a cigarette, a small piece of bread, the last of it, and a drink of water. He had his foot in the stirrup when three riflemen appeared on the bank of the wash and the meanest of them said, "Mister, step away from the hoss or I'll drop you right where you stand."

Flintlock did as he was told, turned and said, "What are your intentions?"

"My intention is to kill you," the mean gent said. "Unless you can convince me otherwise."

"And that ain't likely," the stone-faced gunman beside him said.

CHAPTER THIRTY-SIX

A silent gunman pushed bread and a bowl of beans through the cell door into Viktor's waiting hands. For a few moments the man stood there, sniffed, and walked away, shaking his head.

"How would you smell without a bath for days?" Jane McIntyre called after him. "Tell Hammer we need to bathe."

The gunman ignored that, waved an uncaring hand and kept on walking.

"Son of a bitch!" Jane yelled, all her pent-up anger spiking each word.

She took a piece of bread from Viktor and sat beside Louise Smith, who lay on a cot. The girl's eyes were closed and sweat beaded her forehead.

As gently as she could, Jane put her arm around Louise's shoulders and lifted her head. "Eat some of this bread, Louise," she said. "You must eat."

"No . . . I don't want to eat. I want to die."

"Well, that's too bad," Jane said. "Because I have no intention of letting you die."

The girl's eyes fluttered open. "When . . . when they do it, cut off my head, I mean, will I feel pain? Will my eyes still see when my head rolls on the ground? Will I *know*?"

"I can't answer that," Jane said. "Don't even think about it because it isn't going to happen."

"Your son will save us?"

"Yes, he will. Sam will find a way."

"No, he won't. He won't find a way because there is no way. You, me, Bridie and Viktor, we're all going to die soon. I'd rather lie here in this terrible place and let my life slip away than face the headman's sword." Tears formed in Louise's eyes. "Please, Jane, do me one last favor . . . let me will myself to die."

"Eat the bread and stop feeling sorry for yourself, you damned slut," Bridie O'Toole said, her eyes aglow with rage. "You may live or you may die, like the rest of us, but we're not going to stand by and watch you kill yourself." She snatched the bread from Jane's hand, bent over and shoved it into the girl's mouth. Louise clenched her teeth but Bridie shoved harder, grinding the bread against the girl's lips with the palm of her hand. "Eat! Eat! Eat! Damn you, eat!"

"Bridie, no!" Jane yelled. She pulled the woman away and said, "Viktor, hold her." Louise sat up on the cot. Her mouth was covered in saliva and bread crumbs and blood trickled from a cut on her lower lip. Jane again put her arm around the girl's shoulders and said, "It's all right. You'll be just fine, I promise."

Louise broke free of Jane's arm and lay on her back, tears streaming down her cheeks. "Oh God, how I wish I was dead," she said.

Viktor let Bridie go and sat on the cot. He took the girl's hand, placed it against his lips and whispered, "Viktor will not let anything happen to you. Sleep now and later you will eat." Louise closed her eyes and the giant gently brushed damp hair off her forehead with his massive paw.

Outside the steel gate someone applauded.

Jacob Hammer stood there, smiling in a shaft of morning light that angled from the hole in the mesa roof. "That was most entertaining," he said. He wore a Chinese morning tunic of blue silk. "A scene worthy of Dante's *Inferno,* played out by the damned."

Jane stood close to the door. "Hammer,

303

you've had your little joke, now release us," she said.

The man shook his head. "This is no joke, Pinkerton lady. You must all die, and very soon." He looked at Louise, who sat up on the cot, watching him. "Do not be afraid, my faithless bride. Decapitation by the sword is the most elegant of deaths. It is an exquisite thing and there is only a whisper of pain, there for a moment, and then gone."

"Hammer, you're a madman," Jane said.

"Yes, of course I'm mad, but then the whole world is mad and there can be no great genius without a touch of madness."

"You're not a genius, Hammer," Jane said. "You're a cheap, violent thug who has lasted this long only because you hid yourself away in a wilderness and called yourself the Old Man of the Mountain. In a city, you'd be just another two-bit hoodlum and you'd have been hanged or jailed years ago."

"Perhaps," Hammer said. "But then, was choosing this remote mesa not a sign of my genius? Besides, I am planning a return to the city, where I'll obtain riches and power that a churl like you can't begin to imagine."

"You damned fool, you'll be dangling from a noose within a year."

"Most unlikely." Hammer sniffed. "Hmm . . . this cell will need to be cleaned out after you're all dead."

"You won't kill us, Hammer."

"That is an idle boast, Pinkerton, and now you bore me. But I'll leave you with this thought . . . unlike beheading, burning is a terrible death and it is not quick. I so look forward to watching your last agonies as I dine."

Hammer abruptly turned and walked away. Jane let loose a string of mountain man curses at his retreating back but he seemed not to have heard.

CHAPTER THIRTY-SEVEN

"Do you know why my men didn't shoot you down in the dry wash?" the little, one-eyed man said.

"My good looks?" Sam Flintlock said.

"Hardly," Colonel Alfons Janowski said. "I must warn you not to make any further jocular remarks, sir. Your life hangs in the balance. They did not kill you because you said you were an enemy of Jacob Hammer, and the enemy of our enemy is a friend. Do you understand?"

"Yes, I do," Flintlock said.

"You may be a spy."

"A man with a bird tattoo on his throat does not make a good spy. I don't blend in, if you catch my drift."

"No, you do not, that is certain. But the question remains, where do you blend in? With Hammer's gunmen, perhaps?"

Flintlock shook his head. "No . . . not with Hammer's men. He holds my mother captive and his gunmen killed my best, my only, friend."

Janowski turned to one of his men and said, "Give this man coffee. He has a story to tell and his own life to save."

The colonel and his fifty mercenaries, three regular army soldiers and a few hired mule skinners were camped on the east side of Balakai Mesa. He'd chosen his camp wisely, hidden in a stand of juniper and sagebrush. The trees helped dissipate the smoke from the only fire in camp, where a huge pot of coffee hung over the meager flames.

After Flintlock tried his coffee and built a cigarette, Janowski said, "Now talk, and may God help you if I catch you lying."

"I have many faults, but lying isn't one of them," Flintlock said.

"I'll be the judge of that. Now proceed," Janowski said.

Flintlock recounted his time in the Arizona Territory, his war on Hammer's couriers and the death of O'Hara and the capture of his mother and Bridie O'Toole. He mentioned Louise Smith, adding that she was either Hammer's bride or dead.

When Flintlock finished speaking, Janowski turned to the men who surrounded him, listening, and said, "Did you hear that, gentleman? The Pinkertons were here before us."

This occasioned a babble of comment in half a dozen different tongues and one gray-haired man spoke for the rest when he said, "Just two women?"

Flintlock nodded. "Sometimes two women can be an army."

This brought laughter and after it died away Janowski said, "When my attack on the mesa begins, I can't guarantee your mother's safety . . . Mr. . . . ah . . ."

"Flintlock. Sam Flintlock."

"Do you understand what I just told you?" Janowski said.

"Yes. I understand. I'll make myself responsible for my mother."

"That is, if I let you take part in the attack," Janowski said. "Most of my men were trained soldiers. They know how to fight and follow orders."

"So do I," Flintlock said.

Janowski looked doubtful, but once again Lady Luck smiled on Flintlock as though she'd adopted him as a son.

A tall, thin man with a heroic mustache had just joined the group around the colonel when he saw Flintlock and roared, "Damn your eyes . . . Sam Flintlock!"

Flintlock looked at the man and said,

"Chester Drake. How the hell are you doing?"

"I'm doing fine. I heard you was dead, Sam, so seeing you sitting there is a sore disappointment to me."

"You two know each other?" Janowski said.

"Well, we swapped lead once over to Caldwell way when we were bounty-hunting the same outlaw," Drake said. "You was lucky that day, Sam. My shooting was off on account of too much whiskey the night before."

"And you was lucky my Winchester jammed up," Flintlock said. "As I recollect, by the time I shucked my Colt you were already flapping your chaps over the horizon."

"With the two-thousand-dollar reward money fer Mexican Bob Becerra in my pocket," Drake said, grinning. "Did you forget about that?"

"I didn't forget. I spent quite a while looking for you, Chester," Flintlock said. "For old times' sake. But we never did cross tracks."

"That's because I stayed out of your way, Sam. You always were fast with the iron."

"Mr. Drake, can you vouch for this man?" Janowski said.

"Colonel, Sam Flintlock is an ornery cuss and so mean he'd piss on a widow woman's kindling, but he's good with the Colt's gun and he has sand."

"Then you have the qualifications I require, Mr. Flintlock," Janowski said. "You may join us or ride on. Whatever course you choose, I will not stand in your way."

"I'd like to join you, Colonel," Flintlock said.

"And I'm glad to have you as an auxiliary," Janowski said.

"Colonel, I found six dead men south of here. Were they Hammer's men?"

"Yes, they were. After they identified themselves to one of my patrols, they decided to make a fight of it. A bad mistake." The colonel watched a V of geese fly over the camp, and then said, "Those scoundrels were carrying a hundred thousand dollars, presumably some of Jacob Hammer's ill-gotten gains. Well, that money is now part of the spoils of war and will be distributed among my men, those that survive."

"Don't let Chester get anywhere near that cash, Colonel," Flintlock said, looking at Drake. "He has a habit of taking all the money and then lighting a shuck for the horizon."

Janowski allowed himself a rare smile. "I'll

310

bear that in mind," he said.

After supper that night Colonel Alfons Janowski, who looked pale and seemed to be ailing from his march across some of the most rugged country on earth, called a council of war and outlined his plans for the coming attack.

He gave most of his attention to a scholarly looking, middle-aged man who wore round eyeglasses and a serious expression. Wilfred Griffiths looked like an aging Midwest college professor but he'd fought with distinction as a major in the 1st Kentucky Artillery in the War Between the States. Acknowledged to be one of the best light artillerymen in the nation, he had written several scholarly books on the subject.

"Major Griffiths, I will state my plan in regard to the howitzers and you will make your comments or ask questions after I am done," Janowski said. "Is that clear?"

"Your obedient servant, Colonel," Griffiths said.

"Very well then, I'll begin," Janowski said. "There is a man-made opening in the roof of the mesa that will be the target of your initial bombardment. I will ascend in the observation balloon and relay to you the coordinates before you open fire. Your comments?"

"I have studied the mesa and with the howitzers at maximum elevation I can drop my shells into the opening as planned. Of course, it all depends on the size of the hole."

Flintlock said, "I've been up there and the opening is pretty big."

Janowski was surprised. "Mr. Flintlock, you climbed the mesa?"

"Yes. I was looking for a way to rescue my ma," Flintlock said. "But I had no chance of getting down into the Hammer compound from there. It's a deep hole."

"How deep?" Griffiths said.

"Thirty feet, maybe more," Flintlock said.

"And how big is the opening?"

"It's a circle. I'd say ten paces across."

"About twenty feet?"

"Yeah, about that."

"Major Griffiths, can you hit a target that small?" Janowski said.

"Yes, Colonel. Once I have the coordinates I believe I can."

"Believe you can, Major?"

Griffiths smiled. "I know I can."

Janowski nodded. "Good . . . then that is settled." He turned his attention to a man who wore the blue frock coat of the Prussian army though it was much faded and missing buttons. "Captain Von Essen, any counterattack will come from the north along this valley. You and a thirty-man infantry force will deal with this exigency."

Dieter Von Essen, a tall, robust soldier of fortune who was cashiered from the Prussian army for pilfering funds from the officers' mess, said, "*Mein Oberst,* there is an entrance to Herr Hammer's compound, a narrow pass. We do not as yet know the enemy numbers. Rather than meet them in the open field I suggest we lay siege to the pass and shoot them down as they try to leave."

"Mr. Flintlock, are you familiar with this pass?" Janowski said.

"Yes, I am. It's called Pitchfork Pass and it leads into the compound. It's a narrow arroyo that will allow only two mounted men to ride side by side. Captain Von Essen is correct, that's the place to defeat Hammer's gunmen."

"Then deploy your men outside the pass entrance as you suggest, Captain," Janowski said.

"I'd like to join him," Flintlock said.

"I have no objection," Janowski said. "Captain Von Essen?"

The German smiled at Flintlock. "You are most welcome, *mein Herr.*"

"Then I suggest you march north now and move into position under the cover of darkness, Captain Von Essen," Janowski said. "Much depends on you."

"I will not fail you, *mein Oberst.*"

"Good . . . then we attack at dawn," Colonel Janowski said.

CHAPTER THIRTY-EIGHT

Captain Dieter Von Essen was a hard taskmaster and he drove his men mercilessly on the night march northwest, following the contour of the mesa. By the time he called a halt, half his men, all of them cavalrymen, hobbled on blistered feet. They were now close to Pitchfork Pass and Sam Flintlock volunteered to scout the entrance and the hilly ground opposite.

"Do not allow yourself to be seen, Herr Flintlock," Von Essen said. "We must depend on the element of surprise."

"No one will see me, Captain," Flintlock said. "When it comes to sneaking around in the dark I had a great teacher."

The big German smiled. "You must tell me about him sometime."

Flintlock nodded. "Sometime."

He turned and vanished into the night, the muttering curses of the suffering cavalrymen soon silenced by distance and darkness.

There was an eerie quality to the moonmisted gloom, a quiet so profound Flintlock could hear his own breathing, coming in shorter gasps the nearer he got to Pitchfork Pass. His boots made a soft . . . *crump* . . . *crump* . . . sound on the coarse sand and gibbering things scuttled away from him as he passed. Much closer now . . . close enough to see the torch-lit arroyo cast a rectangle of dim orange light on the ground in front of the entrance.

Flintlock stopped and listened into the night.

He heard the muffled voices of men, talking, laughing, cursing . . . drunken.

On silent feet, walking across rock, Flintlock stepped closer to the pass. The voices were louder, heedless of the noise they made, guards who were not guarding. That puzzled Flintlock. It suggested a breakdown of discipline and of men who no longer felt the need to be vigilant.

Why?

Was the Old Man of the Mountain dead? That seemed unlikely. The guards were lax in their duty but they were still in place and that meant Hammer was still inside.

Then the truth dawned on Flintlock. The

presence of the Pinkertons had scared Jacob Hammer and he planned to pull up stakes. He was leaving, heading for pastures new, probably within days. Since the mesa fortress was soon to be abandoned, the gunmen guards no longer gave a damn. That was the way of human nature . . . and the way hired men thought.

In the end, it didn't matter that Hammer was lighting a shuck, since Janowski's attack would begin at dawn, but were the Old Man's gunmen prepared to defend the mesa to the death? Judging by the guards in the pass, they were not.

It was something for Von Essen to think about.

Keeping to the shadows, Flintlock scouted the low, brush-covered hills opposite the entrance. There was enough cover for twenty riflemen and probably twice that number. He'd seen enough. The guards in the pass were still carousing as Flintlock slipped into the night and made his way back to Von Essen.

Based on Sam Flintlock's report, Captain Dieter Von Essen roused his men and ordered them to march again and deploy in the foothills opposite Pitchfork Pass. There was some grumbling from the horse soldiers who under normal circumstances steadfastly refused to walk anywhere, but even they saw the wisdom of the Prussian's plan. When Hammer's gunmen spilled out of the pass they would be cut down before they mounted any kind of assault. Von Essen had fought in the Battle of Sedan during the Franco-Prussian War of 1870 and it had taught him the futility of attacking entrenched infantry over open ground. He hoped Jacob Hammer had not learned that lesson.

In complete silence, moving singly and in twos, the mercenaries found cover among the hills. Oblivious, the gunmen in the pass grew noisier and neither saw nor heard anything.

Von Essen threw himself down beside Flintlock and laid his ornate sword on the shallow rise in front of him. "Now we wait, *mein Herr,*" he whispered. "How long until dawn?"

Flintlock glanced at the lowering moon. "I reckon three hours, Captain."

"Ach, is it so? A long wait for tired men, is it not?"

"Will they stay awake?"

"I warned them on pain of death to remain alert." Von Essen turned his head and growled at a grizzled man a few feet away from him, "And no smoking, Herr Adams. It is verboten."

The man called Adams grinned. "Pipe's cold, Cap'n."

"Then keep it that way," Von Essen said. "*Mein* own pipe is in *mein* pocket."

"Hope it don't burn a hole in that fancy coat o' your'n, Cap'n," Adams said.

"Like yours, it is cold, Herr Adams."

The gray-haired man winked. "Then keep it that way."

Von Essen sighed and shook his head at Flintlock. "Americans are not Prussians."

Flintlock smiled. "No, Captain, we are not."

He looked at the cold, uncaring face of the moon and wondered if his mother was also looking at the night sky. Was she alive or dead? He refused to even consider that question.

Jacob Hammer woke from a terrible dream.

His silk nightshirt soaked in sweat, he was so disturbed he threw on his robe and walked along dark corridors in search of Dr. Chiang, his personal physician and soothsayer.

Hammer tolerated only two locks in his compound, the one that fastened the iron door of the dungeon and the other that secured his own bedroom.

He burst into Dr. Chiang's quarters and roughly shook the old man awake.

The physician was startled. "What has happened in this house?" he said.

"I had a terrible dream." Hammer said. He dragged the man out of bed. "You must interpret it for me."

Chiang sat in a chair and bade Hammer take a seat in the one opposite. "Did you dream of China again?" he said.

"No . . . I dreamed of men's bodies, many bloody, naked bodies, surrounding me in a field of scarlet wildflowers. I tried to run, but fell down and I could not rise. Then the bodies rose and came toward me, their eyes shining like emeralds, and they chanted . . . chanted . . ."

"Chanted what?" Chiang said.

" 'Cursed . . . condemned . . . doomed . . .' Just that, over and over again." Hammer shook his head. "I woke in fear. My God, it was a terrible dream."

"Then fear no longer," Chiang said. "To dream of the dead brings good luck, and each body represents one year of good fortune. This is the eve of the Hungry Ghost Festival and your honored ancestors visited you in your sleep."

"But why did they chant those dreadful

words?"

"The ancestors predict the fate that will befall your enemies, that they are cursed, condemned and doomed. Oh, what a happy dream you've had!"

Hammer grabbed a handful of the old man's nightshirt and pulled him closer. "Is what you tell me the truth? If you are lying to me, hiding the real meaning of the dream, I'll have your tongue torn out."

"All is true. I would not lie to you. There is no point in concealing the truth. That is like wearing embroidered clothes and traveling by night."

Hammer let go of the physician's shirt and said, "Then I am content that what you told me is the truth, that I will triumph."

"Yes, you will. I will give you a sleeping draft and then you can return to bed and slumber in peace. All will be well."

After Hammer left, Chiang sat for a while, his face troubled. Finally, he rose, pulled a carpetbag from his closet and began to pack.

CHAPTER THIRTY-NINE

Sleepless, Colonel Alfons Janowski awaited the dawn.

Major General Elliot had provided him with a middle-aged infantry sergeant and a couple of privates who had worked with observation balloons during the war. The men assured Janowski that the contraption would be filled with gas and fired up, ready to go just before first light.

Earlier Sergeant Tam Nolan studied the colonel with a measuring gaze, seeing a one-eyed man who was missing an arm and walked with a cane, and said, "Could get bumpy up there, Colonel. The cable is worn and the winch is rusty, hasn't been used since the Battle of Chancellorsville."

"I'm sure I'll manage, Sergeant," Janowski said.

"Yes, sir. I'm sure the colonel will be fine."

"I can calculate the coordinates quickly," Janowski said. "I will not be aloft for long."

"As the colonel says, he will not be up there for long."

"However, there will be snipers. I've detailed a dozen of our best rifle shots to clear the top of the mesa."

Nolan frowned. "Are all these men former soldiers, sir?"

"Yes. All of them."

"In whose army?"

"In a dozen different armies. That tall man you see asleep over there by the juniper was a colonel in the army of the Queen Hazrat Mahal during the Indian Rebellion of 1857 against the British East India Company. And over there, sleeping with his rifle, is Bertrand Giroux. He was in the 1st Regiment of the French Foreign Legion in the Crimean War and was wounded at the Battle of the Alma River in the Ukraine. He carries Russian lead in his back, too close to the spine to remove." Janowski smiled. "I have absolute faith in my men, Sergeant."

"As you say, Colonel."

"I admit they don't look soldierly on parade, but, by God, sir, they can fight."

"They're mercenaries, but I'm sure they'll stand, sir."

"Depend on it, Sergeant Nolan."

"And what of the enemy?"

"They're also mercenaries."

"Hired gunmen, sir. I hate the breed."

"No quarter will be asked or given in the coming battle. Do you understand that, Sergeant?"

"I'm a regular soldier, sir. I'll have no truck with killing prisoners."

Janowski nodded. "Then leave that to my mercenaries."

"Yes, sir."

"You are dismissed, Sergeant."

Nolan snapped off a salute, turned and vanished into the darkness.

Colonel Janowski felt ill. He had shooting pains in his left shoulder and arm and he knew very well what they might portend. Too many wars . . . too many wounds . . . time was finally catching up to him. He glanced at the star-glowing sky and shook his head.

My God, would this night ever end?

The sound of merrymaking had finally ceased in Pitchfork Pass.

Sam Flintlock regretted that his Hawken was with his saddle back in Colonel Janowski's camp. It would be fun to send a .50 caliber ball bouncing around the arroyo and wake everybody up.

Captain Dieter Von Essen was also thinking about the men in the pass, but fun was not in his mind. He had something entirely different in mind . . . bloody, violent death.

"Herr Flintlock," he whispered, his mouth close to Sam's ear. "There may be a way to demoralize the enemy before the battle even starts." He saw the question on Flintlock's face and said, "Do you think the men on guard are asleep?"

"Dead drunk, I'd say," Flintlock said.

Von Essen rubbed his stubbled chin. "I wonder . . ."

Flintlock waited for something further but when it was not forthcoming, he said. "Wonder what, Captain?"

"If all the guards were found dead come morning, would not it shake the enemy to its core? Perhaps it would undermine their will to fight."

"It would make them feel mighty uncomfortable, that's for sure," Flintlock said. "If it was me and I found the guards dead, yeah, I'd be spooked."

Von Essen nodded. "Spooked. Yes, a good American word that I've heard before. Well, we will spook them. I think it's a plan worth trying."

"Only problem is that shooting will alert Jacob Hammer and his gunmen," Flintlock said.

"This is not a task for guns, Herr Flintlock. It's a job for cutthroats."

Von Essen turned to one of his men and whispered, "Bring me the Corsican brothers."

A few moments later a couple of swarthy, muscular men dropped to the ground beside Von Essen and he spoke to them in urgent French, with much pointing to the entrance pass. When he'd finished, the older man nodded and said, *"Oui, mon capitaine."*

The Corsicans bellied forward into the gloom, and Von Essen whispered to Flintlock, "The Giovannetti brothers are good *soldaten,* the same breed as the Emperor Napoleon, and they are demons with the vendetta blade."

Flintlock watched as the two men crouched and made their way across the open ground between the hills and the entrance to the pass. Each held a wicked-looking knife in his right hand, the blade gleaming in the moonlight. Unchallenged, they entered the pass entrance like lethal wraiths . . . and reappeared only moments later, again crouching low as they returned to the cover of the hills.

"There was no one there," Flintlock whispered to Von Essen.

"Yes, the guards were there, *mein Herr.* The blade is quick."

One of the Corsican brothers dropped beside Von Essen, whispered, *"Quatre,"* and then faded back to his post.

"What did he say?" Flintlock said.

"Four. That's how many were sleeping in the pass."

"They killed four men?"

"Yes." Von Essen ran a forefinger across his neck. "Four are now kaput. Their throats were cut."

"That's gonna shake things up," Flintlock said.

"My wish is that it saps the morale of the defenders. Disheartened soldiers are easily defeated." Von Essen put his cold pipe in his mouth. "Like the perfidious French at the Battle of Sedan, where I won the Iron Cross Second Class. Let me tell you about my gallant deeds that day, Herr Flintlock. It will only take an hour or two. It all began . . ."

Sam Flintlock sighed.

Would this night never end?

Chapter Forty

Colonel Alfons Janowski stood by the basket of the observation balloon with Sergeant Tam Nolan and Wilfred Griffiths, the artilleryman.

"I plan to be aloft just before dawn," Janowski said. "Major Griffiths, with any luck I'll be able to give you the firing coordinates early, depending on visibility. I want the bombardment to commence at first light."

Janowski's face was ashen and his voice was weak, labored, as though talking had become a chore. Both Griffiths and Nolan realized that their commander was a very sick man.

"Colonel, let me make the observations," Griffith said. "I have younger eyes."

"Out of the question," Janowski said. "I can't afford to lose you, Major. The howitzers will win this battle for us and there's no experienced artilleryman to take your place."

"Beggin' the Colonel's pardon, but keeping balance in an observation balloon is a difficult task for a man with both arms," Nolan said. "Sir, you'll be holding a telescope up there and —"

"And returning fire, if need be, Sergeant. It's amazing what a one-armed man can do when he rises to the occasion." Janowski smiled. "A little humor there."

Sergeant Nolan stood to attention and said formally, "Sir, I request permission to make the balloon ascent."

"Permission denied, Sergeant."

"Sir, I can judge the fall of shot as well as any man."

"I'm sure you can, but you are a large man and heavy," Janowski said. "I believe I'm correct in saying that I'm the lightest man in this force. I'll be nimble, sir. Fast up, fast down, with no undue strain on the winch."

"But sir —"

"No buts, Sergeant Nolan." The colonel glanced at the still-dark sky. "Be ready to send me aloft in an hour."

A smear of pale light showed low in the eastern sky but there were stars as Sergeant Nolan assisted Colonel Janowski into the balloon basket. He carried a brass telescope, and his holstered French revolver was buckled around his waist. In the pocket of his greatcoat was a notebook, pencil and a large rock.

"If you please, Sergeant Nolan, you may send me aloft."

The balloon was very small, made for a single airman, and a portable, two-wheeled wooden tank lined with copper carried the water, iron and sulfuric acid that supplied enough hydrogen gas to send it aloft. The ascent was rapid and the steel tether cable was taut as a fiddle string when Nolan judged that the colonel was high enough to overlook the top of the mesa.

The morning was still dark, persistent stars still bright in a sky the color of new denim dungarees. There was no breeze but the air held a chill and Colonel Janowski shivered as he swept the mesa caprock with his telescope. He saw nothing but darkness, no darker shadow that would betray the location of the opening. But a fire winked red in the distance, so there were sentinels present, as Janowski had expected. How long did he have before the balloon was spotted and fired upon? He had no way of knowing since it all depended on the alertness of Jacob Hammer's gunmen. His only course now was to wait, his fate dependent on the awakening sun . . .

The sky to the east brightened and one by one the stars blinked out as the light slowly changed. Now Colonel Janowski saw the opening in the mesa top spread like a dark stain as the night shaded into morning. Quickly he scribbled the range and trajectory in his notebook, tore out the page, wrapped it around the rock he carried and dropped it over the side.

Seconds later, the first bullets from the sentries cracked past the balloon, and then as the riflemen found the range, rounds zipped through the canopy and splintered pieces of wicker from the basket.

The winch began to wind Janowski lower just as the first twelve-pounder shells burst on top of the mesa, erupting high Vs of flame, smoke, rock and flying chunks of iron. Janowski saw explosions inside the shaft and he was sure some of the shells had fallen all the way to the bottom and were detonating within the compound. Despite his pain, the little colonel smiled. He was sure the howitzers were bringing a hundred different kinds of hell down on Jacob Hammer and his outlaw band.

And in that, he was entirely correct.

CHAPTER FORTY-ONE

Jacob Hammer woke to the sound of exploding shells and the smell of fire and smoke. He jumped out of bed, just as his house rocked from a shell hit and part of his bedroom ceiling collapsed onto the floor, bringing down with it shattered timbers, thick dust and huge chunks of plaster. Moments later the wall behind his bed burst into flame as the room beyond was ravaged by fire. Fear shivering through him, Hammer ran to his closet and hurriedly dressed in riding breeches, English boots and a white shirt. He crossed a couple of gunbelts across his hips, a Colt in each holster, and ran through a fog of smoke out of the room.

Hammer's house was aflame, its ornate roof caving in many places, and the roaring shells continued to fall. He ran for the door, almost colliding with Dr. Chiang, who carried a carpetbag and looked terrified.

"Help me, Jacob," the physician yelled. "I don't want to burn to death."

Hammer, his face contorted in fury, gritted between clenched teeth, "You lied to me. You told me all would be well." A shell detonated close and the building shuddered, lifting off its foundations. "Is this what you promised, soothsayer?"

"No, Jacob, all will be well," Chiang said. A pool of urine formed around his feet. "We can escape, you and me. There is a way."

"Here is your escape, traitor," Hammer snarled. He shot the little physician between the eyes and didn't wait to see him fall.

His blazing house tumbling around him, Hammer ran outside and into a scene of horror. The whole compound was on fire, flames leaping between the tinder-dry buildings. Heedless of nothing but their own safety, men and women ran headlong for the pass. Hammer saw a young woman with brunette hair clutch at a gunman's ankles, begging him for help. The man kicked her aside and yelled, "I can do nothing for you."

Bodies sprawled everywhere, some of them burned to a crisp, others horribly mutilated by shellfire, and panic-stricken horses, the white arcs of their eyes showing, galloped wildly around the blazing compound and added to the bedlam.

Filled with anger and vindictive hatred, Hammer pushed his way through the fleeing, frightened crowd toward the dungeon. He'd have to escape with the rest . . . but first he'd carry out the executions he'd planned.

The shelling had stopped, but the heat from the fires was intense and clouds of thick smoke broke across the compound like the cresting waves of a nightmare sea. Hammer, both guns in his sweating fists, coughed, choked, gagged, as he staggered toward the cell. So intent was he on his revenge that the tumult around him ceased to register. Now his only desire was to kill . . . destroy the Pinkerton bitches and his unfaithful bride, the authors of his downfall.

Hammer struggled closer to his goal . . . but then a shock.

The iron gate to the dungeon had been blown off its hinges and rubble blocked the entrance. Hammer managed a smile. The sluts had been buried alive. He would have preferred to shoot them, but their crushing deaths under tons of rock was still as sweet as honeyed wine.

But Jacob Hammer did not have time to rejoice . . . as horror descended on him.

■ ■ ■ ■

Out of smoke and fire, Viktor lurched toward Hammer, his face contorted in rage and hatred. The Russian giant's bloody shirt hung in tatters over his hips, revealing his massive chest and shoulders and muscular arms.

Hammer was aware of the steady rattle of rifle fire from the pass. His men had obviously gotten over their panic and were fighting back. Now was not the time to contend with this mindless monster.

"Viktor, follow me," Hammer said. "We're needed at the pass."

The giant ignored that and kept coming, the fingers of his enormous hands spread, ready to grasp . . . ready to kill.

"Viktor, I gave you an order," Hammer said, a spike of alarm in his voice. "Obey me, you dog."

Silently, Viktor advanced, his small, gray eyes glowing, a gargantuan, relentless force of nature burning with the desire to kill the hated man who had so many times abused and humiliated him.

"Another step and I'll kill you," Hammer said.

Viktor ignored him, his shuffling feet closing the distance.

Hammer took a step back and fired.

Viktor took the hit and kept coming.

"Damn you!" Hammer yelled.

He fired both revolvers rapidly and saw his bullets punch great holes in Viktor's chest. Hammer knew he'd scored fatal hits, but the giant didn't flinch. Hammer triggered more shots without effect . . . and then screamed as Viktor's hands found his throat, digging deep into his windpipe as though he wore iron gauntlets.

Jacob Hammer could no longer scream. His eyes popped and his lips drew back in a grotesque parody of a grin. He couldn't breathe. His head felt as though it were about to explode and he knew death was close . . .

Then, the pressure on his throat lessened. He saw the change in Viktor's slackening face, the man's dawning realization that the bullets had taken their toll and his great strength was failing.

Hammer reached up, grabbed Viktor's wrists and pulled them from his throat. He broke free, raised his Colt, shoved the muzzle between the Russian's eyes and pulled the trigger. *Click!* He'd run the revolver dry. But the bullet wasn't necessary. Viktor staggered, said, "Bad man." And collapsed to the ground.

Now the compound was a roaring inferno and its only occupants were the dead and dying. Hammer took time to load both his Colts and then sprinted for the pass, red-hot embers tumbling around him like the snows of hell.

When Jacob Hammer ran into the pass, about thirty men and a few women were crowded together, trapped, unwilling to leave in the teeth of rifle fire and unable to retreat back to the blazing compound. Bullets zipped through the narrow arroyo, ricocheted off the walls and already three dead men had been hit and lay sprawled on the ground.

Hammer's face was grim. They couldn't stay in a pass that was rapidly becoming a charnel house. Every eye turned to him, looking for guidance, and a man said, "The guards had their throats cut. We tried to leave and lost six, seven men in the first volley."

"Who are they?" Hammer said.

"Don't know, boss," the gunman said. "But it could be an infantry regiment out there. We can't show our faces at the entrance to the pass without being shot down." Then, hope in his eyes, "Is there another way out of here?"

"No. No, there's not," Hammer said. A bullet whined off a wall and he instinctively ducked. "Damn it, we can't stay here."

"Then surrender," another, older man said. "The army will treat us decent."

"No surrender," Hammer said. "We'll shoot our way out."

"We've already tried that and all we have to show for it is dead men," the man said.

Hammer looked around and said, "You men there, bring those white women forward, not the Chinese girls. We'll use them as a shield."

The gunmen hesitated and the five women shrank back, fear in their faces.

"Damn it, there are army officers out there," Hammer said. "They won't give the order to shoot white women and it will give us the time we need to launch a counterattack."

The men were still undecided, giving one another worried, sidelong looks and Hammer yelled, "Do you all want to be shot down or burned alive in this death trap? The women are our only hope of getting out of here in one piece."

"Not me," the older man said. "I'm surrendering."

"Then go, damn you," Hammer said. "Put

338

your hands in the air and surrender. Get out! Get out while you still can."

"I'm with you, Dan," another man said. Then, "Let's go."

The two gunmen raised their arms and walked through the smoky pass to the entrance. "We surrend—"

Those were the last words the older man ever spoke as he and his companion were shot down by a fusillade of rifle fire.

"Fools! Damn fools!" Hammer said. "Now bring those women forward."

Shaken by the deaths of their confederates, men rushed to drag the shrieking, protesting women to the front. "Now, listen up," Hammer said. "We men will crouch behind the women until we're close enough to rush the enemy positions. At that point, the women will drop to the ground out of harm's way and crawl out of the line of fire." He looked into the terrified female faces and said, "You've trusted me before and you can trust me now. None of you will be harmed."

But the women wanted no part of Hammer's plan. They struggled to break free even as tongues of fire from the blazing compound licked into the pass and scorching cinders, driven by the firestorm, cartwheeled to the ground.

Hammer glanced over his shoulder at the looming conflagration, and his voice took on a tone of urgency as he yelled, "Now, men! Get behind the women and push them forward. I will lead the counterattack."

Chapter Forty-Two

Sam Flintlock heard someone to his right yell a one-word question filled with uncertainty, "Captain?"

"They're using their women as a shield," Flintlock said. His mother wasn't among them.

"I see it," Von Essen said, his face as grim as a hanging judge passing a death sentence. Then, his one-word answer to the one-word question . . . "Fire!"

Twenty riflemen, conditioned since their youth to obey an order without question, cut loose with a withering volley. All five women were cut down and behind them several men were hit and fell. Then Flintlock heard a man yell, "Attack!"

The Hammer gunmen, their morale shaken, were now a frightened mob. Firing as they came, they made a halfhearted advance on Von Essen's position, but as volley after well-aimed volley crashed into their ranks, they faltered, then broke and fled, leaving half their number dead on the ground.

About a dozen gunmen retreated eastward, only to run into Colonel Janowski's men who'd come to the aid of the detachment at the pass now that the shelling had ceased. The demoralized gunmen raised their hands and tried to surrender but were quickly shot down. Back in Washington, Senator Flood had made it clear that surrender was not an option, and, like Von Essen, Alfons Janowski followed orders.

Sam Flintlock followed his heart.

A column of scarlet-tinted smoke rose from the hole in the mesa caprock like an erupting volcano, and somewhere in that inferno was his mother. Flintlock didn't know if she was alive or dead, but he intended to find out. Janowski was sitting with his back against a rock, and he and Von Essen were deep in conversation.

As an occasional shot rang out and dispatched a wounded gunman, unnoticed, Flintlock rose from his position and walked to the entrance of Pitchfork Pass. He levered a round into his Henry and stepped into the heat and smoke of the arroyo. He walked past the grinning skulls that decorated the walls, and ahead of him the opening that led to the compound was framed by fire, like a side entrance to Hades. Flintlock tied his bandanna around his mouth and nose and plunged into the inferno.

Sam Flintlock walked into a horseshoe of flame.

Directly ahead of him a house burned and on either side of him rows of low, wooden buildings were ablaze. Smoke hung over the compound and he had to step around the blackened bodies of men, a few women and several horses. The women's bodies were scorched beyond recognition and Flintlock, his heart sinking, realized he'd need to search further, perhaps in the buildings once the fires had died. His eyes were red-rimmed from smoke, glowing sparks blistered his face and hands and even with the protection of the bandanna the stench of burning flesh was unbearable. He ordered himself to give up the search and return later . . . before he, too, ended up a blackened cinder.

Flintlock took one last look at the fiery buildings and turned to leave. But then he stopped in his tracks as he heard a groan coming from somewhere to his left where the smoke hung thickest.

"Who's there?" he yelled.

No answer.

"I can't see you, partner. Can you speak?" Flintlock yelled.

The fires were dying down now, having destroyed all they could destroy, but flames still roared and flaming wooden beams crackled and showered sparks into the air.

"Here . . ."

A man's voice, somewhere in the smoke.

"Keep talking, feller, I'm coming."

It dawned on Flintlock that the man was one of Jacob Hammer's gunmen and he'd have to shoot him. He didn't want to think about that. Not now.

"Over here . . ."

The man's voice sounded weak, probably from smoke, and Flintlock headed in that direction. He found a stricken giant. The man lay on his back, his massive chest covered in blood. He'd been shot many times at close range, powder burns visible under the gore. The colossus was in pain, his thick lips peeled back from his teeth, breath coming in short, quick gasps, yet he clung to life, tenaciously surviving by the sheer force of his will.

The man raised an arm and pointed. "There . . . womens . . . you go . . . Louise . . ."

He reached up and with the last of his strength he grabbed Flintlock by the nape of his neck and pulled him close. "Go . . ."

A moment, and then the giant's eyes fluttered closed and with a great, rasping sigh he died.

Flintlock disentangled himself from the man's hand, stood and his gaze followed the direction of the pointing finger. The direction was to the left of the burning house, an area of the compound invisible in the smoke. But the women were over there and Flintlock's mother was one of them. Heedless of the danger from the still-ravenous fire, he sprinted in that direction, his heart hammering in his chest. Could anyone have survived the shelling and the blaze? Sam Flintlock was not a praying man, but he asked for God's help as he ran . . .

Let me find them still alive.

Flintlock almost tripped over a heavy steel gate that lay in front of an arch-shaped depression in the rock face. It looked like a cave of some kind, but if it was, the entrance was blocked by tons of rubble that had fallen from higher up the wall. A sick feeling in his belly, he laid his rifle on the ground and stood close to the tumbled rocks, some of them as large as a beer barrel, and yelled, "Ma! Can you hear me?"

Flintlock realized the desperate futility of that shout as soon as he uttered the words. But there was something he could do. He grabbed a rock, threw it aside, and then laid hands on another.

The pitiless fire mocked him, the smoke did its best to choke him and his hands soon blistered and then bled from the hot sandstone.

But Flintlock worked on, heedless of pain, the mass of rock in front of him now his most hated enemy.

CHAPTER FORTY-THREE

After an hour of removing rock by blistering rock, burned by flying embers, choking, coughing in the smoke, Sam Flintlock had made little impression on the pile of rubble that blocked the cave entrance. Around him the fire was burning itself out, but slowly, like a destructive demon prolonging its own evil existence.

Flintlock had called to his mother many times as he worked, but each time he was greeted by silence. Doggedly, he went back to removing rocks, a relentlessly unending task that was gradually exhausting him.

"Hände hoch!"

Flintlock turned to the harsh Prussian voice. Captain Dieter Von Essen, a revolver in his hand, eyed him through the misting smoke. Behind him eight mercenaries had rifles in their hands and ice in their stare. Von Essen screwed a monocle in his right eye and peered, his thin body bent forward from the waist.

"Herr Flintlock?" he said. *"Sind Sie das?"* Then, in English, "Is that you?"

Flintlock realized he was covered from head to toe in soot. He wiped his throat with his hand, revealing some of the thunderbird tattoo.

"Ach, I thought you'd been killed," the captain said. He holstered his gun. "What are you doing here?"

Flintlock motioned to the rubble. "Captain, I think my mother and two other women are buried behind these rocks."

"Then we must free them, instanter!" Von Essen turned to his men. *"Meine herren,* remove this barrier." He stepped to Flintlock, grabbed his wrists and stared at his bloody, torn hands. "But not you, Herr Flintlock. You have already done enough."

The eight mercenaries stacked their rifles and then worked on the rockfall. As he watched his men work, Von Essen said, "The butcher's bill was low in this battle, Herr Flintlock. We suffered two dead and three wounded."

"And Hammer's people?" Flintlock said. His eyes were glued to the cave entrance.

"Fifty-seven dead, including eight women, two of them Orientals." Von Essen shrugged. "But there may be more bodies in the burned buildings."

"Pity about the women," Flintlock said.

"Ancillary damage is to be expected in war," Von Essen said.

"Any sign of Jacob Hammer?"

"I don't know. I never met the gentleman, but later perhaps you can inspect the bodies."

"If he's among the dead, my mother will be able to identify him. She's a Pinkerton."

The Prussian was puzzled. "What is this . . . Pinkerton?"

"A detective," Flintlock said.

"Ah, that is good, very good," Von Essen said. "There are no female detectives in Prussia."

"Or anywhere else," Flintlock said.

"One more thing, we must add Colonel Janowski to the casualty list," Von Essen said. "He is very ill. His left side is paralyzed and he has trouble speaking. I think this will be his last campaign." The captain smiled. "It is just as well that it ended in a splendid victory. Just between you and me, Herr Flintlock, I do not approve of elderly officers going up in balloons."

"Captain! Over here."

This from a man at the rockfall.

"What is it?" Von Essen said.

"We think we hear something."

Flintlock rushed to the rubble, a question on his face, but a man held a forefinger to his lips and said, "Hush."

Flintlock cocked his head and listened. There it was! A soft scraping sound that came and went. It could mean only that the women were removing rubble from the other side. Forgetful of his tattered hands, Flintlock grabbed a rock and tossed it aside. The other men joined in and after fifteen minutes they'd cleared a small space, enough that Flintlock could put his mouth to the opening and say, "Ma!"

A moment passed and then, "Is that you, Samuel?"

"Yeah, Ma, it's me. Are you all right?"

"I'm fine and so are the others. But did you see Viktor? Just before the cave-in he left to find Jacob Hammer."

"Viktor? Is he a big feller?"

"Yes. He's a giant of a man."

"Ma, he's dead, all shot to pieces."

A long silence, then, "Jacob Hammer killed him."

"He lived long enough to tell me where I could find you. Now we've got to get you out of there."

Fifteen minutes later the women were freed. Like the other two, Jane was soot stained but otherwise seemed in good health. Louise Smith and Bridie O'Toole hugged Flintlock and thanked him profusely, tears of relief and gratitude in their eyes.

"Samuel, you rescued us in the nick of time," Jane said. "Bridie and I were to be burned at the stake today."

"And I was to have my head cut off," Louise said.

Flintlock smiled. "Don't thank me." He brought the Prussian forward. "This is Captain Dieter Von Essen. Without him and his brave men you'd still be Jacob Hammer's prisoners."

The Prussian clicked his heels and bowed over Jane's hand. "And you, dear lady, are Herr Flintlock's mother?"

"Yes, I am, Captain."

"I am honored to meet you, Detective. Your son fought well."

"Thank you. I have no doubt he did."

Von Essen looked around at the smoldering buildings and the sprawled dead. "And now we must get you and the other *junge Damen* out of this terrible place, but first I must ask all of you to perform a distressing duty."

"You saved our lives, Captain," Jane said. "You only have to ask."

"All Hammer's men are dead, but we

can't identify his body as being one of them. Can you help us identify —"

"Yes, we can," Jane said. "His is a face we'll never forget."

CHAPTER FORTY-FOUR

Colonel Alfons Janowski slurred his words from a slightly twisted mouth, but his eyes were as bright and alert as ever. "Your mother and the other women couldn't identify Jacob Hammer?"

"No, Colonel," Sam Flintlock said. "Maybe he burned in one of the buildings."

"Or he escaped," Janowski said.

"Then he's on foot without water and food," Flintlock said. "I'll find him."

"And when you do?"

"I'll kill him."

"The rest of us are returning to Flagstaff, where my men will be paid off by an army paymaster. You were not an official member of this force, so you will not be paid, which is unfortunate. But . . . you will receive a sixtieth share of the hundred thousand dollars we took from Hammer's brigands, around sixteen hundred if my calculations are correct."

"You don't have to pay me anything, Colonel," Flintlock said. "If it wasn't for you my mother would have been executed today."

"But I insist, Mr. Flintlock. You took part in this action and are thus entitled to a share in the spoils of war." Flintlock opened his mouth to object, but Janowski said, "I will brook no argument. Mr. Griffiths, my artilleryman, is acting as paymaster. See him and he'll give you what you're owed."

"Colonel, maybe you should rest up for a spell before you head for Flagstaff," Flintlock said. "You're not well."

Janowski's twisted mouth managed a smile. "My right arm lies on some foreign field and now my left is paralyzed. But Sergeant Nolan assures me he knows a way to tie me on my horse so that I won't fall off and I'm taking his word for that."

Nolan, who kneeled beside the colonel said, "I'll take good care of you, sir."

"There are doctors in Flagstaff," Flintlock said.

"Yes. For me and my wounded and I will bury my dead there." Janowski looked up at the mesa. "I've given orders that Hammer's dead be taken into the compound and laid out in a respectful manner. The army engineers will be here later to restore this part

354

of the mesa and they can deal with the bodies then." The old man was tiring and Nolan scolded him for talking so much, but he rallied and said, "Mr. Flintlock, you must never speak of this action. My mercenaries are sworn to secrecy and the soldiers —"

"It never happened, Colonel," Nolan said.

"Good. Let Jacob Hammer's criminal enterprise be buried in the mesa with his dead and forgotten," Janowski said.

"Louise is leaving for Flagstaff with Colonel Janowski and his men," Jane said. "He says he'll make sure that she has enough money to travel east where she has kin."

"What about you, Ma?" Flintlock said.

"Bridie and I talked it over and we feel it's our duty as Pinkertons to see this case through to the end."

"And that will be when we see Jacob Hammer dead," Bridie said.

"After I told the colonel about Viktor's bravery, he agreed to take him to Flagstaff for burial," Jane said. "He promised he'll receive the same military honors as his own dead."

Flintlock nodded. "The big feller died a hero, that's for sure."

Bridie O'Toole watched bloody corpses being carried into the mesa and said, "Let's

355

get away from here. I've seen enough of Pitchfork Pass to last me a lifetime."

Flintlock nodded. "We'll go get my horse and see if we can round up mounts for you and Ma."

By the time Flintlock and the women walked around the mesa to the horse lines, the howitzers had already been taken apart, ready for loading onto the pack mules. The empty shell casings had been picked up and the observation balloon and its winch had been placed to one side and would ride on the sturdy, two-wheeled gas wagon. All evidence of the artillery bombardment was gone. Only the thin drift of smoke from the hole in the mesa caprock remained and even that was rapidly dissipating in the wind.

During the shelling, horses had stampeded from the Hammer compound and Flintlock had no trouble finding mounts and saddles for Jane and Bridie O'Toole and packhorses to carry the food and ammunition that a grateful Colonel Janowski had bestowed on them as well as the sixteen hundred dollars that he'd given Flintlock.

As they rode away from the mesa and its horrific memories, Jane suggested they head for the warm-water seep where Flintlock had been introduced to Pears soap. "I need to wash off the stench of Hammer's cell," she said, and Bridie readily agreed.

"And then we hunt for Jacob Hammer," Flintlock said. "He could be anywhere by now. How the hell —"

"Language, Samuel," Jane said. "There's no need for profanity."

"All right, Ma, then how the heck do we find him?"

Jane answered without hesitation.

"Samuel, hate is a terrible burden to bear, and right now I fancy that it's driving Jacob Hammer. The only way he can free himself from it is to destroy the objects of his hate. Louise Smith is out of reach, but he still has us, and he hates us with a passion that by now is eating away at him like a cancer."

"Then we don't have to find him?" Flintlock said. "He'll come to us?"

"I guarantee it. That's why we'll return to the hot spring and make ourselves visible."

"I don't like that much, Ma," Flintlock said. "You plan on making us targets."

"Exactly, Samuel. Clever boy, you catch on fast," Bridie said.

"We'll be targets, but we'll also be wary," Jane said. "The thing to do is to make Hammer overconfident, because an overconfident man can make mistakes. He only has to make one . . . and then I'll kill him."

"Or I will," Flintlock said.

"We'll see," Jane said.

CHAPTER FORTY-FIVE

Jacob Hammer had gotten as far away from Balakai Mesa as his wounded left leg would allow. He had no water and no horse, and as he sat in the shadow of a rock wall and watched blood stain the sand under his thigh, he knew that his chances, like his luck, were fast running out. But the will to survive burned bright in the man, its flames fueled by his hatred of the Pinkerton women and the man with the tattoo on his throat.

Hammer would not let himself think about dying until he'd exacted his revenge on those three . . . enemies. Then a thought struck him — what if they were gone? What if that very morning they were somewhere drinking coffee, laughing over the destruction of all his plans while he sat, wounded, in the sun and suffered? He shook his head, clearing his negative thoughts. No, that would not be the case. By now the army, if it had been the army and not some ragtag bunch of bounty hunters, the lowest trash on the frontier, had discovered that his body was not among the dead. Would they come looking for him? No, the army would assume that without a horse or water he'd perish in the wilderness. And bounty hunters would take what loot they could find and leave. They had destroyed the settlement and that was what they'd been paid to do. Searching a hot, barren wilderness for a single fugitive would not enter into their thinking.

But the Pinkertons would think differently. And the tattooed man, the one they called Sam Flintlock. They would not leave until the job was done and Jacob Hammer, the Old Man of the Mountain, was dead. Their own hatred for him and all he stood for would drive them. Hammer's smile was grim. Let them come, let them find him, and he'd be ready.

He took stock of his situation.

By his best estimate he was about three miles northwest of the mesa in rough and broken country dominated by high walls of red sandstone and deep gulches. He'd seen no sign of water. The bullet that hit him had taken a furrow of flesh out of his thigh but had not struck bone. The wound bled, but it was not serious, though his leg had stiffened up and made walking difficult. He'd lost his rifle, but still had his Colts and filled cartridge belts. He'd never met anyone faster than he was on the draw and shoot and considered himself more than a match for Flintlock and his women.

But Hammer had no horse and no water and that worried him.

He tried standing. His wounded leg supported him pretty well, but how far he could walk on it was a question that troubled him.

What was that?

The faint sound of a steel-shod hoof on rock.

Had his enemies found him? If so they'd pay dearly for their boldness.

Hammer backed farther into the rapidly narrowing shadow of the rock wall and drew both his Colts. His mouth was dry and his eyes burned from the sunlight, but he was ready.

The sound of hooves came closer. It sounded like only one horse, not three as he'd expected. Maybe it was only one of the women. Perhaps Flintlock and one of the Pinkertons had been killed or wounded in the fight. Hammer smiled. A lone Pinkerton woman. Now, that opened up a world of delightful possibilities. Of course, it could be a cavalryman or a bounty hunter. Either way, Hammer was relaxed, confident he could handle either situation.

A few moments dragged past and the sound of hooves grew closer. Then a man's voice. "Damn you, water mule, for the most stubborn critter that ever was. I don't aim to haul you all the way to Canada and there's the truth of it."

A bearded man pulling a mule behind him walked onto the flat, sandy area that led to the rock wall where Hammer stood in shadow. As the man walked closer, the balky mule fighting him every inch of the way, Hammer stepped out in plain view.

"Whoa, you startled me there," the bearded man said, halting in his tracks. "What are you doing all the way out here?"

"I could ask you the same thing," Hammer said.

The man smiled. "I'm an explorer, on my way to Canada, but I got lost. Fact is, I get lost all the time. Name's Lon Stringer and this here is my water mule."

"Why do you call it that?"

"Because he can nose out water from ten miles away."

"I could use some water," Hammer said.

"Traveling light, huh?" Stringer said. "Here, you're wounded."

"Shot myself by accident, drawing down

on a cougar."

Stringer nodded. "That can happen. I've never been much a one for gun handling my ownself. Like you, I'm not much good at it."

Hammer found that amusing, but didn't let it show. "Water?" he said.

"Oh, sure."

Stringer took his canteen from the water mule's pack and handed it over. "There you go, Mr. . . ."

"My name is Jacob Hammer."

"Right pleased to meet you, Jacob —"

Hammer saw the man's face change as his name rang a bell with him . . . an alarm bell, judging by Stringer's stricken expression.

Hammer took a swig of water, and another and then he wiped his mouth with the back of his hand and said, "Heard that name before?"

"Can't say as I have," Stringer said.

"Lying in your teeth, aren't you?"

Stringer managed a smile. "Well, maybe I've heard folks mention it a time or two."

"What folks?" Hammer said.

The bearded man shrugged. "Oh, I don't know. Just folks."

"Like Pinkerton detectives, maybe?"

Stringer shook his head. "Don't know any

of them."

"How about a man with a bird on his throat?"

This time Hammer knew he'd struck a chord, though Stringer denied all knowledge of such a man. "I think a man with a bird on his throat is a thing I'd remember," he said. "Here, let me take a look at that leg."

"My leg is doing fine," Hammer said. His smile was chilling. "You're not doing fine, explorer man."

"I mean no harm," Stringer said.

"Did Sam Flintlock send you? Did he ask you to spy me out?"

"I don't know anybody by that name."

"You're a damned liar."

"Sorry you feel that way. Well, now me and the water mule got to be moving on, see if we can get unlost and then go find Canada."

"You're not going anywhere," Hammer said. "Where is Flintlock? Does he have two women with him?"

Stringer shook his head. "I don't know the man."

Hammer drew and fired. His bullet hit Stringer's left shinbone and dropped him.

"Where are Sam Flintlock and the Pinkerton women?" Hammer said.

Stringer's face was twisted in pain but his

eyes blazed defiance. "I don't know him."

Hammer fired again, and this time Stringer's right shin splintered and the little man cried out in agony.

"Where are Sam Flintlock and the Pinkerton women?"

"I . . . don't . . . know . . ."

"Mr. Stringer, you'll never walk again, but you can still do your exploring from a wheelchair," Hammer said. "Where are Sam Flintlock and the Pinkerton women?"

"Damn you, go to hell," the little man said.

Hammer fired another shot, this time into Stringer's left thigh.

"Where are Sam Flintlock and the Pinkerton women?"

Stringer was in serious pain but he had sand. His teeth clenched, he said, "I don't know."

A bullet clipped three fingers off Stringer's left hand.

"Where are Sam Flintlock and the Pinkerton women?"

But now the little man was incapable of answering, blood pooling in the sand around him. But he looked up at Hammer and whispered, "Take care of the water mule . . ."

"You're not fit to live, you traitorous dog,"

Hammer said.

And he shot Lon Stringer, explorer, between the eyes.

CHAPTER FORTY-SIX

The hot-water seep was as Sam Flintlock remembered it, except that it was a little deeper and a few degrees cooler. His mother and Bridie made bathing and clothes washing their first order of business while he was banished and told to stand guard at a distance. When it came his turn to take a bath Flintlock pointed out that he'd washed all over not a week before and still smelled of Pears soap and Sarah Bernhardt.

Later Flintlock scrounged as much wood as he could from the trees that grew here and there and built a fire. He made no effort to keep the smoke to a minimum since his purpose now was to draw in Jacob Hammer . . . if the man was still around.

Jane was sure Hammer was still in the area and would take the bait, but Bridie had her doubts, voicing the hope that Hammer had crawled away and died somewhere.

But it wasn't in Flintlock's nature to wait

for the man to show up and attack at a time of his choosing. If he was out there and had gone to ground, Flintlock aimed to find him.

"Sam, you're a grown man and although I'm your mother I'm not going to tell you what to do, but I think you're putting your life in danger," Jane said. "We're in a good defensive position here and we can wait him out."

"I won't let Hammer pen us up, waiting for him to strike at his leisure, Ma," Flintlock said as he swung into the saddle. "I'm going out to shake the bushes. I'll be back before dark." He smiled. "Don't wait up."

"There will be no sleep around here until Hammer is dead," Jane said.

"Then let's hope I kill him today and we can all get some shut-eye," Flintlock said.

"Be careful . . . son," Jane said. "I'll worry about you."

"I can take care of myself, Ma," Flintlock said. "Old Barnabas and his cronies taught me a thing or two about how to stalk and kill a man."

"Your grandfather lost seven men, eighteen horses and a wagon in one expedition to the Cache Valley in the Idaho Territory," Jane said. "Take what he taught you with a grain of salt."

"He never told me that," Flintlock said.

"He never told you a lot of things," Jane said.

There was a slim possibility that Jacob Hammer had returned to the scene of his crime at Balakai Mesa and was holed up there nursing his wounds, if he had any. It wasn't likely, but Flintlock decided it was a place to start.

A thunderstorm was piling up massive ramparts of black clouds to the south as Flintlock reached Pitchfork Pass. The place was deserted. He dismounted, slid his rifle from the boot, and led the skittish buckskin into the arroyo. The big horse smelled death and as Flintlock led him deeper into the pass he became more and more agitated and constantly tossed his head, the only sound in that dark, soundless space the chime of his bit.

Yellowed, grinning skulls still adorned the walls of the pass and once a pack of rats scampered around Flintlock's feet, like himself, heading for the compound.

Hemmed in on three sides by blackened, burned-out buildings, the floor of the compound was littered with dead, swollen bodies with blue faces, some with open eyes that stared at Flintlock but saw nothing. There was no sign of army engineers and

369

the corpses still lay where they'd been dumped by Colonel Janowski's mercenaries, the stench unbearable in this arena of death. Only the busy rats moved and the only sound was their sated squeaks and Flintlock's labored breathing. He turned away from the dreadful scene and led his horse into the pass. It was all too obvious that Jacob Hammer wasn't there. The man belonged with the rats because he was one of them . . . but even he shunned that place.

Sam Flintlock breathed deeply of the clean morning air as he mounted the buckskin and rode east. Distant thunder rumbled as the storm rolled closer and lightning spiked among the clouds and Flintlock cursed himself for a fool for even coming here. But he rode on. Jacob Hammer had not escaped to the east where he would have run into the mercenaries. He must have escaped during the battle at the pass and headed west, but where he'd gone after that was anybody's guess. Sickened and depressed by what he'd seen at the mesa and disheartened by the vastness of the landscape ahead of him, he let the buckskin have its head. Perhaps the horse would lead him to Jacob Hammer.

■ ■ ■ ■

Probably to keep ahead of the approaching thunderstorm, the buckskin picked its way northward, into broken country cut through by numerous dry washes and fantastic rock formations. After an hour, Flintlock drew rein at a sandstone overhang that promised protection from the now-teeming rain. He dismounted and led his horse into the shelter, ate some jerky then smoked a cigarette. The storm was violent but brief, and the sky was clear blue when Flintlock again mounted and continued on his horse's northeastward track. Wishful for coffee, another hour and he'd call it a day and head back to camp.

But after just thirty minutes the buckskin raised his head, his ears pointed forward, scenting something he did not like in the newly washed air. Flintlock eased the Winchester from the boot and kneed the horse into a walk. Ahead of him a sand-bottomed dry wash skirted a stand of juniper and piñon and then headed in the direction of a high rock wall. The big buckskin was uneasy, and Flintlock leaned over and patted its neck.

"What is it, boy, huh?" he said. "What do

you smell?"

And then his own answering thought . . . *You smell a rat.*

Flintlock drew rein, swung out of the saddle and followed the wash on foot, his rifle at the ready. Behind him his horse had found some graze and took no further interest in the proceedings. It wasn't a cougar, then, so it had to be some other kind of animal . . . or a man. Was that man Jacob Hammer?

Warily, Flintlock stepped forward, every nerve in his body stretched as taut as a fiddle string. His eyes scanned the landscape ahead, the wash snaking away from him, the rock wall . . . where a naked man stood watching him.

Without thinking about it, Flintlock instinctively threw himself to the ground, the Winchester coming to his shoulder in a single, swift movement. He expected to hear a shot, feel the impact of lead striking his body. But it never happened. The man just stood there, his back against the wall, his arms bent as though his hands were on his hips. Flintlock got to his feet.

"Identify yourself," he said.

No answer.

The rifle at his shoulder, Flintlock stepped forward and then froze in his tracks. There was something about the man that was familiar . . . and something else . . . the man's eyes were open, staring, but he was dead.

Now Flintlock stepped closer and looked at the lifeless face of Lon Springer.

The little explorer's body had been all shot to pieces. The torrential rain had washed away most of the blood but the wounds to his legs, hand and head stood out in dreadful relief against the whiteness of his skin. Springer had died a painful and undignified death. The body had been stripped and then propped up against the wall, and under his armpits two rocky projections caused by erosion helped hold him upright.

Flintlock shook his head and said, "Lon, who did this to you?"

The dead man couldn't answer that question, but Flintlock could . . . the little explorer had been murdered and his body desecrated by Jacob Hammer.

What really sickened Flintlock was the fact that Hammer did not leave the body for him to see. He had little reason to believe that Flintlock would come this way and admire his handiwork. No, the monster had done it for his own gratification, a grim hunting trophy he'd mounted for display and amusement. In that moment of truth, Flintlock knew he faced a great evil that must be destroyed, even at the cost of his own life. Such a demon as Jacob Hammer must no longer be allowed to cast his malevolent shadow on the earth.

CHAPTER FORTY-SEVEN

"I found a place where a rock face had split apart and I put him in there," Flintlock said.

"I suppose that's as good a resting place as any for an explorer," Jane said.

"I don't think Lon Springer was a very good explorer," Flintlock said. "He told me he kept getting lost all the time."

Jane smiled. "Explorers are always getting lost. Didn't David Livingstone get lost in darkest Africa before Stanley found him and showed him the way home?"

"That Livingstone feller was lucky it was Stanley," Flintlock said. "Jacob Hammer found Lon."

Bridie O'Toole said, "Sam, are you sure it was him, Hammer, I mean?"

"It was him, all right," Jane said. "Think about it, Bridie. Who else would kill a man bit by bit and then display his naked body?"

"The death of a thousand cuts," Bridie said.

"Or a version of it, using a gun."

"Samuel, do you think Hammer knew that you had met Lon before?" Jane said.

"I'm sure he did. I think that's why Hammer killed him."

"And now he'll try to kill us," Bridie said.

"Yes, Bridie, yes, he will," Jane said. "Starting tonight we'll sleep in shifts. I'll take the first four-hour watch, Samuel the second, and, Bridie, you the third."

"How do we know when our four hours is up?" Bridie said. "We don't have a watch."

"Yes, we do," Flintlock said. He reached into his pants pocket. "Captain Von Essen gave me this, said he took it off the body of one of Hammer's gunmen." He passed the watch to Jane. "It's a Waltham railroader and a good timekeeper."

Jane smiled. "The spoils of war, huh?"

"Yeah, just like the sixteen hundred dollars in my saddlebags."

"What are you going to do with all that money, Samuel?" Jane said. "Providing I allow you to keep it. It is stolen, after all."

"It was stolen from the thief who stole it in the first place, Ma. That makes it legal in my book."

"I'm sure if I look hard enough I'll find some logic there," Jane said.

Bridie said, "What about it, Sam? How

are you going to spend the money? You can buy me a present if you like."

"Maybe I'll do that," Flintlock said. "A present for you and Ma. But right now, my thinking is that I might set myself up in the dry goods business. I think I would prosper in that profession."

"A laudable ambition, Samuel," Jane said. "Dry goods would be a vast improvement on what you are presently, a lawman of sorts today, an outlaw of sorts tomorrow."

"Outlawing is a tough business. Me and O'Hara once tried the train-robbing profession, but we never did cotton to it . . . too much competition from the likes of Jesse and Frank and them. Tried bank robbing for a spell one time, but quit that real quick after we saw a citizens' posse string up Stuttering Steve Clifford. Hung him in a barn up El Paso way and it took ol' Steve the best part of a morning to choke to death, and all the time his pet hog was licking his toes."

"Well, if all that didn't teach you a lesson about the perils of lawlessness, nothing will," Jane said.

"You're right, Ma. All things considered, I'll be better off selling dry goods," Flintlock said. "But not in this territory, not west of everything."

■ ■ ■ ■

Wood was hard to come by, but during his first watch he stoked up the fire, a beckoning beacon to bring Jacob Hammer closer. He really didn't expect the man to attempt a night attack, but there was always a chance he might try it.

At midnight by his watch, Flintlock rose and stretched and then took up his Winchester again and patrolled around the rise. At its western end the bluff broke off abruptly and there was a sheer drop of about twenty feet that ended at a narrow, U-shaped rock formation. He stepped back from the edge. If a man fell over there he'd land fast and hard and if he didn't kill himself, he'd suffer some broken bones.

Somewhere out among the canyons coyotes yipped, and with them was Jacob Hammer. Was he even now staring at the distant, blinking firelight, biding his time, waiting to take his revenge on those he hated? It was probable, no, more than that, it was highly likely. Flintlock glanced at the sleeping women and wished this was all over, done and finished, Hammer dead and his ma and Bridie wiring from Fort Defiance for further instructions. That was his wish, but the reality was that as long as Hammer breathed his ma, Bridie and himself were in terrible danger. A shot could come out of the darkness at any time and find its firelit target. It was a worrisome thought.

Flintlock roused Bridie O'Toole at two in the morning. The woman woke instantly and sat up, fully aware of her surroundings. "Anything happening?" she said.

"The coyotes are hunting and making a racket, and I heard an owl. But apart from that, nothing," Flintlock said.

Bridie rose to her feet and picked up her rifle. "Get some sleep, Sam." Her voice sounded hollow in the quiet.

"I'm not much of a sleeping man," Flintlock said. "Wake me in a couple of hours."

"No, I'll wake Jane at six. She's a Pinkerton and she aims to do her fair share. Let me have the watch."

Flintlock passed over the Waltham and Bridie said, "Sam, do you think he'll show?"

"Tonight?"

"Tonight, tomorrow, will he show?"

"I think he will."

"Think?"

"All right, I'm sure he will. But by day. Not night."

Bridie smiled. "He'll want to see our faces

when he kills us, huh?"

"He'll see our faces, but it's the last thing Jacob Hammer will ever see."

"Is he good with a gun?"

"I don't know. But to have survived this long in a violent business, I imagine he's better than most."

"Better than you, Sam?"

"That remains to be seen, but I doubt it." Flintlock grinned. "I'm pretty fast, you know."

"I'm keeping you up," Bridie said. "You'd better turn in."

Flintlock tossed some sticks on the fire and then sought his blankets. As he stretched out his mother spoke from the darkness. "How good is he, Samuel?"

"Real good, I imagine."

"I imagine that, too," Jane said.

CHAPTER FORTY-EIGHT

Jacob Hammer knew he was a dead man.

He'd seen gangrene before, in China, seen it many times, and smelled it . . . the vile stench of rotting meat.

The wound on his thigh had turned black and it oozed pus and the pain was intense, unbelievably intense, like no pain he'd ever felt or ever imagined. Later today, tomorrow, his whole leg would become black and poison his blood and kill him.

If Dr. Chiang had been here he could have cut off the rotten leg, sawed it off just below the hip and given him a chance of life. But he'd killed Dr. Chiang because the man was a traitor and a liar, a soothsayer who could not predict his own death and the death of the man who'd given him a home and made him rich.

In the end, Hammer knew he'd been surrounded by treachery, blackhearted betrayal. Chiang, curse him, had been one of the traitors, but the two women Pinkertons and the man called Sam Flintlock had been the worst of them.

Hammer ordained they had to die before he did . . . and their deaths must be as painful and disgusting as his own.

Oh, he knew where they were. He'd seen their fire not far from where he lay in the shadow of a rock and watched the mule eat the last of the oats from the sack he'd found in its pack. The mule was a deceitful, traitorous wretch and when this was over and his enemies dead, he'd shoot the foul beast between the eyes.

But for now, he needed the stubborn brute. It would carry him to his destiny.

Hammer had cut open his riding breeches to allow the leg to swell. There was no chance of removing his boot. His lower leg was swollen inside the leather and the pain would be too much to bear and might incapacitate him. He had to be able to walk, and silently at that.

It would cause him terrible pain, but Hammer had to find out if he could still walk. Still hobble. Slowly, carefully, he got to his feet and put weight on the rotting leg. Sweet Jesu! He felt pain that was beyond pain, lightning bolts of searing agony that jolted through his entire body.

He clenched his teeth against a scream and willed the pain to pass, but it did not. Gasping now, sweat staining his shirt, he took one step, tried another, and fell hard on his side. Now there was no holding back the scream. He rolled on his back and shrieked and shrieked until his parched mouth and throat could shriek no longer. Then a blackness overcame Hammer and he fell headlong into a hellish, scarlet-streaked pit that had no bottom . . .

Jacob Hammer woke to bright sunlight. He'd been unconscious, but for how long? Judging by the position of the sun in the sky, no more than an hour. But now the die must be cast. The deaths of the Pinkertons and Flintlock must be tonight. By tomorrow he might be unable to get to his feet. By tomorrow he might be dead.

A pipe of opium would remove his pain, dream him into a better place, but he had none. All he had was the faithless mule . . . his only ally.

He lay on his back and smelled sun-warmed rock and the ever-present stink of his corrupting leg. How simple it would be to get his gun and blow his brains out and end his suffering. But that was out of the question. The Pinkerton women and Sam

Flintlock must not go unpunished. Their treachery and deceit was too grievous a sin.

Now . . . he must get out of the sun.

A great discovery!

If he lay on his back and pushed with his good leg he could cover ground, slowly and painfully to be sure, but enough that he soon reached the shade of the massive rock and his canteen.

Hammer drank deeply, then formulated his plan.

After several minutes, he finally nodded, satisfied. Yes, it would work if he played his cards right and got a little luck on his side. Certainly, he could kill one of them easily and probably all three . . . and now that was the only thing that mattered.

Jacob Hammer, a man dying by degrees and in pain, closed his eyes and waited for the twilight time before the darkness, kept alive only by his insane compulsion to kill.

Covering the ten yards that separated Jacob Hammer and the mule was a nightmare of torment. Hammer made the agonizing journey on his back before he got to his feet and placed his arms across the animal's back to support his weight. He and the mule stood like that for several minutes, while Hammer fought back rising nausea and endured torture that felt like a brawny lumberjack hitting his wounded leg over and over again with the honed edge of an ax. Hammer smelled the stink of his own sweat and the decaying meat stench of the gangrene and he fought down the urge to scream and scream and never stop. But he endured. The madman knew that failure was not an option.

Climbing onto the bony back of the mule was almost too much for Hammer, but he succeeded because uppermost in his mind was his vision of the two women and Flintlock sprawled dead on the ground, their bodies abused and violated in ways that, despite his pain, still had the ability to amuse and excite him.

He urged the mule forward, a short-barreled Colt shoved into his waistband at the small of his back, his shirt pulled over the revolver to conceal it.

His stubbled face white as ash, dark shadows in his sunken cheeks and eye sockets, surrounded by the stench of rot, Jacob Hammer looked and stank like the Angel of Death.

CHAPTER FORTY-NINE

Sam Flintlock had stripped the area surrounding the rise of wood. The fire still burned but it was a pale yellow shadow of its former self, barely managing to keep the coffeepot simmering.

"He's not going to show, is he?" Bridie O'Toole said. "I think he's dead."

"Could be," Flintlock said. "Come first light I reckon I'll ride out again and take a look-see."

The stars were bright, a crescent moon was on the rise and the country around them was bathed in a spectral, mother-of-pearl light that silvered the coats of the coyotes prowling the canyons. There was no sound, only the faint crackling of the fire and the soft rise and fall of Jane's breathing as she slept.

Flintlock poured himself coffee and then stood beside Bridie again.

"You should be sleeping, Sam," the

woman said.

"I will, soon," Flintlock said. "Strange kind of night."

"Eerie. Is that the word, *eerie*?" Bridie said.

"Don't know," Flintlock said. "I've never heard it before. What does it mean?"

"Spooky."

Flintlock nodded. "Yeah, it's spooky, makes me think of ha'ants and boogermen and such." He took a sip of coffee, took time to build a cigarette and then said, "I can tell you a spooky story."

Bridie smiled and shook her head. "Please don't. When I'm on guard by myself I don't want to think about ghosts."

"It's not about ghosts. It's about a hat."

"A hat?"

"Yeah, a Stetson hat." Flintlock lit his cigarette and breathed out smoke as he said, "Want to hear it? Keep you from getting bored."

"You've got no intention of turning in, Sam, so let me hear it. And if it's real scary I'll never forgive you."

"It's not real scary, but it's mighty strange. It all started a few years back, in the winter of '78, as I recollect. There was a ranch by the name of the JW over to the Texas Trinity River country and one of their top hands was a puncher by the name of Donny Powers, a nice-enough feller when he was sober. Well, come one Friday night Donny decided to go into town and have a drink or two and maybe a woman."

"What kind of woman?" Bridie said, frowning her anticipated disapproval.

"A fancy woman."

"A whore?"

"Yeah, that kind of woman."

"Well, Donny just went down in my estimation. Every time a man lies with a loose woman Our Lady sheds a tear. The nuns taught me that."

"Are you trying to spoil my story on purpose?"

"No, I'm not. So, Donny rode into town . . . and then what happened?"

"He had a few drinks, but the saloon was dead so he decided to head back to the ranch."

"I should hope so," Bridie said.

"The trouble was, he'd only been on the trail for an hour or so, when a thunderstorm blew up, a ripsnorter and a humdinger as the JW punchers described it later."

"Poor Donny," Bridie said.

"Yeah, poor Donny, because he got struck by a lightning bolt that killed both him and his hoss, a bay mare that was reckoned to be the best cutting pony on the JW. Old Joe Wilson, the owner of the ranch, sure mourned the loss of that mare."

"Is that it?" Bridie said. "Is that the story?"

"No, that's not it. I'm closing in on the rest of the yarn now, what you might call coming up on the crux of the matter. By the way, this is good coffee you made, Bridie." He dropped his voice to a whisper. "My ma makes lousy coffee."

"Go on with the story, Sam," Bridie said.

"Where was I? Oh yeah, well, next morning after the storm cleared, they came and took away Donny's body and the dead mare. But here's the thing, when the lightning hit him, Donny's hat was blown off and it lay there on the trail and nobody touched it."

"Why not?"

"I'll tell you why not, because Texas punchers are the most superstitious critters God ever put on earth and they figured Donny's Stetson was a bad-luck hat and they wouldn't go near it. For years that old hat lay on the trail and for years the JW hands would ride a mile around it, wouldn't even look at it." Flintlock tossed out the dregs of his coffee. "As far as I know, Donny's bad-luck hat is there still and likely it will always be, unless one day a big wind comes up and blows it away."

Bridie nodded and said, "I wouldn't pick that hat up, would you?"

"Hell, no. I want no truck with bad-luck hats. Did I spook you?"

"No. When you study on it, it's a kind of sad story," Bridie said.

"I guess so, sad for Donny Coombs and sad for the bay mare. Now I'll go find my blankets."

"Sleep well, Sam."

"I sure will," Flintlock said. "Telling that spooky hat story has plumb wore me out."

CHAPTER FIFTY

Bridie O'Toole put the Waltham back in the pocket of her skirt. It had just informed her that it was three o'clock, the darkest hour of the night. On all sides of her stretched the silent land, bathed in wan moonlight. To the north flashes of heat lightning throbbed in the sky, obliterating the stars, and now a rising wind guttered the flames of the campfire and raised sparks around the sooty sides of the coffeepot. Jane and Flintlock seemed to be sound asleep, cocooned in their blankets.

Bridie yawned, stood and held her rifle loosely in her left hand. She looked around her but saw only the gleam of moonlight on rock and black pools of mysterious shadow. The silence was so profound, so vaguely disturbing, that she sang the old Irish tune of "The Female Highwayman" under her breath.

Silvy, Silvy, all in one day,
She dressed herself in man's array,
A sword and pistol by her side,
To meet her true love she did ride.

There was a sound below her, Bridie was sure of it . . . the clink of a steel horseshoe on rock. Or was she hearing things? She stepped closer to the edge of the rise, softly singing her song, her rifle at the ready.

She met her true love all on the plain,
"Stand and deliver, kind sir," she said,
"Stand and deliver, kind sir," said she,
"Or else this moment you shall die."

The song faded on Bridie's lips. Was that a groan? A man in pain? Or was it the whimper of a horse wounded in the battle at the mesa?

She looked over at the sleeping Jane and Flintlock, wondering if she should raise the alarm and wake them. No, she wouldn't do that. Suppose it turned out to be nothing, just the sound of a coyote or something? Sam Flintlock would tease her, tell her that she'd been spooked by his stupid hat story. That was unacceptable and Bridie made a decision . . . she was a Pinkerton and Pinkertons don't run for help at every turn. There was something down there in the darkness and she must find out what it was. She had it to do.

Stepping carefully, Bridie O'Toole took the gradual slope from the ridge, stopping often to listen into the night. She heard nothing. Now convinced that her mind had been playing tricks on her, she reached the flat and whispered, "Who's there?"

No answer.

She walked forward a couple of steps and then, scanning the darkness in front of her, her eyes put form to the sounds she'd heard . . . a man wearing a bloodstained shirt lying over the neck of a horse . . . no, a mule.

"Are you wounded?" Bridie said, stepping closer.

Then two events happened very fast . . .

Bridie made out riding breeches, English boots and hair seamed with gray and in a moment of horrified realization she saw that the man was Jacob Hammer. A split second later, Hammer's left arm shot out in a sweeping motion and backhanded her viciously across the face. Stunned, the woman staggered and triggered off a round that went skyward. Her head spinning, she fell on her back and Hammer threw himself on top of her.

Bridie was dimly aware that Hammer had screamed horribly when he hit the ground, but from pain or rage she did not know. But now the man grabbed her by her hair and she felt the cold muzzle of a gun shove against her temple.

"Help me, bitch, or I'll kill you," he said, a gasping, primitive snarl shot through with pain. Bridie, wincing as Hammer clawed his strong fingers deeper into her hair, said nothing. "Help me to my feet or I'll blow your damned brains out," the man said.

"Let me go," Bridie said. "I'll make sure that you're given a fair trial."

"Don't talk to me of trials," Hammer said. "You and Flintlock and his mother are the ones on trial . . . and you've been found guilty and sentenced to death. Now get me to my feet or I kill you right now."

"Bridie!"

Flintlock's voice.

But Bridie's head had cleared and she was standing, Hammer leaning heavily on her, his left arm wrapped around her shoulders. The man's breath was hissing through his teeth and he was obviously in agony, but the muzzle of his revolver never left the side of Bridie's head.

"Stay back, Flintlock, or I'll scatter this sow's brains," Hammer said.

"Let the girl go, Hammer," Flintlock said. "You're finished. It's over."

"If I'm finished, then so is she. Now drop that rifle."

"Sam, shoot him!" Bridie yelled.

"No! Don't shoot, Samuel," Jane said. She stood beside Flintlock. "He's insane and he'll kill her."

"I deserve to die," Bridie said, tears staining her cheeks. "I'm supposed to be a Pinkerton but I let him take me. It was easy for him."

"You are a Pinkerton, Bridie," Jane said. "Now you must be brave."

"Shut the hell up, all of you!" Hammer yelled. "Flintlock, drop the rifle or the slut dies. Make up your mind because you're fast running out of time."

"Seems to me that you're the one running out of time, Hammer," Flintlock said. He hesitated a moment and then dropped his Winchester.

"Now, you and the other whore slowly back up the slope," Hammer said.

He tightened his muscular arm around Bridie's neck and the woman cried out in pain. "Help me follow them."

"Damn you, Hammer, you're dying on your feet," Flintlock said. "Best you make your peace with God."

"The hell with God and the hell with you. Now back up, all the way to the top."

Bridie tried to wrench herself free, but again Hammer's arm tightened on her neck and she sobbed in sudden pain. "Support my weight or I'll tear your damned head right off your shoulders."

"Bridie, do as he says," Jane said.

It took several minutes for Hammer to reach the top of the rise and by the time he got there, Bridie O'Toole's head was bent over at an odd angle, her face a mask of suffering. Hammer backed his way past the campfire and then stopped. "Flintlock, bank up the fire. I want to see your face when I shoot your mother."

"Do it, Samuel," Jane said. "Don't argue with a madman."

Flintlock stared hard at Hammer and said, "Mister, you better hit with all six cartridges in that Colt because I'm going to walk through all of them to get to you and wring your neck."

He stepped forward and then halted in surprise as Hammer screamed, high-pitched shrills that shattered the quiet of the night.

"No!" the man shrieked. "Not now!"

He staggered back, his face ashen as the gangrene infection finally affected the tissues of his brain. His enormously swollen leg collapsing under him, he clung desperately to Bridie.

"Noooo . . . not now," he screeched. "I must live . . . I must . . ."

He triggered a shot, aiming at Jane, but the bullet went yards wide. He fired again and again, missing with each shot. Flintlock advanced on him, his face a mask of fury.

Hammer fired at Flintlock then stumbled backward, Bridie still in the viselike grip of his arm. Yet another step back . . . and then a frenzied wail as the man reached the edge of the rise, lost his footing and toppled over the edge screaming, dragging Bridie with him.

Flintlock grabbed a flaming brand from the fire and he and Jane hurried from the ridge to the U-shaped rock at the bottom of the drop.

Hammer lay on his back, his face contorted with pain, and Bridie lay a couple of yards away, unconscious but alive. Jane kneeled beside the woman as Flintlock held his makeshift torch high and stared down at Hammer.

"Kill me . . . kill me . . ." Hammer said.

Flintlock shook his head, his merciless face like stone. "I'll do nothing to ease your pain, you dirty son of a bitch." He turned to Jane. "How is she, Ma?"

"She's got a pretty good bump on her head, but she'll be fine."

Jane looked at Hammer. "In the end, you acted like the two-bit crook you always were."

"I should've killed you" — Hammer grimaced as he was hit by a spasm of pain — "when I had the chance."

"And now you never will," Jane said. "Ain't that a shame."

Flintlock picked up Bridie in his arms and carried her back to the rise. Neither he nor Jane looked back at Jacob Hammer.

Hammer was still alive, but barely, when Flintlock and the two women rode down from the rise. His back was broken and he hadn't moved. Jane had filled a spare canteen at the seep and now she dismounted and walked to the dying man. She dropped the canteen beside him and said, "Take a drink now and then, ease your road to death."

Hammer's eyes were glazed, his face unnaturally white. His ravaged body stank. "Woman," he said, "am I in Shanghai?"

Jane shook her head. "No, you're in hell."

CHAPTER FIFTY-ONE

A relic of the recent Apache wars, the orderly buildings of Fort Defiance were surrounded by a sprawling village of adobe dwellings and thatched, wattle-and-daub jacales. The headquarters building was flanked on two sides by the enlisted men's quarters, a sutler's store, adjoining that the quartermaster's store, a blacksmith's shop and stables. A flagpole stood in the center of the parade ground, the Stars and Stripes hanging limp in the still morning air. Fort Defiance would win no prizes for beauty. It was hot, dusty, neglected and run-down.

A cavalry corporal left the headquarters building, crossed the parade ground and stepped into the sutler's store, a dark, dingy establishment owned by Reuben Horn, its equally dark and dingy proprietor.

The corporal's boots thudded on the wood floor as he walked to the counter where the two Pinkerton women and the man with the big bird on his throat stood, eating cheese and crackers.

"Your answer just came in from the Pinkerton Agency, ma'am," the soldier said, handing a slip of paper to Jane. "And I hope it's the news you've been waiting for."

"Thank you, Corporal," Jane said.

"Your obedient servant, ma'am." The corporal gave a snappy salute and left.

Jane read the wire, read it again and Bridie O'Toole said, "Well, what is it?"

"We've got our orders," Jane said.

"Don't keep us in suspense, Ma," Sam Flintlock said. "What does it say."

"I am ordered to New Orleans to investigate a man named Giuseppe Morello and his criminal organization. I have to wire for further instructions when I arrive."

"And what about me?" Bridie said.

"You're ordered back to Chicago. That's all it says," Jane said.

"I won't do office work," Bridie said, looking crestfallen. "I'm a detective, not a filing clerk."

Jane smiled. "I'm sure the agency has something else in mind, Bridie. By now they know the valuable role you played in bringing down Jacob Hammer, and if they don't they soon will because I will tell them."

Bridie hugged Jane and said, "I knew I

could depend on you."

Reuben Horn, a man with black hair, black eyes and, if the talk around the fort was correct, a black heart, stepped behind the counter. He stared at Flintlock for a few moments and then said, "You're Sam Flintlock, ain't you?"

"That's the name," Flintlock said.

"Heard you're doing a job fer the army, riding out this morning."

"Word gets around," Flintlock said.

"It's a small fort," Horn said. "What are they paying you to go out on the scout?"

"Enough."

Horn waved a hand, dismissing that last. "Two dollars a day and your grub ain't enough."

"Maybe so, but I've nothing better to do."

"Man you're being paid to find is a friend of mine, goes by the name of Jasper Davies. Ain't that so?"

"That would be the man. Stole a pair of army mules."

"That's neither here nor there," Horn said. "I'll pay you ten dollars not to find him."

"Ten dollars. Sounds like Davies is kin."

"He's kin to a skunk," Horn said. "But now and again he does work for me. I set store by him and I don't want him to spend

401

the next year or two scratching his name on a cell wall. I need him here."

Flintlock shook his head. "Sorry, mister, I'm being paid by the army to do a job and I'll do it. First come, first served."

Horn's face turned ugly. "Tattooed man, if you catch up with Jasper, it will be better for you if you don't bring him in . . . if you get my drift."

"You threatening me?" Flintlock said.

"Maybe I am, maybe I ain't. Let's just say that this here cannon on my hip ain't for show."

"Samuel, let it go," Jane said. And then to Horn, "If you make any more threats against my son, I'll report you to Lieutenant Colonel Brand. Now, what do we owe you for the stale crackers and dried-up cheese?"

"I reckon you all ate a dollar's worth," Horn said. He smiled. "Brand is an idiot and an Indian lover. He don't scare me none."

As Jane and Bridie hustled Flintlock out of the door, Horn called out after him, "Remember what I told you, tattooed man."

Sam Flintlock rode out of Fort Defiance two hours before noon with Sergeant Clive Britton and two troopers. Britton, a grizzled veteran of the Apache wars, was a talking man.

"Sam, afore we left the word around the fort was that Reuben Horn put the crawl on you."

Flintlock's eyes were fixed on the sandy trail ahead of him. "Who told you that?"

"Horn put it out, said your ma saved you from a whipping."

Flintlock shook his head. "The man is a liar."

"He's all of that," Britton said. "But Horn is a dangerous man to cross. He's mighty slick with the iron. If I was you, I'd be careful around him."

"Let's catch Jasper Davies first, and then I'll study on it."

"What did he tell you?"

"About what?"

"About Davies. Jasper is a friend of his."

"He offered me ten dollars not to find him."

"And will you take it?"

"I reckon not. I've picked up Davies's tracks already. He's heading south."

"Jasper isn't too smart, but he's a sure-thing killer," the sergeant said. "He's a dark-alley man and him and Horn go way back. About ten years ago, they beat it out of Fort Worth ahead of a hanging posse and then, don't ask me how, Horn got himself a job here in the Territory as an Indian agent with Davies as his assistant. With their dirty thumbs on the beef and flour scales, they starved the Apaches for years and when Geronimo and the rest of them were packed off to Florida, Horn opened his sutler's store using the profits he made from dead Mescaleros."

"Sounds like a real nice feller," Flintlock said.

"He's poison and so is Davies," Britton said. "He may put up a fight."

"I doubt it," Flintlock said. "His kind never do, Clive."

For a while the four men rode in silence, the rocky landscape around them shimmering in the heat. After a while Flintlock drew rein. He dismounted and scouted the ground around a stand of juniper and New Mexican pine and said, "Davies sure isn't in a hurry. He dawdled here, smoked a few cigarettes and then went on his way again. Judging by the mule dung, he's no more than an hour ahead of us."

"Probably Horn already has a buyer for them mules," Sergeant Britton said. "My guess is he told Davies to ride out a ways and then halt at a place where they could meet up. Horn didn't think the army would go after Davies after our scout died of the consumption a month ago. He didn't count on you taking the job." Britton turned his head and looked at Flintlock. "Here, why did the colonel offer you the scout job anyway?"

"He'd heard my ma mention my name and he remembered stories that I was a bounty hunter who ran with a half-breed Apache," Flintlock said. "He said I was in the right place at the right time." He smiled. "But the cook at Fort Defiance could follow this man. He's making no attempt to cover his tracks."

"Well, I couldn't track him," Britton said. "I was never much of a hand at it."

"You really think Horn was in on the theft of the mules?" Flintlock said.

"You can bet the farm on it, Sam. Them two are responsible for most of the thieving and horse stealing around here, and now and then a killing and robbery, if the truth be known."

After an hour Sam Flintlock reached the northern rim of the Defiance Plateau, riding into high land covered with juniper, pine and grama grass. There were also thick stands of yucca and Gambel oak as well as serviceberry and squawbush. The ancient

405

cliff dwellers and later the Apaches and Navajo had gathered food there, but had left no marks on the land.

Sam Flintlock smelled traces of smoke in the air and said to Sergeant Britton, "We're close." He turned to the young troopers. "You boys better get your carbines ready."

The soldiers looked to their sergeant and Britton said, "Do as he says."

"I suggest you give the order to dismount, Clive," Flintlock said. "We'll go on foot from here."

Britton left one soldier with the horses, and Flintlock led the way through the pines. He stopped and then in a whisper he said, "I'll go ahead and try to surprise him. Clive, you hear shooting come a-running."

The sergeant nodded and he and the trooper waited while Flintlock glided through the trees on silent feet, as O'Hara had so patiently taught him.

Jasper Davies had made camp in a clearing and sat by a hatful of fire, boiling coffee in a tin cup. The two mules and his mustang grazed nearby and showed no interest in what was happening around them. Flintlock took stock of Davies. The man was small, wiry, with a badly cut shock of black hair. He wore a belt gun and a sheathed knife at the small of his back. Davies's face was pinched, mean and thin-lipped and his duds were shabby and ill fitting, as though they'd once belonged to a bigger man.

Flintlock wiped sweat from the palm of his gun hand on his pants, pulled his Colt from the waistband, took a deep breath and stepped into the clearing.

"Git your hands up, Davies," he said.

The man snapped his head around, saw Flintlock and blanched. "What the hell . . . ?" he said.

"On your feet, Davies," Flintlock said. "Do it now!"

The little man rose slowly and said, "What the hell are you?"

"Just a scout come to take back the army's mules and the ranny that stole them."

"You ain't taking me back to Fort Defiance," Davies said. "They'll hang me."

"Heard of a man getting hung for stealing a horse," Flintlock said. "But I never heard tell of a man getting hung for stealing a mule."

"Two mules," Davies said.

"Never heard of a man getting hung for two mules, either," Flintlock said. "Now unbuckle that gunbelt with your left hand, let it drop and take a step back. Be quick about it. I'm not a patient man."

Jasper Davies was thinking about making

a play, figuring his chances. Flintlock could see it in the man's eyes and he didn't much care for it.

"Don't let it even enter into your thinking, Davies," he said. "I can drill you square before you clear leather. Now, unbuckle the belt, like I told you."

"Who the hell are you, mister?" Davies said. The speculative light was gone from his eyes.

"Name's Sam Flintlock."

"The Texas bounty hunter?"

"The same."

"I ain't gunfighting you, mister."

"No, you ain't. Now drop that belt before I drop you."

Davies's left hand moved toward his belt buckle . . .

And then disaster.

A shot came from the trees and Davies's thin chest seemed to cave in from the impact of the .45-70 bullet. The little man shrieked in pain and surprise and fell, dead when he hit the ground, his twisted face in the fire, boiling hot coffee beading his thick hair.

Flintlock dragged Davies from the fire and turned him onto his back, but the man was as dead as he was ever going to be.

The young trooper stepped out of the

pines, his Springfield carbine in his hands. He had a round face, freckled like a sparrow's egg, and looked to be all of sixteen years old. "He was going for his gun," the boy said. "I saw it plain. Oh God, did I kill him?" He was white as a sheet and looked as though he was about to puke.

Sergeant Britton stepped beside Flintlock and looked down at the body. "Gun's still in his holster," he said, flat, toneless, making no accusation.

"I've never killed anyone before," the trooper said. His eyes were red. "But he was going for his gun. Sergeant, I seen it plain."

"Sam?" Britton said.

Flintlock looked at the trooper, way too young to be a soldier in any army.

"Davies was going for his gun," Flintlock said.

Britton grinned. He slapped the youth's back and said, "Private Corcoran, you done good."

"Sergeant, I don't feel so good."

The trooper ran into the trees and retched and Britton smiled at Flintlock and said, "The first one is always the worst."

Flintlock nodded. "Let's hope he doesn't have to kill another."

"He's a soldier, killing goes with the job," Britton said.

"I'm sure Private Corcoran is aware of that now," Flintlock said.

Under a sky ribboned with scarlet and jade, Sam Flintlock and the soldiers rode into Fort Defiance with Jasper Davies's body slung over the back of his mustang. The two troopers each led a mule, and Colonel Brand watched the procession from his office window and then stepped into the square, his tunic unbuttoned and a cigar between his teeth.

Sergeant Britton drew rein and saluted his commanding officer. "Two mules, property of the United States Army, recovered and the thief killed while resisting arrest."

"Unfortunate," Brand said. He looked at Flintlock. "Did you kill him, Sam?"

Flintlock shook his head. "No. Private Corcoran did."

"Private Corcoran saw Davies draw down on scout Flintlock and to save scout Flintlock's life Private Corcoran discharged his rifle and killed Davies."

Brand nodded. "Well done, Private Corcoran. Sam, you owe this young soldier a debt of gratitude for saving your life."

"Seems like, Colonel," Flintlock said.

Brand nodded. "Well, carry on, Sergeant Britton. A drink with you, Sam?"

"Just as soon as I see to my horse," Flintlock said.

"Good. I look forward to it, and I have a proposition for you."

CHAPTER FIFTY-TWO

Flintlock led the buckskin into a stall and was brushing him down when Reuben Horn walked into the stable. He stood hipshot against a post, tilted his head a little to one side and said, "I'm trying to figure what kind of fool chooses not to heed a fair warning. I told you not to come back here with Jasper Davies and you ignored me and brought him in dead."

Flintlock laid down the brush and turned to face Horn. The sutler was relaxed, confident of his gun skills and he had little regard for Flintlock. Contempt was obvious in his eyes.

"Pity about Jasper," Flintlock said. "But if you don't want to get shot, don't steal the mules."

"Is that supposed to be funny?" Horn said. "I don't like saddle tramps making fun of my friends."

Flintlock's face hardened as he stepped

away from the buckskin.

"Mister, it's pretty obvious to me that you're looking for a fight," he said. "If that's the case, shuck your pistol and get to your work."

Horn's smile was not pleasant. "Is that an invitation to open the ball, tattooed man?"

"I couldn't make it any plainer."

"Then here beginneth the lesson."

Reuben Horn went for his gun . . . and instantly understood three facts as he cleared leather. The first was that he'd badly underestimated Sam Flintlock. The second was that the tattooed man was fast, faster than he'd seen before. And the third, and the most appalling, was that the bullet that had just crashed into his chest had killed him.

Horn staggered, staring bug-eyed at Flintlock as he tried to bring up his gun. But he had no strength in his arm . . . no strength at all.

As for Flintlock, never a man to leave well enough alone, he fired again, and again, his bullets smashing Horn to the ground, where the man died, straw in his beard and the smell of horseshit in his nose.

Flintlock stepped through gray gunsmoke, glanced at Horn's sprawled body and walked to the door of the stable. He attracted a swarm of soldiers. Leading them was the stalwart figure of Colonel Brand.

"Flintlock, what the hell happened?" he said.

"I shot Reuben Horn. He's back there."

Brand brushed past Flintlock, stared at the dead sutler for long moments and then said, "How did it happen?"

"He took offense that I brought in Jasper Davies."

"And you shot him?"

"He showed his displeasure by drawing down on me."

"Damn it all, Sam, you were lucky. Horn was good with a gun."

Flintlock nodded. "He showed some promise."

Brand stared at Flintlock as though seeing him for the first time. Then, "You men there, take Reuben out of here. He's upsetting the horses."

A gray-haired officer, wearing a captain's shoulder boards on his fatigue blouse, glanced at the body as it was carried past him, shifted his gaze to Flintlock and said, "Colonel, do I arrest this man?"

"No, it was a clear-cut case of self-defense," Brand said. "Davies drew on Mr. Flintlock."

The captain looked surprised. "Davies was

good with a pistol."

"Not quite good enough, it seems," Brand said. "Carry on, Captain Brooke. Sam, I'll see you in my office."

Lieutenant Colonel Brand handed Sam Flintlock a glass of whiskey and said, "Cigar?"

Flintlock took the makings from his pocket and said, "I'll smoke this, if you don't mind, Ben."

"Go right ahead. Some of my men are much addicted to the Texas habit, rolling cigarettes, cigarettes, all the time. I never could take to it. There's nothing like smoking a good cigar."

"Reuben Horn sold me this tobacco," Flintlock said. "Funny old world, isn't it?"

"Not funny for him," Brand said.

"Good bourbon, Ben."

"Horn sold me that, too. It's Old Crow, not the usual frontier firewater."

Flintlock built and lit a cigarette and then said through a cloud of smoke, "You have a proposition for me, Ben?"

"Ah . . . I had, Sam, not I have," Brand said, looking uncomfortable. A white moth flew around the oil lamp on the colonel's desk and made a *tick . . . tick . . . tick* noise on the glass chimney. "It was my intention to offer you a post as my regimental scout, but I've had a change of heart."

"Why?"

"Because you seem to attract trouble, Sam, like . . . well, like the lamp flame attracts that moth. You've only been on the post a few days and already I have two dead men on my hands. Good Lord, man, how many bodies will you stack up in a month, or a year?"

"I wouldn't have taken the job, Ben," Flintlock said. "But I will say this . . . I'm not by nature a troublemaker."

"And I'm not saying you are, but it seems that badmen just naturally find you. Maybe it's because you're fast with a gun, I don't know, but I need a scout, not a shootist." Brand poured more Old Crow into Flintlock's glass. "Sam, no hard feelings, I hope."

Flintlock smiled. "Of course not, Colonel. I hope you find your scout, especially one that stays sober, at least some of the time."

Brand raised his glass. "I'll drink to that." He and Flintlock drank and the colonel refilled the glasses. "Your mother is a fine woman, Sam, so here's a toast to the ladies."

"To the ladies, God bless them," Flintlock said.

"We're not ladies, we're Pinkertons," Bridie

O'Toole said. "A woman can't be a lady and a detective at the same time."

"Well, you and Ma look like ladies," Flintlock said. "A pair of fine ladies."

And as his mother and Bridie stood at the open door of the stage that would take them to the rail depot, that was the truth. The officers' wives had gotten together and donated clothing for Jane and Bridie, who were happy to shed their worn and stained skirts and shirts for dresses, shoes and dainty hats.

Jane said, "Sam, about what happened last night . . ."

"Horn drew down on me, Ma," Flintlock said. "I didn't have any choice."

"Son, I know you didn't, but this violent life you live is leading you nowhere."

"I'm a bounty hunter, Ma. That's what I do."

"And now and then, an outlaw."

"Ma, I —"

"Samuel, you're getting older and you no longer have O'Hara to watch your back," Jane said. "How long before one of those men you hunt proves to be faster on the draw than you, or a lawman arrests you and sends you to prison for the rest of your life?" The woman's voice was pleading. "Samuel, turn away from all that and settle down someplace, marry a nice girl and earn a respectable living. Hang up your gun before it's too late. I don't want my only child to die before me."

Bridie said, "Listen to your mother, Sam. Look at you standing there in dirty buckskin with a revolver stuck in your pants. You don't look like Jane's son, you look like a dangerous frontier desperado. I think I've gotten to know you these last weeks, and I know you can do better."

"Samuel, you played a noble and courageous role when you helped take down Jacob Hammer," Jane said. "Now let that be your swan song."

"I'll study on what you've said, Ma," Flintlock said. Then, "I always thought I might prosper in the dry goods business."

"Yes, Samuel, you've told me that before," Jane said. "And if you feel that's where your future lies, then do it before it's too late."

The stagecoach driver climbed into his seat, leaned over and said, "Five minutes, ladies. We got a schedule to keep."

"Ma, what about you?" Flintlock said. "I'll worry about you in New Orleans."

Jane smiled. "Detective work isn't quite as dangerous as that business at Balakai Mesa. I'll be fine. But don't follow me to New Orleans, Samuel. I'm a Pinkerton and I need to do my job alone. Do you understand?"

"Then how do I get in touch with you?"

"You can write to me care of the Pinkerton Agency, 80 Washington Street, Chicago, Illinois."

"Here, Sam," Bridie said, handing Flintlock a slip of paper. "Last night, I wrote the address down for you. I knew you'd want it."

"Ma, about New Orleans, I —"

"No, Samuel. I can't have you following me around the country. You must live your own life. We'll meet again, I promise."

"All aboard, ladies," the stage driver said.

Jane kissed her son on the cheek and said, "Until we meet again, Samuel."

Bridie did the same and then Flintlock helped them into the coach. He was relieved to see a tough-looking soldier was already aboard.

A whip cracked and the coach lurched into motion, six horses in the traces.

"Wait!" Flintlock said.

The coach gathered speed and Flintlock raced alongside. Jane stuck her head out the window, and he yelled, "My name! Ma, what's my name?"

"Your father's name was Archibald Dinwiddie," Jane said. She waved a hand. "I'll tell you about him one day."

Flintlock watched the coach disappear in a cloud of dust and then he stood in the middle of the parade ground, head bowed, his face stricken. He couldn't believe his ears, but there was no mistake . . .

After all those years of searching, his name was Sam Dinwiddie.

The hurt was almost too much to bear.

His head snapped up as he heard a sound . . . there it was again . . . uproarious laughter in the wind that sounded suspiciously like O'Hara and wicked old Barnabas . . .

In Austin, Texas, six weeks later, Sam Dinwiddie stepped into the store of Elias Appelbaum, Gentlemen's Clothier, and his instructions were straightforward, "I need everything from the skin out, twice over."

If Appelbaum was intimidated by the man in the buckskin shirt with the big bird tattoo on his throat he didn't let it show. He took the measuring tape from around his neck and said, "Certainly, sir. Let me just take your measurements." He studied Sam Dinwiddie with a critical eye and added, "Something in a clerical gray for the city, I think, and a Scottish tweed for more informal, country wear. Will this be cash or charge?"

"Cash on the barrelhead," Sam Dinwiddie said. "And I want to look like I'm the proprietor of a dry goods store."

Several hours later, after swift alterations were made to ready-to-wear garments, Sam Dinwiddie admired himself in the Appelbaum full-length mirror. He wore a clerical gray ditto suit, elastic-sided ankle boots, a white shirt with celluloid collar and red tie and a fine derby hat. A pair of kid gloves completed that vision of sartorial splendor and Sam was mightily pleased, and so was Elias Appelbaum.

"You do look splendid, sir," the tailor said. "The . . . um . . . high celluloid collar covers most of the . . . um . . . most tastefully done bird. Does that present a problem?"

"No, it does not, Mr. Appelbaum."

"And the . . . um . . . gentleman's previous garments . . . does he . . . um . . . wish to retain them?"

"Burn them, Mr. Appelbaum."

"Burn them, Mr. Dinwiddie?"

"Yes, burn them. I have no further use for them."

"I am so relieved to hear that, Mr. Dinwiddie. They are rather . . . um . . . worn."

"I wish to thank you for your excellent

421

tailoring, Mr. Appelbaum. I feel like a new man."

"And, if you don't mind my saying so, you look like a new man, Mr. Dinwiddie. You're going to be quite the young man about town."

Watching his grammar, Sam Dinwiddie said, "Now, Mr. Appelbaum, before I leave, can you direct me to an emporium that sells Pears soap? Sarah Bernhardt swears by it, you know."

AFTERWORD

Indian Springs, Kansas, May 1903

The Logan Brothers stage rattled to a halt outside the Indian Springs depot, followed by its attendant dust cloud. A gray-haired lady opened the door and stepped into the street with a supple gracefulness that belied her age. She looked up at the driver and shook an admonishing finger. "Mr. Logan, be careful of my luggage, now, you hear? I have breakables in the suitcases."

"Yes, Miss McIntyre," the driver said. "I'll treat them like they was made of crystal."

"I should hope so," Jane said, "since that's what's they're carrying."

Matt Logan carefully unloaded Jane's two carpetbags and a pair of matching leather suitcases and laid them on the sidewalk.

"Now, Mr. Logan, someone to help me carry these to my son's store, if you please. They are heavy."

"Yes, Miss McIntyre," Logan said. "I'll

send out a boy toot sweet, as the Frenchmen say."

"Is that what they say?" Jane said. "Well, I need a strong boy, mind, with a modicum of intelligence. I won't have my son see my luggage carried by a cretin."

"A strong, smart young feller comin' up," Miss McIntyre," Logan said. He disappeared into the stage depot.

Jane waited on the sidewalk and frowned her disapproval as one of those newfangled, steam-powered horseless carriages belched into town and drove noisily down the main street, trailing dust from its wheels.

Jane shook her head. A horseless carriage, indeed. That was a foolish fad that would never catch on, great, deafening brute of a thing that it was.

A towheaded boy of about fourteen stepped out of the depot and joined Jane on the sidewalk. He touched the brim of his peaked hat and said, "I'll carry your luggage, Miss McIntyre."

Jane nodded. The boy looked strong enough and he was polite. That would do for now. "Now, a carpetbag under each arm and a suitcase in each hand. Yes, that's right, you've got the hang of it. But be careful, I've got breakables in the cases."

"Yes, Miss McIntyre," the boy said.

He seemed to handle her luggage with ease and went up in Jane's estimation. "Now, can you point out my son's store? His name is Samuel Dinwiddie."

"Why, Mr. Dinwiddie's store is right across the street," the boy said. "To the left of the church. See, it says, 'Dinwiddie and O'Hara, Dry Goods.' "

"The place with the red, white and blue bunting outside?"

"That's the one, Miss McIntyre."

"What's that sign above the door? I can't read it from here."

"It says, 'Welcome Home, Ma.' I guess that means you, Miss McIntyre."

"Yes, yes, it does mean me." Jane said. "And Samuel never forgot the gallant Apache, did he?"

"I guess not, Miss McIntyre," the boy said. But it was obvious that he didn't know what she was talking about.

Sam Dinwiddie stood on the sidewalk outside his store, grinning, as Jane walked closer. On his right was his pretty wife, on his left his tall son and beautiful daughter.

Sam left the sidewalk to greet his mother, his arms outstretched. "Welcome home, Ma," he said.

And Jane smiled. Yes, she was home . . .

Home with her family where she belonged.

ABOUT THE AUTHORS

William W. Johnstone is the *New York Times* and *USA Today* bestselling author of over 300 books, including the series The Mountain Man; Preacher, the First Mountain Man; MacCallister; Luke Jensen, Bounty Hunter; Flintlock; Those Jensen Boys; The Frontiersman; Savage Texas; The Kerrigans; and Will Tanner: Deputy U.S. Marshal. His thrillers include *Black Friday, Tyranny, Stand Your Ground,* and *The Doomsday Bunker.* Visit his website at www .williamjohnstone.net or email him at dogcia2006@aol.com.

Being the all-around assistant, typist, researcher, and fact checker to one of the most popular western authors of all time, **J.A. Johnstone** learned from the master, Uncle William W. Johnstone.

He began tutoring J.A. at an early age.

After-school hours were often spent retyping manuscripts or researching his massive American Western History library as well as the more modern wars and conflicts. J.A. worked hard — and learned.

"Every day with Bill was an adventure story in itself. Bill taught me all he could about the art of storytelling. 'Keep the historical facts accurate,' he would say. 'Remember the readers, and as your grandfather once told me, I am telling you now: be the best J.A. Johnstone you can be."

The employees of Thorndike Press hope you have enjoyed this Large Print book. All our Thorndike, Wheeler, and Kennebec Large Print titles are designed for easy reading, and all our books are made to last. Other Thorndike Press Large Print books are available at your library, through selected bookstores, or directly from us.

For information about titles, please call:
(800) 223-1244

or visit our website at:
gale.com/thorndike

To share your comments, please write:
Publisher
Thorndike Press
10 Water St., Suite 310
Waterville, ME 04901